Logically Stupid,
That's Love

Logically Stupid, That's Love

Shikha

Srishti
PUBLISHERS & DISTRIBUTORS

SRISHTI PUBLISHERS & DISTRIBUTORS
Registered Office: N-16, C.R. Park
New Delhi – 110 019
Corporate Office: 212A, Peacock Lane
Shahpur Jat, New Delhi – 110 049
editorial@srishtipublishers.com

First published by
Srishti Publishers & Distributors in 2016

10 9 8 7 6 5 4 3 2 1

Dedicated to my "Life ki Battery" and "Love ki Factory"
guys, Suman & Parth for being Logical or Funny
as time deems, but Lovable throughout.

Acknowledgements

For my first book, I spent many hours thinking whom I need to thank for a wonderful life. And then there were many who made to the list in the course of my journey as an author.

My husband Kumar Suman and son Parth who deal with my idiocracies the most. I wish God keeps showering patience on them, and I keep bringing my characters to life.

I don't mean to sound self-pompous, but next thanks go to my parents Mr. Vipin & Mrs. Shobha Mehra for providing the ingredients that make me a go-getter.

My brother Vishal, and his family, Jisha & Romir for being a part of all my insane ideas unconditionally.

I'm thankful to almighty for a loving family, super-crazy fun friends, acquaintances I made in the publishing world and admiring readers I earned.

It was one exciting experience to be published with renowned publishers, Srishti. Thanks for dealing with my nitty-gritty naggings and making me more cognizant with the book world in India.

Suhail Mathur at Book Bakers, for such a lovely cover page that depicts the story so beautifully.

Dipankar Mukherjee at Readomania, for being my beta reader and helping me chisel my story even better.

Thanks to Emenox media group with whom I've signed the film deal of my first book. For making happen the moment every author wishes for in less than a year of the book's release.

My school buddies at Bal Bharti Public School, Brij Vihar, who are and will always be part of my cherished childhood memories.

For my friends for life Deepa Wahi, Swati Aggarwal, Shweta Purohit, Tanurima Dey, Charu Khurana, and Priyanka Agarwal for never being judgmental in judging the mental in me.

One page can never be enough to thank the people in your life for making it worth living.

Thank you, God, for everything!

Life-changing events

My Boss and his daughter – Jabse dono mile hain,
life ki lagi padi hai

"Good times, here I come," proclaimed soon-to-be twenty-four Kartik Brar as he breathed Mumbai's air jumping out of the train. His dream vacation was about to begin. A tall, wheatish, handsome and fiercely confident young man, he lifted his backpack with a jerk and wore it on both his shoulders. He strolled whistling to catch a local train to his friend's place in Malad on a sunny afternoon in August 2002. Kartik had earned his MBA in Marketing from IIM Kolkata three months ago. He hailed from Amritsar and also had a B.Tech in computer science to his credit.

Kartik was here for a vacation, and inevitably, his memory leaped to a few months back, recalling hanging out with friends on the hostel's terrace for a late night booze party.

◆

"Kartik, you aren't going for campus placements?" asked his friend Govind.

1

"I'm not interested in running someone else's business," Kartik said without doubt.

"Hang on! Are you planning to start your own venture?" another friend asked, shaking his head, trying to absorb what was being said.

"I'm not there yet," Kartik sighed. "But yes, a small company which I can take places." He gulped a big sip of his beer.

"I think I saw something like that on the notice board this evening," said Govind nodding his head sloshedly.

Kartik gripped Govind's shoulders.

"Do you remember what?"

Govind burped and smiled foolishly, "I don't even remember my name right now." The friends laughed jocundly.

Realizing that he was too drunk, he waited until morning to stroll to the notice board on his two feet.

His eyes scanned all the notices on the board before landing at the low-left corner where the high-right key of his success story was pinned. He called the gentleman late in the morning. The person, soon after the initial conversation, emailed him several questionnaires to assert his marketing skills. Being thrilled at Kartik's responses, they fixed an appointment in one of Kolkata's restaurants and scheduled it a week later.

Kartik walked in well-dressed, shoes-polished, clean-shaven, with neatly-combed hair and a folder in his hand. But he wanted his confidence to do the talking.

A medium built, mostly-black-haired-but-a-grey-streak man, appearing to be in his late forties walked in. The grip of his handshake spoke a lot about the mettle the man possessed. "Let me introduce myself once again."

Both got seated.

"I'm Ajit Khurana. I have worked with India's top IT companies for over twenty-three years. Technical expertise is my forte, and soon the world is going to know my name."

Kartik's confidence appeared timid in front of his to-be-mentor's.

"I have developed a tool that can revolutionize data-warehousing."

Pride filled Ajit's face. He continued, "It needs extensive marketing, so it creates a stir it deserves."

Kartik nodded, "Where do I fit in? How can I help you?"

Ajit joshed, "I want you to plan and drive the entire marketing campaign."

Kartik was stunned. "Sir, I'm a fresher. It's too much responsibility, and I'm not sure if I can handle it."

Ajit looked at Kartik, unblinkingly.

"I like your honesty, but you sounded more confident on the phone and in your answers. You seem to be unsure about your potential now."

"Absolutely not, sir. I could have chosen to join any bank or insurance company had it been about money instead of passion. But from what I hear, it's twenty-three years of your sheer excellence. Coincidentally, that is my age."

"I too could have picked up a marketing agency had it been about money," Ajit interrupted. "But I want someone young who feels the same rush about my dreams. For whom it's about proving oneself to the world."

Kartik's chest broadened. "I will not disappoint you, sir. Please give me this job."

"Again, young man. I'm not here to offer you a job. I'm here with a question." Ajit thumped the table lightly. "Do you want to carry the burden of my dream along? Do you want drown in my passion?"

Kartik heaved and answered with utmost certainty. "Yes, sir. It's my mission as much as it is yours."

Ajit smiled and said, "After your MBA, take a vacation at my expense as the joining bonus."

"I'll join next month, sir. Vacations can wait."

"No! After two years of hardship, you need a little break before a lifelong series of hardships." Ajit said smiling. Kartik nodded.

"I always wanted to go to Goa. I think I'll go there in August around my birthday."

"That's great then," Ajit said. "What a coincidence! I'll be in Mumbai in August with my family to attend my niece's marriage. Why don't you come to Mumbai and then drive to Goa? It's worth an adventure. I'll ask my secretary to make the car and hotel bookings."

"You don't have to bother," Kartik hesitated at his offer.

"As I said, your vacations are at my expense." As if remembering something suddenly, Ajit gently slapped his head. "We haven't talked about your paycheck."

Before Kartik could speak, Ajit completed the statement. "It will be incentive based. Your paycheck will have different figures each month, based on your performance. I will be more than pleased to sign a higher amount each time."

Kartik smiled smitten by the zeal Ajit exuded. The ambitious young man was surely looking forward to kickstarting his career under Ajit's leadership for it to shape up as he always dreamt it would.

♦

The train halted at the Malad station. Kartik hired an auto to reach Govind's place just to discover that he'd been diagnosed with tuberculosis the evening before.

"I called up your home last evening, but you had left by then," said a feeble Govind.

Kartik patted his shoulder. "We'll go some other time. Take care."

"I'm sorry. I spoiled your programme."

Kartik patted him again and told him to rest. He moved towards the phone in the living room. Very few people could afford mobile phones that time. Ajit could, Kartik couldn't.

"Hello, sir. It's Kartik Brar here."

"Hello, young man. Hope you've reached Mumbai?"

"I have sir, thank you. But my friend is unwell. I called to request for the cancellation of my reservations."

"That's not done. You must go even if your friend can't."

"Alone would be no fun. I'm confused."

Ajit sighed. "Well! Spending time alone at times does wonders. Your journey shouldn't be affected by such reasons."

"Fine, sir. Yeah, I think I'd still like to go."

"Very well," Ajit said. "My secretary was unsure about your Mumbai address, hence the rental car will arrive in the hotel I'm staying at. It's where my niece is getting married tonight. Come late at night and drive to Goa..."

Ajit was interrupted momentarily by a sweet girlish voice; all Kartik heard was 'Dad'.

"As of now, get some rest. You must have had a long journey, and another lies ahead."

Ajit gave him the hotel's address and hung up. Kartik slept at Govind's house for the rest of the day so that he'd be ready to drive in the night.

He boarded a Mumbai local once again, being convinced that the vacation he deserved must be enjoyed. After all, he was heading to Goa to get high and jump into action that didn't require Govind anyway.

The action had been missing ever since he post-graduated. A girl Ruchira of his class had struck perfect wavelength with his idea of quality time. Though his friends addressed her as his girlfriend, he kind of let that be rather than give away details of their arrangement. Kartik always found the concept of a 'girlfriend' highly annoying, and when he witnessed his friends with their girlfriends, that further sealed his philosophy. It's not that he was commitment-phobic, but just too particular about his breathing space. Ear-piercing long phone calls, chocolate day, teddy day, rose day blah-blah day was beyond him. He wasted minimal time on anything that wasn't about his career, and never let anything ride on him. He cherished his male friends' get-togethers where he could be himself, let loose, talk rubbish, and drink without being stared at.

Ruchira was a little miffed over his missing the campus placements, but then he didn't appreciate the discussion as they weren't supposed to be discussing each other's career choices. And when Kartik Brar, one of the top five of the batch, picked up something called DataMagica (which was googled by everyone in class but none found a hit), their parting was far from tearful, and rather cheerful for her.

He had reached the hotel a couple of hours earlier, and even the barat had just arrived, so he was strolling lazily to kill time. He looked down from the lobby to the garden area where the marriage function was being held.

After some time, the bride was escorted to the altar where the groom was waiting for her anxiously. Kartik was watching through the glass door from half-a floor above.

Kartik's eyes were aimlessly wandering and froze on one of the bridesmaids. She was walking right next to the bride wearing a golden lehenga and was one of the most beautiful girls he'd ever laid eyes on. Sparkling blue eyes, snowy white glowing skin, and an electrifying smile with nearly perfect curves held Kartik's attention for the next one hour and thirty-eight minutes, scanning her from head to toe at least a hundred and thirty-eight times. Kartik's experience adjudged that it couldn't be more than twenty-one years since this fairy had fallen from paradise.

Kya malai se lagti hai yaar, haath lagane se hi maili ho jayegi.

Kartik followed her every movement – cheering the exchange of garlands, light dancing, giggling with other girls and rolling her eyes in a peculiar cute fashion when a groom's friend approached her. Another thing his experience could ascertain – definitely a metro girl.

Itne variety ke soaps hai market mein, maili ho bhi gayi thodi si toh kya hai.

A lady wearing a violet sari walked over and whispered in her ear. She turned swiftly to the lady annoyingly. Just then, a hotel attendant came over to Kartik, realizing that he'd been waiting since long. Kartik averted his gaze to inform the attendant that he was waiting for somebody. And when his gaze returned, she had disappeared from the party.

Kartik made a face and walked to the payphone in the lobby to call Ajit.

"Your car for Goa should arrive shortly. It's an SUV. I'll come over to the reception when they reach." Ajit hung up.

"Who's going to Goa?" Ajit's wife Alka asked, draped in a violet sari.

"I'll tell you later. We have some serious issue to address right now."

Ajit and Alka were standing in their hotel room where they were being confronted by their beautiful blue-eyed daughter Sahana, dressed in a golden lehenga.

"How could you even think that?" Sahana asked, angrily folding her arms.

"Every girl needs to be married one day. I'm doing exactly what I should be doing?" Ajit answered.

"I'm in my second year of college; just twenty years old. Why is my marriage your only concern?"

"Because you have no interest in academics. You're just wasting your time partying and loitering around with your loopy friends. So if I have a good marriage proposal for you, then why not!" Ajit insulted Sahana in his signature style for being aimless in life.

"Just because I'm not a nerd, does not imply I have no right to enjoy my youth."

"Well, the family I zeroed in for you are even bigger party animals than you. You'll get to party all your life."

"Enough dad. You're getting offensive."

"Then cut it short."

"I'm not getting married and that's it."

"You are and that's what it is."

Ajit's phone rang. The car had arrived. "Yes, he's in the lobby. Needs to drive to Goa." The agent also told him the car number, and Ajit repeated it to confirm. It caught Sahana's ears.

"I'll be at the lobby soon," Ajit hung up.

"Alka, we need to meet the groom's parents tomorrow morning in Mumbai itself. Hope Sahana puts up a decent show. Prepare to be a good wife, daughter-in-law and mother, if nothing else."

Sahana's face turned red in anger, being disgraced so apparently by her father.

Alka followed Ajit out of the room, trying to resolve their conflict.

Go Goa Gone

Sahana moved to her luggage hurriedly and packed some clothes and cash in her backpack. She picked a blanket too. She secretly crept out of the hotel from the service delivery route to reach the parking and spotted the car that was all set to zoom into Goa. And what luck, it was unlocked!

Being an SUV it had enough space for her to hide at the back. Sahana covered herself with the blanket.

Kartik greeted Ajit in the hotel lobby, and the agent also walked up. "Sir, the car is open and is parked on the left-end."

Kartik took the keys, gripping them hard with excitement. He had no idea that on this trip, where he had set out alone, he'd be joined by a beautiful co-traveller. Kartik took charge of the steering wheel. Sahana edged when the car roared. She lay straight while the car steered out of the hotel so that she would remain unnoticed. Slightly palpitated, slightly confused and severely offended, Sahana had run away.

The ride to Goa was slightly bumpy, long and tiring. Kartik, who loved driving otherwise, was mildly irritated of having to travel alone and with music being his only known companion. 'Red Bull' was doing the trick to keep him going. Sahana conked out peacefully after a few kilometres, the slow music serving as a lullaby. They reached Goa at 10.00 a.m.

"Good morning, sir. We're pleased to have you," the attendant at the hotel greeted him as he opened the door of the car. Kartik greeted him back and stretched his arms to relax his stiff joints.

"Are you alone, sir?" Kartik nodded and picked his backpack on the adjacent seat, yawning.

As he reached the gate of the hotel; he was alarmed by the attendant's shriek. "What's the matter?" asked Kartik.

The attendant was puzzled and was pointing at the car's back door. "Are you sure you're alone, sir?"

The car door was pushed from the inside. Kartik shook his head hastily to believe the scene in front of his eyes.

A high-heeled sandal came out, followed by the hem of a golden lehenga. Kartik's heart missed a beat recognizing the lehenga he had seen over a hundred times the previous night while fantasizing the legs underneath them. Soon she emerged out wholly, causing the missed heartbeat to bounce back. She picked up her belongings and the attendant stood there stunned, though still doing his duty. "Good morning, ma'am. We are pleased to have you."

The gatekeeper whispered into Kartik's ears. "Sir, wives never allow their husbands to holiday alone."

Kartik returned to his senses with that statement. He whispered back. "Not my wife. But I like your idea; holidaying alone is a bad option."

She walked up to Kartik recognizing his checked shirt she'd seen a few times the previous night. She said smiling, "Thanks for the ride. You drive very well."

As she walked past him, the breeze of cold air brushed by him. He turned on his feet under the whirlwind of her aura, walked behind her to the reception, captivated in her allure.

She was enquiring about available rooms and trying her luck with discounts. Kartik surfaced his reservation papers and collected the keys to his room for the next five days. He still stood there until she was given a room. She had cash to last for just two days. Breakfast was complimentary.

Kartik saw her again in the breakfast area; he was still in a state of disbelief. Okay! Now there was good and bad news. Good being that girl appeared exceptionally tall to him in the morning when standing close, just an inch shorter than him; after removing 4-inch heels, she had come down to 5'7". That was just apt. The bad news was that the long plaited hair had reduced to neck length. There's no way she could chop them herself in the car. It was fake for sure.

She took a seat right in front of him. "Hi, I haven't thanked you properly. Thanks again."

Kartik smiled. "Pleasure is all mine. Had I known, I would've ensured your journey was more comfortable."

"It was great; I slept most of the way. I like your choice of music."

He wasted no time to open up. He extended his hand, "Kartik Brar."

She shook the hand warmly. "Sahana. Nice to meet you."

She withheld her last name realizing that he must be important to her dad; else he won't have arranged a car for him.

"So, were holidays a last minute plan?" Kartik asked.

She laughed lightly, "Yes, kind of."

"Are your friends joining you soon?" he asked.

"No, just me. How about you?"

"Well, I was ditched by a friend in Mumbai. I'm alone too."

Not a bad idea to piggyback. Firstly I save money; secondly I'll be safe as I can always use my last name as the defence in case he turns harmful, Sahana thought to herself.

"It's not safe for a girl to be roaming around alone here," Kartik said as if he had read Sahana's mind.

"Is it?" she heaved a sigh artificially.

"Yes, of course."

"What should I do then? Stay in my room?"

"No!" he exclaimed, "That's not safe either."

"Oh!" she gulped. "Should I go back?"

"No. Now since you've come, you should see the place."

"I don't get it," she frowned animatedly. "You just said it's not safe," she paused. "Alone."

He nodded, "Don't be alone," he blinked. "Be with me."

She smiled blissfully. "Thank you so much. It's so hard to find good guys like you these days."

He smiled stupidly.

They shared their room numbers and Kartik briefed her about the plan for the day, which was to head to a beach in the evening after a nap.

Back in Mumbai, Sahana had left a note that she was at her friend's place in Mumbai. She was safe and would be emailing daily, which she did. Ajit refused to pay any heed to her foolish blackmail, dropped back an email stating no one was worried and that she was free to party as long as she wanted. Ajit and Alka travelled back to Delhi a day later as scheduled. Ajit blocked Sahana's credit and debit cards too.

Kartik and Sahana walked along the beach; Kartik was really impressed with her style. She street-shopped to be rightly dressed for the beach and wore a loose jumpsuit. Kartik had his camera in his hand all the time to capture the beauty of Goa.

"This is beautiful," he said.

"Yeah!" she inhaled the sea breeze. "That's the only thing Delhi doesn't have."

"Delhi!" he smiled, "I guessed so."

"Where are you from?"

"Amritsar. Studied engineering from Delhi and followed by an MBA from Kolkata. Work brought me to Delhi again three months ago."

"That's impressive," she raised her brows. "You're quite a scholar."

"Not really. But yes, investing sincerely in the early years of one's life lays the foundation for a lifelong career," he said and she nodded, impressed again.

"How about you?" he asked.

"Ahhh! Nothing as studious as yours." She smiled. "I'm a second-year student of Philosophy at Delhi University," she seemed more proud of her credentials than him.

"Miranda?" he asked.

"How did you guess that?"

"Just a vague guess." He smiled sheepishly.

The rest of the evening was spent in light-hearted banter. Kartik stole many glances at her. He paid for the dinner.

◆

The next day, late in the morning, Kartik was lazing around the poolside. His eyes dazzled watching Sahana walking towards the pool in a red swimsuit with her legs draped in a yellow sarong. Sahana caught him staring and he quickly averted his eyes. She threw the sarong aside and jumped into the pool; he gazed at her again as he wouldn't be caught while she was gracing the water.

In the evening, they went around the city to visit a few other tourist destinations. Kartik was determined to mingle better with the beautiful co-traveller.

"So, apart from studies what keeps you busy?" he asked while idling on the beach.

"Well! Studies too don't keep me busy. I'm accused by my father of having an aimless life." She said while applying sun-block lotion on her arms.

"Your aim could be different from his."

"No, he's right. I have no aim truly."

He was confused. "What are your plans in life?"

"No plan," she looked at him. "I see my dad working tirelessly for his goals; he's exerting himself too much. I want to save myself that trouble."

He smiled and said. "You didn't read your father right in that case. Reaching your goals is an accomplishment that brings happiness beyond compare."

She replied smiling, "One thing I know for sure today. All great minds think alike. You sounded so much like my dad."

"On that note, I should shut up. Anyway, it's not the right place and time for philosophies," he exhaled air from his mouth upwards to blow his hair. "So, do you have a boyfriend?" Kartik came to the point.

Sahana was caught by surprise and shook her head to answer in the negative. "I wouldn't be holidaying alone if I did."

Kartik narrowed his eyes. "It's a little hard to believe. I always thought all Delhi girls have boyfriends."

She laughed lightly. "I did have one last year for about two weeks, but then..."

"Then?"

"I mean, all boys really want just that one thing."

Kartik smiled mischievously. "They were not consulted when earth's rules were being laid down. So it's not actually their fault," he took his first step to flirt.

Sahana wasn't very surprised; she was used to boys trying their luck every now or then. "Well! If something wasn't done right when the earth was being created, it doesn't mean girls should pay the price a million years later too."

"It's nothing like paying the price. It's being as natural as nature wants you to be."

"I'm so used to such cheesy statements; trust me they don't work with me."

"Then let's make it simple," he passed naughty smile. "What works with you?"

Sahana sat slack-jawed for a considerable amount of time. "Does that mean it has to begin from the mouth?" Kartik came forth in full colours. Sahana zipped her mouth instantly and rolled her eyes. She acted very pricey on day two as well.

But in reality, Sahana found Kartik very different from the boys around her in Delhi. His handshake had nothing to do with flaunting a Rolex; conversations weren't pompous about the last foreign vacation, and there was no annoying, expensive car key swirling on the index finger.

A checked shirt and a pair of jeans, a Timex sports watch, a sense of pride only about his merits, a simple boy trying to impress a girl using his wit, and most surprising to her – the only boy she ever met who was handsome but appeared completely unaware of the fact.

The next morning, she was notified by the receptionist about the checkout time. Sahana said she'd get back with an answer after breakfast.

In the breakfast area, she was a little disturbed to see Kartik trying to flirt with another girl. She shamelessly sat on the same table. Kartik was surprised.

"I thought you left today. You had booked the room for just two days, right?"

"I don't remember saying bye."

She gave the other girl a side look; that girl left saying, "Catch you later."

Sahana looked at him with a little disgust after she left. "You guys are all the same. Characterless!"

"Excuse me?"

"You change sides like *thali ka baingan*."

"My dear," he paused, "I'm on a vacation and not in a spiritual workshop to enhance my character."

"Still, there should be some loyalties."

He narrowed his eyes, "Were you jealous when you saw me flirting with another girl?"

Sahana trembled, "No, and why should I be? But I really thought you were nice."

"I'll still, be nice. I'll drop you to the bus stand and then flirt with some other girl."

Sahana said fumbling, "I'm not going back today. I wanted you to take me to the market to withdraw some money."

Kartik informed her about ATM in the hotel lobby. "No, the money is with my father's friend. He's a jeweller."

Kartik agreed to take her there. Sahana sold her gold earrings to get some cash. She extended her stay for next three days hoping to get a ride back to Mumbai in Kartik's car.

Kartik dialled that other girl's room from the reception.

"Sahana yaar; I'm taking this girl Monica out today. In case of any…"

His sentence was cut short, "How could you?"

"I seriously thought you were leaving today."

"But I'm not. And anyway, you have an SUV, up to eight people can fit in it."

"Are you crazy? Don't you get the hint? Why do you think I am taking her out?"

"Holy smokes!" she exclaimed, "Is that the only thing guys have in their minds?"

He blew air in his hair again, "I'm not here to discuss Mars v/s Venus, but to relish Mars lying on Venus."

Sahana stood quietly and clearly unpleased. She turned to leave for her room as Monica arrived. Kartik felt bad for some reason that he couldn't put in words.

Monica held his arm, smiling naughtily. Kartik passed a weak smile though, realizing the simplicity of Sahana behind her sexy clothes. And for sure, Sahana was a thousand times more attractive. The impact Monica had on him for a few moments evaporated as soon as he saw Sahana again.

"I need you to excuse me, but I patched up with my girlfriend," he truly wanted Sahana to be his Venus for the trip.

Monica said a few choice words and walked away stomping her feet. Kartik waved goodbye to her and flew to Sahana's room and knocked.

"Come let's go. Goa is waiting," he said.

Sahana smiled, "I promise I won't disturb the two of you."

Kartik's raised his left brow, "Only two of us are going."

"Why, she found another Mars?"

"No, I think you're hotter, Venus."

Sahana smiled broadly, "Good you realized that."

They left the hotel to go and explore Goa.

In the evening, they decided to go to a hippy party at the hotel's beach.

Sahana wore a halter-neck black dress; her white skin shone even brighter due to the contrast. With that, she unintentionally hit the final assault on Kartik's temptation.

"Can I buy you a drink?" Kartik asked staring hard. She waved no.

"Why?"

"I don't drink with boys."

"Bartenders are also mostly boys; so if you can drink one made by a guy, you can consider drinking with a guy too."

"Nice try, but it's still a no."

"I'm buying one from the same counter. So I'm at equal risk."

She turned to him rolling her eyes; he handed over the bar menu to her.

"Look here," he pointed at the menu giving her a naughty side look, "Sex on the beach?"

She passed a pressing smile. "One Virgin Mary please."

"And a beer for me please," he added.

As she took her first sip she said, "Happy?"

Kartik stared with little bewilderment, "Excuse me?"

"Happy?"

Kartik passed a sweet smile, "Happy since birth."

"Thanks. It's the first time a guy has bought me a drink."

"Really? Hard to believe that."

She nodded. "I never accepted one, to be honest. You're the first one who could persuade me," she smiled. "And thank you for being so kind throughout."

Kartik slid closer to her and whispered into her ears, "You should also consider being kind."

She sighed. "Just because you gave me a ride to Goa, you think you can have a ride on me? Do I look so easy to get?"

He shook his head. "But being optimistic isn't a sin."

"You sure have a way with words," she said raising her brows at the highly impressive pick-up line.

"And you sure have a way with looks," he said admiringly. "I always wanted to come to Goa, but I never knew that I'll end up seeing something better than Goa."

"On that note, your looking at that something else is very apparent."

"And still you've been with me since three days."

"Because known devils are better than unknown."

"Am I known?" He touched her around the waist and pulled her closer. She slid away gently and continued enjoying her drink while Kartik stared unabashedly.

"Can you please stop ogling me?" said a mildly annoyed Sahana.

"No," Kartik said on a dime. Sahana rolled her eyes and started walking away. Kartik jumped to walk backward, facing her. She struggled hard to stop blushing, but it was futile.

After a few minutes, Kartik made another attempt. "Do you dance? This is the least I can look forward to." She smiled and nodded. Her skills helped Kartik pick up some 'classy' steps.

◆

Day four was going on fine until evening time. Four guys approached Sahana on the beach, assuming her to be a foreigner, while Kartik was taking photographs some distance away.

"Can we help ma'am? You seem alone. Do you want to be escorted somewhere?" The guys said almost in chorus.

Sahana got a little scared as they stared at her shamelessly.

"I'm fine, thank you," she said stepping back. "*Aap apna kaam kijeye.*"

All four men surrounded her. Sahana was looking around for Kartik, but he wasn't in sight.

"Oh! You are desi," one on them said trying to touch Sahana's hand. She hit his hand away. "India has also started manufacturing goods of international quality."

The man at the back tried touching her waist.

Sahana was trembling out of panic. Her eyes moistened with tears of fear. Kartik came to her rescue just at the right time.

He pulled her out from behind; for a moment she assumed it was one of the men. "Leave me. Don't you dare!"

Her eyes then fell on his face. "Kartik!" she said and started sobbing. He asked her to step away and turned to the men.

"Excuse me guys, but you've got to behave," Kartik said.

"Don't lecture us. We, like you, were also looking for some fun."

"But not without permission. It has a very filthy word for itself otherwise."

"Relax," one of them patted Kartik's shoulder. "Everyone has their own tactics."

Kartik pulled his hand down, "I think it's sorted now. Please carry on and leave her alone."

"We thought she's alone. But seems we are too late," one of them winked, and they all walked away laughing.

Kartik walked to Sahana, who was still very uneasy. "It's alright now."

"Had you not come on time, or what if I had been here alone?" she said with a trembling voice.

"But neither happened."

"How can they be so shameless?"

"That was shameful for sure," he smiled to cheer her up. "Not their fault, you're so beautiful."

"Beauty is sure a curse," she was mad. "I just pray they all have beautiful daughters."

"Arrey!" Kartik's mouth dropped, "Having a daughter isn't a curse."

"But it will be for all the guys who don't respect women," she ranted in anger.

"See, all women can't be our mothers or daughters. We guys look for other relations."

Sahana finally smiled a little.

"And as for me, I would love to have a daughter someday."

"Interesting," she rolled her eyes in her signature style.

"But she has to come out of a hot mother," he winked and they chuckled.

Kartik didn't make any attempt to flirt with her that day after her experience with the men.

However, it was fated to be a bad day for Sahana. While lazing on the beach late evening, she accidentally drank a double-dosed cocktail. She was still dizzy while opening her eyes next morning. All she remembered was a spinning head and then collapsing.

She stared hard at the ceiling to get her vision right. She panicked and sat up crossed legs on the bed the next moment.

She looked around manically and felt marginally better to discover it was her room and all her clothes were on.

She covered her face with both her hands to calm her heavy breathing. After few minutes, she walked around the room and found a note on the table.

"Hey, hope you slept well and are feeling better. See you at breakfast @ 10. Kartik."

Her eyes filled with joyful tears as lips stretched in a smile realizing the values of the mischievous boy she was hanging out with.

"Thank you," she said very humbly at the breakfast table.

"No big deal; you aren't heavy to lift."

"But still thanks; I might have created a scene."

"No, you seem to be a decent boozer." They both laughed aloud.

"Thanks again."

"Enough," he said. "Consider saying something that would be more meaningful than thanks."

"Like what?" she narrowed her eyes.

"Happy Birthday."

"Is it your birthday today?"

"No. I'm just making it up," he passed a wary smile.

She extended her hand to wish him, "Wish you a very happy birthday. Treat on me today."

"You're late. I'd already planned to turn twenty-four in style this year."

"Twenty-four...hmm.... I guessed so."

"Yeah right, and you're twenty one."

"Twenty," she said and frowned. "Do I look older than I am?"

He knew these were the most difficult situations to deal with, "No, I mean...I'm not that great at guessing. When will you turn twenty-one?"

"On 25 December."

"So you're closer to twenty-one than twenty. I wasn't really off the mark," he said tongue in cheek.

She smirked, "Whatever, let's enjoy this 'twentieth' day of August."

Kartik had reserved entries for the beach bonfire party where some local band was to play all night long. The price was a little high, but Kartik thought it was worth an experience. The entry was only for couples, and he wasn't planning to go alone anyway.

It was an eventful party attended by a handful of couples. Until midnight, mirthful music had been playing with a lot of dancing around the bonfire. Kartik and Sahana also danced joyfully, coming closer, falling for each other with every passing song (but with a radically different mindset).

Later, some light music was requested by a few lovebirds to set the mood. They began to cuddle in each others' arms as the singer sang romantic folk songs.

Sahana felt a little awkward sitting next to Kartik, but he wasn't. For him, it was the perfect time for another and probably last attempt.

"Thank you," he whispered in her ear moving closer and his one hand at a little distance from her back.

"For what?" she turned her neck a little just to find his face very close to hers.

"For the beautiful time in this beautiful place."

"I should be thanking you rather; it was almost imposed company."

He shook his head, "Pleasure is all mine; I'll remember this trip forever."

"And imposed expenses too."

"Few things are priceless. And then you didn't eat much anyway."

She smiled, "I particularly wanted to thank you for yesterday. I still cringe thinking what would have happened had you not shown up on time. And I'm so glad they left so peacefully."

"Do you know what I told them?"

She shook her head.

"Simply that a lady shouldn't be touched without her permission," he moved his face even closer. He removed the strands of hair from her face, titillating her. "Do I have your permission?"

Sahana turned her face as he brought his lips closer; they fell on her cheek. He moved his hand to hold her waist, caressing it and engaged his other hand turning her face back to him. Sahana's eyes were cast down; she was hesitant, yet in agreement.

"I have never even hugged a guy," she said softly, hugging herself on the waist with hairs flying on her face.

"There's always a first time," he whispered near her ear.

She turned slowly to meet his eyes, "And why should you be my first time?"

He smiled being even more helplessly smitten with the beauty and wit of this dame. Her short flying hairs in the alluring breeze made him even more jumpy with enticement. "Ever been this late out with a guy, alone?"

She softly shook her head. He whispered again, "So first time?"

She nodded lightly.

"Ever ran away with a guy?" She smiled wide, and that answered.

"Another first time," he said amorously. "Ever felt like being with someone before?"

Sahana's smile shrank because that was a revelation of why so many first times had happened in the last five days. Despite Kartik's playfulness, she did see an adorable guy she was failing to resist. The first titling, the first spurt of restlessness, the desire of being without someone, first going weak in the knees. And that first craving for being hugged, touched and kissed. But how was she to say this? She just smiled in her heart for being lucky of being a little less impatient than him for sealing the moment with an imprint of the heart.

She turned her face once again when he tried to kiss her, though this time he pulled her close, and her turned face rested on his shoulder resulting in a gentle hug. He rubbed his nose in her hair, tickling her. She gently rested her hands on his shoulders.

"Shall we head back to the hotel?" he said amorously.

"Nobody will move from their positions!"

A sudden, harsh voice broke Kartik's thoughts and certainly of many around. The police had raided, thinking it to be a rave party.

Everyone began revolting at the allegation. The organizers of the event tried explaining, but the inspector was adamant. Men and women were split up and scrutinized thoroughly. Few were yelling at the police under the influence of alcohol, further strengthening police's suspicion. Organizers struggled for five hours to negotiate with the inspector and convince him that party was drugs clean. It was 6.00 a.m. when it was all finally settled.

Kartik ran to Sahana, "Let's rush to the hotel; we need to leave in another hour. I have a train to catch tonight."

She nodded, and they hurried to the hotel.

Sahana packed quickly and was in the lobby even sooner than him. His eyes were red from the sleepless night.

"I can drive for some time; you may want to catch some sleep," Sahana said when their car arrived at the hotel's gate.

"You can drive?"

"You can put me to test for a few minutes."

He gave her the charge of the steering. And after fifteen minutes when she turned to ask him how she was driving, she was amused to find him sleeping with his mouth open. Sahana smiled and continued driving for the next five hours without a break, to ensure they reach Mumbai in time.

Kartik woke up and realized they had travelled half the distance, and found Sahana extremely stressed. "Hey, thanks, yaar."

"You woke up? Can we afford to take a short tea break?"

Kartik turned his wrist to check time, "Yes, we can. But a short one."

She nodded.

After the tea break, Kartik took control of the steering and Sahana slept for the next three hours. Kartik drove very fast; there was only an hour left to reach CST when Sahana woke up. The car rental agent was there to take the car; the payment had already been settled.

Temptation realized

"Do you have a reservation?" Kartik asked when Sahana tried to get into the train as well.

"I had, but I lost that paper," she made an excuse.

"You remember the coach? PNR number?"

"No."

"How can you travel then? You can go to the booking counter there and check if there are seats and if not, get one for the next train."

She stood quietly, scratching her head. "Any problem?" he asked.

She appeared a little embarrassed and passed a hesitant smile. "I'm out of cash."

Kartik pulled out his wallet. "Don't worry about that."

They hurried to check if there was a tatkal ticket available, but they were exhausted too. Sahana was worried and her embarrassment grew. "Please, I have to go tonight. I don't know anyone in the city."

Kartik smiled no less than an angel, "Come with me in that case. We'll see what can be done."

She joyfully nodded and followed him. Kartik checked with the TC, but the train was full. The TC however suggested that she could buy a regular ticket if Kartik was fine sharing his 2-tier AC seat with her.

Kartik nodded his head, "That looks like the only option."

She smiled feeling relieved. Kartik stepped down from the train to get her ticket. Sahana, in the meantime, pulled out her mobile phone and switched it on for the first time in the last six days. She called her mother to inform her that she was coming back by the Rajdhani and would reach Delhi the next morning.

The train started soon. Kartik had an upper berth and other three seats in their space were occupied by a family. A young eight-year-old was in the adjacent berth. The family slept early and even pulled all the curtains. Kartik waited until 1.00 a.m. to try his luck one last time.

He moved closer to Sahana, who was sitting resting her chin on her knees deep in some thought near the wall. She turned to him instantly and smiled. "You aren't asleep yet?"

"No guy can sleep if someone like you is sitting so close to him in a cramped space," he whispered coaxingly.

"You haven't given up yet?" she whispered too. He shook his head.

"I think it will be rude if you don't consider being nice. We just have that moment missing from our trip," he said resting his hand on her waist and pulling her closer.

"Kartik, my name is…"

"Snow-white," he interrupted. "I always knew that was your real name," he moved his other hand over her hair. "And I think I should be rewarded with some of your charm."

"It's not the right place," she said restlessly.

"Leave that to me."

"You'll behave yourself."

He nodded instantly.

"Just two minutes, only hands and your eyes closed," she laid the rules.

Kartik couldn't believe what he had heard; his heart was dancing with excitement. He moved his wrist to set a two minutes alarm on his watch.

He pushed her to the extreme corner, with her facing the wall. He then took her shirt off, but let her tank-top be. He pulled a blanket and covered both of them together.

He moved his eyes around to confirm that everyone was asleep. It was almost absolutely dark; the only light was that of his watch that set his two minutes rolling.

His hand moved around her belly for a few seconds and gradually he dared to reach the core of his attention for the last six days. Sahana sat numb as his fingers went over her. After forty seconds of playing around over her tank-top, Kartik slid his hand under it. Sahana bit her finger to refrain from making any noise.

Kartik treated Sahana with utmost delicacy. The two-minute alarm beeped, and Sahana breathed easy. Kartik's hands were still resting on her chest. She tried to bring them down. He whispered "Another two minutes, please." She shook her head in refusal.

"Please. Didn't it feel amazing?" She drowned in his desires as this continued seven more times until she stopped his hand in the middle of the eighth two-minute alarm. So two minutes of agreed intimacy lasted for seventeen minutes. He followed none of the rules: he violated the time limit, his eyes were open, but he couldn't see her front that was facing the wall. He put lips on her neck and exposed shoulder.

He gently turned her around. Her eyes were closed, and she was moving her hand around to get hold of her shirt. He held her hands and pulled her closer and rested her arms on his shoulders. He leaned forward to kiss her; she turned her face away. He tried two more times, but she refused nonverbally. She opened her eyes after a minute.

He softly pushed her to the corner again, this time facing him. She shook her head. He set his watch on a two-minute alert again; she gently pushed him away, expressing displeasure over not following the time-limit. He kissed her hands to make her believe that he'll follow this time; she closed her eyes. Kartik removed his shirt and vest, coming very close to her, her bosom touching his chest. She sat frozen again. Kartik removed both her garments under the blanket to rest his eyes and body on her beauty. He started the alarm and in the next two minutes, he broke all the rules.

He stopped immediately when his watch dictated. He moved up to Sahana's face that she was hiding with her hands. He locked her one index finger with his and tried to pull, but she released his finger to keep her face covered. He then held her wrist to pull down her hand. He had to lug it hard.

Sahana's face appeared from behind her palms reflecting the crimson hue of mixed emotions with her eyes shut tight. Her breathing was heavy, and she was slightly shaking too. It took her a while to pull herself together.

And as he moved away, Sahana snuggled in the blanket turning to the other side. She hurried to put her clothes on. Kartik rushed to the bathroom. There arrived a station and he bought some juice for both of them. Sahana was still a little uncomfortable when he returned. He passed her the juice and sat close to her.

"Do you mind sharing your phone number?" he asked.

"Do you plan to date me?"

"It would be my absolute honour. But I can't date anyone. I've committed myself to my future, and I can't do justice to a relationship at this point in my life and career."

She smiled at his honesty and rested her head on his shoulder. "Then why would you want my number?"

"To catch up with you sometime."

"To buy me a drink?"

He rubbed his nose gently on her hair, "To get cozy with you."

She looked up at his face. "Do I look like that kind of girl, whom you'd call to get cosy with at your wish without feeling any need to commit to a relationship?"

"That's not what I meant," he turned to her and held her face. "All I meant was to ensure that you stay in touch and be with me until a time when I'm prepared for a relationship. I promise you'll be my first girlfriend."

Sahana's emotions filled her eyes. She put her two fingers over his lips and kissed them. She embraced him close, dropping some pearls from her eyes over his shoulders.

"You're very special Kartik. I'm not sure you'll call or not. But be assured, you'll always be remembered," she wept softly. "You are officially the first man of my life."

He held her close; he couldn't answer her. He had no answer. She passed on a feeling that was alien to him. He had never felt this heavenly before; it felt much greater than the nineteen minutes of intimacy. *What the hell is happening to me? Did she believe me?*

She relaxed her hug after a few minutes and rested her head on his shoulder. She fell asleep in some time. Kartik found no sleep that night; he kept looking at her beatific face. Just her face.

The train reached Delhi at its scheduled time. When everyone was preparing to disembark, Sahana said abruptly. "I've been told scholars always carry a pen."

He smiled and pulled out a pen from his bag to prove her right.

"And paper too?"

He shook his head.

She pulled his hand forward and wrote her number on his palm.

As they walked out of the train towards the exit of the station, an angry voice called her name.

"Sahana!" yelled her enraged father.

Kartik paled as Ajit Khurana stood in front of them. Alka calmed him down, "We can talk at home, please."

Sahana stood with her eyes lowered, Kartik's eyeballs almost out of their sockets. She stood scared; he stunned. She stood with her one foot over another, he wanting to put his foot in the mouth.

Ajit turned to Kartik. "What are you doing here?"

Despite shaking legs, Kartik managed to answer, "Well, we had seats nearby. So we were walking out together."

Ajit believed him; he had no reason not to.

"Please excuse me, Kartik. I'll see you in office in two days. I have a critical personal issue to resolve right now," Ajit said. Kartik nodded.

"Get inside the car, Sahana," he dictated. Alka held Sahana and they walked to the car. Ajit followed.

Kartik stood there for a long time; bulldozed. He raised his head to the sky and murmured a few slangs; he then opened his palm to see her phone number. He took a deep breath and firmly balled his fingers into a fist. He walked out of the station, slowly recovering from the aftershock of the bomb blast he just suffered in his head, heart and hormones.

Not with my boss's daughter.

Till they met again

Time glided even swifter than a jet for Kartik with only the certainty in life being the entry time at office, and not the exit time, leave alone meal times and leisure times. Kartik kept going no less than a warrior.

In October, DataMagica hit the market. Kartik made several initiatives to popularize the tool. His suggestions like giving a three-month free trial to potential clients particularly did wonders. He also persuaded Ajit to take a few risks like selling at a lower price and training the users at the company's expense. Subsequent licenses of the tool were purchased at the desired price that enhanced profits.

DataMagica received a great response. It was a service for data storage and business reporting for middle-sized companies primarily, at a much lesser price than established market products. Kartik also ensured that the tool gets published in all technical magazines and is noticed by potential buyers.

Ajit was simply amazed at the kind of ideas Kartik kept churning. He too helped Kartik in improving his presentation skills and etiquette. Kartik was improving with every passing month, and so was his paycheck.

With his increasing influence in the company and over the owner, his position was threatened occasionally. His age triggered jealousy and conflicts. Samar Gahlot, the finance head who brought in fifteen years of experience, was particularly miffed with Kartik's aura. Ajit always stepped in favour of Kartik, but diplomatically, reassuring his faith in the young man's potential, while applauding Samar's experience in his domain.

Life was moving in full swing.

Kartik was not pleased with the hustling-bustling city of Delhi. He, belonging to a smaller town, disliked travelling ever since day one. Staying in hostels was different, he realized. He had always lived close to the office to cut short his commuting time. By the middle of the second year of his career, he had moved into a two-bedroom apartment of his own on a bank loan and purchased a second-hand car.

He never found peace in Delhi; Amritsar was his only hope to have some relief. His only good times were with his family and the nonsensical booze parties with his childhood friends.

No girls, no vacations; Kartik worked tirelessly round the clock. Young, ambitious eyes never complained of being deprived of sleep.

◆

It was late September 2004 when all department heads were in the boardroom to review quarterly results. DataMagica had gone international early that year adding a lot of visas to Kartik's passport and frequent flyer passes.

"This is far more impressive than I could ever project," said an elated Ajit. "Thank you all for your efforts in placing

DataMagica on the map of the IT industry in less than two years." Everyone clapped. "And a special mention to be made of Kartik Brar."

The applause got louder while Samar made a face.

"Sir, a two-year anniversary calls for a huge celebration," said HR head Garima Varshney. Garima was of medium height and a slightly plump young girl with a gregarious personality and an ever smiling face.

Everyone supported her and insisted on a huge party with families.

"That's a great idea. Garima, please plan something grand," Ajit said and took his seat.

"Sir, you should suggest a venue. Most of us are outsiders," Garima said.

"Ahh!" Ajit sighed. "I'll ask my daughter."

Kartik smiled at the mere mention of Sahana. A few cherished memories flashed across his mind.

"Does she party very often?" Samar said.

"Until two years back," he smiled. "But then I threatened her that I'd get her married off if she didn't take her life seriously. But then she's my daughter, being a rebel runs in her veins. She ran away to her friend's house when we were in Mumbai for a family function, and returned home six days later."

Kartik suppressed his laughter while everyone else smiled.

"So it is not just us, you're tough at home too," Samar joked.

Ajit laughed, "Maybe yes. But it worked, and I too learned that marriage should only be discussed at the right time with this generation."

◆

Two days later, Ajit returned to Garima with Sahana's recommendation of a venue. Invitations were sent out to the entire board of directors and next level of managers. Families were invited specially.

The party was in the lounge of one of the top hotels. The entire team was impressed with boss's daughter's choice. Kartik was highly excited as he was going to meet Sahana after two years. A little hesitation also crept in, for he had never contacted her after that night. He was unsure about the impression it had left on her.

Kartik was sitting in the bar area when Ajit walked in with his family. All his bachelor colleagues were instantly attentive as the boss's beautiful daughter walked in wearing a stunning green party dress. The married ones too, though they could not do more than steal glances. Not their fault for it was a sight of perfection. Her hair had grown from a little below the neck to a little above the waist mercifully. Her persona seemed to have glorified further.

Pulkit, who reported to Kartik, was gazing too hard, sitting next to him. Kartik didn't quite appreciate that.

"Behave yourself. She's our boss's daughter."

"How does that matter?" Pulkit said.

"It matters. We need to be respectful towards his family."

"Huh!" Pulkit hushed his argument away. "What crap! And I'll respect her too," he stared harder.

"And she's a very good friend of mine," Kartik finally said.

Pulkit lowered his eyes. It's an unsaid protocol between boys that no one would try their luck on another's 'good friend'.

Kartik then turned synergizing all his six senses on Sahana. He started walking with a feeling of excitement and fear, fighting each other within him.

Sahana's eyes that were also searching around, fixed on him as he approached. She smiled warmly, overthrowing Kartik's fear. He returned the smile, and as his hesitation shrank, his footsteps gained momentum.

Sahana noticed what Kartik missed registering in the mirror; the wonder the two years had done to his personality. The transformation of a boy to a young man culminated into a perfect depiction of the mythological figure of the Indian male. Kartik looked even more charming with his killer looks coupled with a supernal smile.

Ajit very warmly introduced Kartik to his wife as a genius. Sahana smiled at her dad's admiration for him. Since Ajit knew that he had meet Sahana before, he asked him to introduce her to others.

"Long time no see," Sahana said when they moved away from her parents.

Kartik just smiled, "You want a drink?"

"I don't drink when my parents are around."

"Mocktail?"

She nodded. They grabbed their drinks and sat down to talk.

"So how's life, Sahana?"

"Good."

"You must have graduated this year."

"Yes."

"What next?"

She chimed with pride. "I'm preparing for MBA."

His eyebrows rose, "That's kind of a 360-degree turn."

She noticed his disbelief, "You think I can't make it?"

"Sure you can. And you will. But I wasn't expecting that answer."

"You must have been expecting 'nothing' as an answer."

"Not really, but maybe fashion designing."

They laughed lightly. Ajit's eyes fell on them. Strangely, they seemed like old friends catching up. But he didn't give it much heed.

"You never called me up?" Sahana said suddenly.

He scratched his nose and sighed before answering. "You're my godfather's daughter. No matter how much I wish, I can't call you to make out with."

She smiled crookedly. "Are you trying to tell me I'm the kind of girl a guy shouldn't call if it's not about making out?"

"Not at all. But I thought even if I'd call with the right intention, it will never be perceived that way. It has more to do with my impression on you."

She blinked her eyes, "Wow. Dad seems to have induced some classiness in you."

"He has enhanced it," Kartik said. "Someone else in his family had actually induced it."

They shared a warm smile.

"So, how's life at your end?" she asked.

"Going well. Too busy with work."

"That implies too much happiness, as a certain scholar told me two years ago."

"Not really. I mean the sense of achievement is very high, but I don't feel as happy as I did a couple of years back," he sighed. "I told you in Goa that vacation would have been perfect had I had an SLR camera," he paused. "Today I have it, but there's no time for a vacation. Maybe you were right, a goal in life stresses you."

She smiled back. "Take a vacation."

He shook his head.

Their focus moved to Ajit's thank you speech. Loud music started right after and the dance party kickstarted.

"Kartik," she smiled. "If I assure that your call won't be misunderstood. Will you call me up?" She paused.

He nodded.

"You may want my number again in that case."

He pulled out his cellphone, "This is my fifth handset in the last two years. I'm a gadget freak. Yours was the first number I ever saved. And same SIM is moving forward."

"Really?" she smiled emotionally. "Then I think you should dial that first number of your phone, which perhaps could also be the only number you never dialled."

Kartik again got that alien feeling watching her get emotional. He nodded smilingly and tried to switch the mood she was sinking in.

"By the way, you've become even sexier."

"Excuse me?"

"The dress is too decent," he paused, "but looks good on you."

She opened her eyes wide as Kartik flashed his rustic shade. "By the way, do you actually drink moonlight?"

"I'll tell dad to work on you better. Someone is still highly gross when it comes to girls."

"He may ask you how do you know?" he smiled mischievously.

She sighed, "That reminds me, hope you never told him?"

"What?" he freaked.

"That I ran away to Goa."

She seemed miffed, "What else?"

He shrugged his shoulders teasingly and smiled impishly.

She shook her head, "You're too much Kartik."

"You still want me to call?"

She nodded her head lightly, blushing sweet.

Coffee with Kartik

It was the Saturday after when Sahana received her much-awaited phone call from the yet unknown number.

"Hello," she said.

"Hi there."

She was happy as a child, "Kartik?"

"Yes, your highness." He smiled too. "Hope I didn't bother you."

"Take it easy. You can't keep up the act of finesse for more than two minutes."

"You should appreciate it has at least reached two minutes in two years."

They laughed.

"So what were you doing?" he asked.

"Struggling!" She phew-ed, "These graphs drive me crazy."

"Are you looking at our company's financial report?" he joked. "Well, they drive me crazy too."

Laughter again.

"No, these mock-test graphs. I'm sure they'll drown me again."

"You should know your strong areas and focus on them; since you have already appeared for the exam last year."

"I know. English is the only thing I'm banking on. I had some luck with data sufficiency, but data interpretation is a mess," she frowned.

"Hmmm."

"Don't you think so?"

"Well, that's the only thing that helped me to make it to IIM."

"That's a distant dream for me."

There was a short silence with same thing jumping on their minds, hoping the other one would say it first. Kartik finally did, recalling she was the one to make the first attempt at the party.

"If you want I can help you."

Sahana blushed and replied, "When?"

"Tomorrow late morning."

"Where?"

"You tell me."

"I'll text you the coffee shop details."

"Great then, tomorrow at 11.00 a.m. Sounds good?"

"Sounds perfect."

She wore a kurti with a loose patiala salwar, punjabi jootis and long earrings with her hair neatly plaited as she entered the coffee shop. Sahana surely had an essence of his soil that day, and it didn't go unnoticed.

After the niceties, Kartik asked her to pull out a mock test.

"You seem to have taken my suggestion about your dress seriously."

"Yes." She gave a pressing smile. "Particularly today, so that you can concentrate only on teaching me."

He raised the brow, "Not just looks, your words too are vibrantly rustic today."

They smiled before looking at the book.

Kartik's calculation skills were much faster than hers. She had been saying him to pace down almost throughout the session. She finally screamed, "Go slow!"

The others in the coffee shop turned at them.

"Sahana, you should keep your volume low while saying double meaning words in public."

Sahana stressed her mind to find an answer to that.

"Leave it. We can't study." She tried pulling her paper back.

Kartik calmed her down.

"See, for a pie graph it's really required to see from all angles, even before you read the questions."

Sahana turned the paper in several directions. Kartik rolled his lips between his teeth to avoid laughing at her, "That's not what I meant by all angles."

She looked up seriously, not realizing that she was being mocked at. Kartik then elaborated on various graphs in accordance with her pace.

They were almost done when there began a discussion over the coffee bill.

"No please. You paid many bills for me in Goa. Let me get this one," Sahana asserted.

"That's not happening. And anyway, it was my idea."

"But you came over to help me."

"My pleasure."

"But you might have had other weekend plans."

"Weekend plans? What does it look like?"

They chortled.

"No girlfriend?" she asked smiling, crossing fingers under the table.

"I'm a classic example of how people are unable to hold their temptation momentarily, and end up paying for years," he sighed and continued. "I'm in such a deadlock situation here. I promised somebody that she'd be my first but I can't ask her; I can't ask someone else either. Phew!"

She narrowed her eyes, "You seem to be regretting your promise. In that case, I am setting you free so that you can ask someone you want."

"No. I'm good. I anyway still don't have time on my clock, and a day on my calendar for a girl."

"You sure?" she asked.

He nodded.

♦

Then there was silence again for months. Sahana thought of letting Kartik chase his dream with full focus. He avoided her so that she'd focus on her studies.

It was March 2005 when Kartik's phone buzzed with Sahana's call. She had made it to a B-School in Nagpur and had enrolled for MBA in HR management. She wanted to treat him for lunch. He promised to come only if he got to pay the bill without any argument; she agreed.

They met as gleefully as always, and Sahana came to her point very soon. "I found a solution to your girlfriend issue."

He smiled.

"Your vow says I have to be first, but doesn't really say for how long," she paused. "So, you can date me for a month, or maybe for a week and then you can break up with me to move to the next one."

Kartik was perplexed. "And why would I break up with you?"

"Any damn reason. Maybe that you just don't like me anymore."

"And you'd believe me?"

She smiled sprightly. "If you can say it; I'll believe it."

"I can't say it."

"Can't say what?"

"That I don't like you."

"So, it implies..."

Kartik blushed, "It implies that you're all set for your MBA in HR."

She smiled askew.

Letters – 10 ml Love

That night Kartik kept tossing and pained his pillow to such an extent that it jumped out of the bed to save its life. Kartik finally pulled out Sahana's picture from his Goa album that he had secretly clicked when she was watching the sunset. He stared at it and it aroused different feelings: confusion, titillation, admiration and his alien feeling.

God gives courage to few right people at very wrong times. Kartik was that one right person God chose pretty often.

Kartik picked up his phone and typed out an SMS.

kbrar.asr@gmail.com, wrt 2 me whnever u need help with studies. Good Luck!

God also gives courage to few wrong people at very right times. Sahana was that one wrong person God chose even more often. She wrote an email to Kartik.

Sahana: *Just studies? U mean only whn I'm stuck in assignments? U r so kind always Kartik*

Kartik: *No, wrt to me otherwise as well. Abt place, college, frnds etc.*

Sahana: *Thanx. That sounds more of a frnd. I'll wrt whn I reach. Any tips for hostel life?*

Kartik: *Just enjoy. It's 1 exp to cherish. Bt b safe, don't jump coll wall lte nght.*

Sahana: *Ok, if u insist :)*

Kartik: *Take care. Best of luck!*

Sahana: *I'm nt gng to a war. Anyways thnx for ur wshes.*

Sahana: *Reached Nagpur safe and sound. Mom and Dad left this morning. Place is good. Hostel is reasonably clean, and only coolers are allowed, no AC. Isn't that an adventure already?*
My roomie is a Bong girl. She looks the bookworm types. Just shared a 'Hi' since mrng. not talking much. She has even marked a border in the room, must be diplomat's daughter. God, she stares like boys.

Kartik: *Good you reached safe, and already having an adventure :p*
Don't worry about your roomie, she must have had bad experience in a hostel earlier. Give her some time. you both will be friends soon.
And why the bloody hell if someone's staring it has to be attributed to boys?

Sahana: *You were right, she's been in hostel for 4 yrs already. How do you always knw so much abt girls?*
But she is much bolder than I assumed. She not only stares, but also smokes like boys. She does in little balcony outside the room and I've insisted on spraying freshner after tht. Chiii!

Kartik: *It's not abt girls or boys. Those who've been in a hostel and have not had a good exp with a roomie always draw a border.*
Smoking is bad, but don't complain abt her. Your room freshner shud suffice.

Sahana: *Hey! I've been chosen as Ms Fresher unanimously by seniors. My roomie ended third; she isn't even talking to me ever since. She's now even marking the border in balcony railing where we hang our clothes to dry. She's soo unfriendly. Chii!*

Kartik: *Oho Ms Fresher. Congratulations!! So you have a whole list of admirers in the college already.*
Don't worry abt ur roomie, you'll find many such in ur journey of life. Let her do her bit, she's just jealous of you.

Sahana: *Haina? Even I think she's jealous. But why? We aren't competing in any sense. I'm HR, she's operations. What's her basic problem?*
Anyways, howz life at ur end?

Kartik: *Sorry for not being able to wrt for two mnths, lot of travel and new customers. Life's busy, but no qualms.*
Howz it gng with ur roomie? It shud be settled by now.

Sahana: *Don't be sorry, I knw u r a busy man. I tried calling on ur bday but phone was switched off. I assumed you must have been out of India. How was ur day?*
I've started ignoring her as a problem. She actually jumps coll walls, She's just so...Chii!!

Kartik couldn't stop himself from calling Sahana up the evening he received this email. She pinched herself to make sure he was really calling her. They talked at length about life, and his birthday. It was his first ever long call to a girl. To his utter surprise, far from being tedious, it was rather delightful.

◆

A week later, Monday was a crazy day at work for Kartik. Five new projects were kick-starting at a same time; it was a hectic day rolling out the plans. Late evening, he walked into the meeting room where Ajit was awaiting the status. Kartik, after finishing his part, sank in his chair closing his weary eyes, and Garima walked in to discuss on team resources. Realizing Kartik had too much to do already, Ajit took over the conversation.

Kartik's ears perched hearing Ajit's words on clock awareness, "It's already 7.30 now, so we can only speak to the concerned people tomorrow morning."

Kartik opened his personal emails in a hurry. Sahana usually wrote at about 5 p.m. after her classes. Kartik blushed reading Sahana's email.

Sahana: *Hey, our skit won the first prize in the inter-college drama competition. I played the female lead. Many in the audience said that I look like Aishwarya Rai! Do I? I never heard that from you. Maybe they are just making it up. Had I, you would have told me. Right?*

A fatigued man was suddenly injected with life inviting unbelieving expressions of the audience around. When Kartik found four eyes scrutinizing his face, he haphazardly checked whether his laptop was connected to the projector.

The other two were thoroughly entertained at his nervousness.

"Take it easy, we didn't read anything," Ajit said jokingly.

"Nothing as such, sir," Kartik said as he closed the email.

"You never told me about your girlfriend," Ajit said.

"I don't have one, sir. How can I talk about a non-existent being?"

"Why?"

"Well, sir," Garima interfered, "he thinks he doesn't have time and a state of mind for a relationship; so why agonize anyone with his weirdness?"

Kartik fisted his palms under the table at Garima's useless repetition of his words about his personal life. He had told her that as a cautionary measure in case Garima had any interest in him. He wasn't very pleased with her echoing those words to Sahana's father.

She left the meeting after a minute.

"Sir, nothing of that sort. I'm a very simple person. And I'm a firm believer of woman liberation," Kartik said to repair his post-Garima's image. "She was being extreme."

"I know, few grapes are sour," Ajit winked, "You're frustrating her."

"No, not at all. Just a good friend. And I respect her a lot."

"That's impressive," Ajit said. "Or maybe it's this letter girl who you fantasise about."

Kartik sat quietly, giving no answer. Ajit would be the last person in the entire milky way (beyond a shadow of doubt) Kartik would discuss his fantasies of his letter girl.

Kartik: *So u act too? Multi-talented! Ignore ur roomie if u r unable to make frnds with her. Stay positive. But I'm so impressed with her jumping the walls!*

Sahana: *Don't be impressed! How come that is impressive? People these days have no hold on their desires.*

Kartik: *Arreee! Ask her how happy she must be. Now I think u r being jealous of her :p*

Sahana: *Cut the crap! Why wud I be jealous? And anyways jumping the college wall isn't my kind of thing.*

Kartik: *Yah! Yah! You would rather elope in a stranger's car when your dad mentions marriage :D*

Sahana: *You know that?? Well!! My dad arranged that car. I had as much right on it as you did.*

Kartik: *Oh! Oh! So u knew that. In that case u should have told. Ur dad arranged my room too ;)*

Sahana: *Well! It's all luck. This Bong had it as her destiny to be my first roomie :P*

Kartik was bombarded with official work in the following months. Diwali vacations followed, which took Sahana to Delhi and Kartik to Amritsar. The next email she got was in the middle of December.

Kartik: *Hi there. Howz life? & howz ur roomie?*

Sahana: *Life's good. We won the inter-college dance competition too. Roommie is okay, nothing grt. I have many friends now, so her being hostile doesn't bother me anymore.*

Kartik: *Wonderful, that's the best approach. Dance too, but I'm not surprised this time. By the way, how r your studies going? U NEVER write about that.*

Sahana: *They are alright. Dad will get my MBA degree in another 1.5 years. I'll be your colleague at DataMagica then. Happy?*

Kartik: *Looking forward to it.*
Happy since birth ;)

Kartik travelled a lot taking DataMagica places, in the true sense of the word. His conflict with Samar also grew visibly. He kept belittling Kartik's proposals for overall organization growth and not just marketing. Samar would erupt whenever Kartik tried to make a suggestion on improving the handling of finances.

For Kartik and his loyal friends at work, Samar was always a crapehanger whose energies were centralized on negativity.

The company grew and they moved to their own newly constructed office of seven floors. Kartik for obvious reasons was very popular among girls at the office.

His trips to Amritsar became less frequent; his mother came at times to live with him to ensure his well-being. Back home all his childhood interests also started getting married off. His mother zeroed down on a few girls for Kartik, but he declined outrightly, though he attended their wedding parties to dance mirthfully with his childhood friends.

◆

Four fully boozed friends – Happy, Honey, Jolly and Bobby – under the starry moonlit sky in old Amritsar were remembering a girl next door who drove away as a pretty bride a night before.

"Razoo," said Honey and burped.

"As if you loved her," teased a drunken Bobby.

"I did," Honey cried artificially. "She was in class nine and I in ten. I truly loved her then."

Jolly shook his head cinematically. "I never knew this." He hiccupped. "What went wrong?"

"Went wrong? Someone's evil eye fell on my twentieth first love," said a swinging Honey. "My only mistake was to send this bastard Happy to talk on my behalf."

Beer spurted out of 'Happy' Kartik's mouth, "Bro. Trust me I went with your proposal, but she held me real firm, and so lovingly."

He crossed his hands around himself and laughed wickedly.

"It's not fair to upset girls. I too fell in love with her for the next seventy minutes." Everyone guffawed.

"We all loved Razoo," Bobby declared.

"She was no less than an angel," Jolly hiccupped again. "She could read in your eyes what was running in your mind."

"And always granted it without asking," Happy added.

"You bastards," Honey pointed a finger at them while his body shook. "You're mocking at my true childhood love. My true feelings for fifteen days of class ten."

"Just for fifteen days? I had feelings for Razoo every fifteen days," Jolly laughed.

"Mine was every week before I went away from home nine years back," Happy fuelled Honey further.

Honey's pointed finger at Happy was now shaking, "You scoundrel, you'll know how it feels when your girl will also be taken away by someone!"

Happy faked shivering in fear.

"Chill, bro. She was for each one of us. We all have a feeling of loss today," Bobby patted Jolly's back.

"Cheers to Razoo!" the boys said in unison.

A possessive MBA intern

It was an evening in April 2006 when all the senior associates gathered in the big hall in the company's basement to hear the new management structure.

Official announcements on positions were being made as the company was planning to go public. The position of the Chief Finance Officer went to Samar, Aman Sinha was announced as the Chief Technical Officer. And most applauded announcement of the evening was Kartik being declared the Chief Operational Officer. Marketing, HR, and Admin were to be under him. Ajit withheld the Chief Executive Officer title and remained the overall boss.

Samar fumed at the announcement since as per protocol, if the CEO is not in office, the COO would be the ultimate boss. Ajit calmed him down stating it would never happen. But can anyone see the future?

With time, Ajit had discovered the ravenous nerve of Kartik. His greed for a glorifying career was lucid in all his actions. Ajit knew which strings were to be pulled and when to get the best out of him. Ajit had also started paying him higher incentives on sales. Kartik's salary was a highly confidential matter of the company. Ajit played his card of giving the second most influential post of the company to him officially to keep him running faster and thriving harder.

It was a great day for Kartik as the same morning he'd received the delivery of his brand new car.

He went home excited, only to find out that his cook wouldn't be coming. He had no option but to rustle up something himself. He dialled a special number, kept his phone on speaker and started cooking.

"Hi darling," he said.

"Hi, dear. What were you doing?" A female voice answered.

"Missing you, what else?" Kartik said playfully. "I have two pieces of great news for you."

"Wow."

"The first is that our new car is here and you'll be the first lady to get a ride."

"I'm already looking forward to it," she said joyfully.

"And another is that today I've been officially been announced as the COO of the company."

"COO?"

"Leave it. I've been promoted; to make it simple for you."

"God Bless you!" she paused. "So are you getting a raise as well?"

"Why do you always ask about my salary?"

"Well, your Papa only gets happy when there's a salary hike. I can't relate to your COO, head, toe, blah blah."

"Maa, you're impossible. You are such a mood spoiler," Kartik was vexed.

"Mood spoiler! For heaven's sake Happy, use this charm on some pretty girl and give me a friend in the family. You men have sucked all the colours out of my life."

"There you go again, you're getting fanatic about it."

"You'll be twenty-eight soon; start thinking about planning a family."

"Mom, I called to give you good news and you're talking rubbish."

"Allow me also to call all our relatives and give them the good news."

"Phew!" he sighed, "I'm disconnecting the phone now."

"No way. Listen to me," she paused. "Tell me what kind of girl do you want?"

Their discussion lasted for a few minutes and he finally gave in.

"Give me a year and we'll talk about it," he said.

"But should I not know what kind of girl will catch my boy's eyes?" she asked smiling.

Kartik stood silent and a face that had caught his eye about four years ago flashed in front of his eyes. No other face ever since then had won his attention; he was still truly captivated by her charm.

"Good night, Maa. We'll talk later," said Kartik. He felt life was good.

◆

The next day, while driving to office, Kartik saw the post office's red mail van while waiting at the traffic signal. He smiled recalling a game of his childhood, where they would cross fingers and make a wish watching a mail van; then observe silence until they'd see a black car for that wish to be granted. For some reason Kartik did cross his fingers and looked around; a big black car crossed the road right then, even before he could make a wish.

Ajit requested Kartik to come over to his cabin.

"I have a weird task for you, and I'm afraid you can't say no," Ajit opened the discussion.

"Let me know, sir," Kartik replied humbly.

"We have an MBA intern joining today; who has to be made to feel important," Ajit sighed animatedly.

A luxurious car stopped at the gate of the office; a high-heeled lady in a business suit started walking towards the reception.

Kartik's knitted his brows. "Sir, anyone can take care of an intern. I have many other important tasks at hand."

"I know Kartik. But she needs to sit with top management so that she can flaunt it in her college."

She took an elevator to reach the seventh floor where top management's cabins were.

Kartik had by then realized what wish has been granted by mail-van-black car combination, without spelling the wish. There was a knock on the door.

Sahana entered the room smiling, and her eyes sparkled seeing Kartik. They greeted each other. Concealing their excitement and keeping their faces straight was as tough as it could get for two longing hearts.

Soon, all three of them walked out of Ajit's cabin and Sahana was introduced to the rest of the staff. While all C*Os of the company had their cabins at the corners of the floor, the rest head of departments sat in big cubicles in the middle.

"This is Garima, our HR head. You must have met her in the party last year," Ajit said. Sahana shook her head. "Didn't Kartik introduce the team at the party?"

Kartik got a little nervous, "I couldn't get hold of many of them at the party, they were so engaged dancing."

"I see. No problems. Do that now," Ajit smiled at Kartik and moved back to his cabin. Kartik then took Sahana around and introduced her to all the major associates, except Samar.

"By the way, you didn't write to me that you'll be doing your internship here?"

"Surprise!" she replied smiling.

Sahana's excitement diminished a tad as she learned that Kartik would be travelling for the next two weeks.

Sahana had to work closely with Garima, and to ensure she felt important, she accompanied the team to all discussions related to the HR department. Garima was very cordial with Sahana and guided her well in areas like recruitments, staff welfare, conflict resolution and people management in general. But what didn't go down well with Sahana was when during one coffee break after a week, Garima opened up with her and admitted having a crush on Kartik.

Sahana restricted her mingling with Garima after work. When Kartik returned and each time he came over to Garima's seat for a discussion, Sahana who sat next to her passed visibly unpleasant expressions to him. The forementioned continued for another week.

"Hi Garima. How're you doing?" Kartik came over to Garima's desk smiling warmly.

"Great. How about you?" she replied jovially.

"I have this urgent task for you. But before that, I'm sorry for always throwing emergencies at you."

"It's my pleasure. And if it's not an emergency I can handle, then I'm not important." Her smile broadened. Kartik laughed lightly, unaware of the fuming Sahana.

"I just forwarded you an email where a female team-member has accused her lead of being biased towards guys in the team. I want you to confirm allegation before we take any action."

"Oh, that's bad. Let me get to it straight away."

They checked the email together as Kartik grabbed a chair between Garima and Sahana. She hurried to the fifth floor with a team member wherefrom the project was executed.

Kartik turned to Sahana then, who pretended to be busy but was actually annoyed. "Good morning," he said politely.

"Good morning," she replied without turning to him.

"Doesn't seem to be a good one for you."

She did turn finally, "It is."

"Are you mad at someone?"

"Not at all. And even if I am, you shouldn't bother yourself with less important people around."

His eyebrows rose, "You're certainly not one of them."

Kartik's phone rang. It was Garima. He answered.

"Refrain from speaking to the project lead; you may just want to confirm with few more female team members."

He paused to listen to her, "Exactly my dear. You're such a genius."

He hung up.

Sahana said abruptly, "She reports to you. Whatever you'll tell her stands as an order. There's no need for you to sugar-coat it."

He blinked to believe. "We all work together, Sahana. And creating the right working atmosphere is very essential."

"I know that. But that doesn't call for being unnecessarily sweet. You can really be less mushy. Consider giving bathing in honey syrup a miss."

"Mushy? Honey syrup!"

"Precisely. 'Yes dear,' 'had you not been around.' Such lines sound so filmy."

"Are you trying to tell me my management style isn't appropriate?"

"It's not your management style in question; but your selection of words which is diabetically sweet."

Kartik was a little shaken; he did get the core issue but was thoroughly confused on how to handle it. Garima returned to Kartik's rescue after giving instructions to junior HR, and Sahana again passed weird expressions while they discussed the matter at hand.

After noticing her unfriendly expressions for a few days, Kartik finally brought it up with her in his cabin. "Do you have any problem with Garima?"

"No."

"You don't look very happy with her?"

"She isn't my friend."

"But she's a great HR manager. You'll learn a lot from her."

Sahana's eyes opened wide, "You seem really impressed."

"Yes, I am. She's a friend and an outstanding employee."

"I'm sorry to have caused discomfort to your friend," she gave a wry smile.

"Sahana, you need to grow up. It's an office; you must behave nicely. You can't make your dislikes be so obvious. It disturbs the harmony of teamwork."

Sahana sat still. "Trust me, dear, you're just starting your career, don't burden yourself with hard feelings," he paused. "And it anyway doesn't suit you."

"What do you want me to do?"

"To smile, chill and bubble," he asserted. "And do exceptionally well in your performance and return as a full-time HR manager after a year. And above all, spread positivity. That is what your personality is all about. The others should also know how spirited a person you are."

Sahana's smile returned, and triggered Kartik's too. "And if there's anything I can do to make it better for you, please let me know."

"Maybe you can take me out for coffee," Sahana cleared his confusion over her displeasure. "You should treat me better."

Kartik almost blushed. "It's an office, Sahana."

"Maybe after office."

"Ajit sir won't appreciate it."

"Doesn't matter."

"It does matter to me."

"And only to you. You're the only one creating a fuss about it."

"Sahana, grow up."

"Kids drink milk; coffee is for grown-ups." She said as she rose from her chair. "And I think it should be a wilful invite."

She walked out of his cabin leaving him speechless.

The rest of the day Sahana tried to make up with Garima and showed more sincerity about work. Early in the evening, she got an SMS, "*After off 2 late 4 coffee; dinner?*" Sahana smiled.

Sahana commuted with her father to office. She made an excuse of a friend's birthday and stayed back. She waited until 7.30 p.m. for Kartik to finish his work.

"You work too late," Sahana said while they walked towards the parking lot.

"I'm leaving early today for you."

"How sweet!"

Sahana took a seat, and Kartik smiled as his promise to his mother to be the first lady in his car got shattered so winsomely.

"So where should we head to?" he asked.

"You tell me. You must have some favourites around here."

"You won't like that. It's not high class."

"You need to stop taunting me with the high-class remark. I've had enough of it."

"You're getting so cranky these days."

"Because you're testing my patience." She said fisting her palms.

Kartik turned to drive, "Okay. Let me pick then; good food for sure."

She smiled, and they had a good time. Kartik dropped her back home stopping a few metres ahead and asked her to call when she entered the house. She did.

The importance of
being Sahana

Sahana's spirits lifted manifolds at work from the next day onwards. She also conducted few pieces of training for new joinees on communication skills; it was her forte for sure.

Kartik also devised a plan to ensure Sahana felt important for the company and special for him. He allotted fifteen minutes daily to discuss her HR section, which though could be avoided, but shouldn't be. Sahana wasn't very pleased until fifteen minutes were made thirty. Kartik made time for the evening's coffee by shortening his lunch-time.

For two weeks, the meetings went pretty well. In ten minutes, they wrapped up the work related discussion; the rest of the time was spent talking about everything under, and even above the sun. Sahana mostly preferred listening to Kartik's hostel life and MBA experiences. She also talked about the NGO she was associated with that worked for kids, and how much she adored kids.

Sahana noticed Kartik's peculiar way of moving his pen when he was thinking. He held it horizontally with his little and index finger giving an upward thrust with the two middle fingers as if counting two; and then a seesaw and another count of two.

Another thing in office was Kartik's alternate Friday hang-out party with his friends in the pub nearby. Sahana wasn't very surprised to discover Kartik being the most notorious one and pulling everyone's leg.

Miffed with the sugary formal decency of their coffee meetings, Sahana added a pinch of spicy indecency. Before the meeting she headed to the restroom just to unbutton her shirt's button, and hide it with the file while walking towards the COO's room. Kartik was very tempted to bring it to her attention, but he just could not do it. He was sure it was not deliberate, but it did play around with his thoughts. Soon he realized that someone like Sahana couldn't have made that mistake. Whenever he'd seen her around office, the button always behaved itself.

It was during one such meeting at the end of her second month of the three months of internship that Ajit walked into the cabin.

Kartik stood up to greet Ajit. He wondered about Sahana's open button. Sahana whose back was to her father seemed nervous. Kartik astutely engaged Ajit in giving a file while she quickly buttoned her shirt and turned smilingly at Ajit.

"Good that we are all here together, Dad. I have an important thing to discuss."

"Important?" Ajit teased.

"Yes." Sahana raised her shoulders, "It's about my reputation at my college."

What kind of reputation would an 'only-culturally-active' student have?

"Then for sure it's unimportant," Ajit joked.

Sahana passed a rueful smile. Ajit laughed and held her shoulder, "Tell me, ma'am, what can we do?"

"That sounds better." She smiled. "I've promised that someone from our company will come over for a guest lecture this year. And it has to be a good guy, not just anybody."

"Ahaa," Ajit said. "I'll come in that case."

Sahana's smile shrank., "Of course you can come, but it's an MBA college, and there would be stream-specific questions. Your experience is rich but still you're MS in Computer Science and not an MBA."

"Hmmm," Ajit said thoughtfully, "Then I'll ask Samar to go."

"Chiii," Sahana said instantly.

"Sahana!" Ajit said shocked. Kartik laughed out lightly.

"I'm talking about my reputation and you are thinking of sending Samar!" Sahana said with mild irritation.

Ajit sighed again and looked down to think. Sahana turned at Kartik passing a nano-second long wink.

"I'll go, sir. It'll be a good opportunity for me as well," Kartik said hastily, to avoid another wink.

"You sure?" Ajit asked.

"Very much," Kartik confirmed.

Sahana smiled and passed him a nano-second wink again. Kartik was frightened; his reputation mattered a lot to him. He didn't appreciate Sahana's stupid act. He even slightly regretted his coming so far with her. *If just a wink can give me shivers, how can I even dare to think of talking to sir about us? And why is she so dimwit always?*

◆

Ajit was hosting his birthday dinner five days later. Alka as always kept it a homely affair, making all his favourite dishes.

"It's your luckiest day of the year," Sahana teased Ajit at the dinner table while the food was being served.

Ajit laughed lightly, "Every dog has its day."

Sahana playfully slapped Ajit's hand, "Oh, when is Mumma going join us from the kitchen? It's so hard to resist the food."

"Will take some time, I'm expecting three more dishes," Ajit said gleefully.

Ajit's phone buzzed with a few birthday wishes. Sahana sat resting her one hand under her chin and staring at the kitchen door.

Unconsciously her other hand started playing with a spoon, an upthrust at a count of two and then a swing at another count of two.

◆

Three days later Ajit spoke to Kartik before leaving for Europe.

"How is Sahana doing at work?" Ajit asked.

"Very well, sir. Her excellent communication skills are helping many."

"Glad to know that," he paused. "But please ensure she doesn't get too involved. I do not want her to join the company."

Kartik was confused. "But why? Usually, people love their kids showing interest in their businesses."

Ajit smirked. "Sahana's a delicate darling. It might just be a temporary phase; she isn't accustomed to working hard."

Kartik stood quietly as Ajit continued, "And I have plans for her so that all her interests, tantrums, and expenses are taken care of. I plan to get her married as soon as she completes her MBA into a reputed business family of the city."

Kartik said as he listened to his boss, "Sir, she may have some other plans for her life?"

"Thankfully my daughter doesn't have a boyfriend. My wife keeps a close eye. She just has some stupid girls as friends, which is manageable. I'm sure she won't run away this time," he paused. "And you know what the best part is? The guy has seen Sahana around in family parties; he's very keen on her. What more could I ask for? She gets a life she's used to and a husband's love." Ajit smiled blissfully.

Kartik battled hard to pretend being unaffected.

"Please take care. It's anyway just two more weeks," Ajit said while Kartik stood there realizing that he met none of Ajit's expectations for his son-in-law.

"Have a great trip, sir. We need your expertise to kick start BI consulting. I'll manage the rest."

"Yes sure, once the technical details are final, you need to take over."

"Gladly."

As they walked out of Ajit's cabin, their eyes together fell on Pulkit, who was staring at Sahana. It angered both, yet Kartik wanted to save Pulkit any major trouble and reached out to his pocket to buzz him. Pulkit then did something that couldn't be pardoned. Sahana dropped a pen and bent to pick it up. Pulkit's eyes dared to dive into her shirt.

"Pulkit!" Ajit called out sternly.

Kartik turned at Ajit and stiffened watching him so enraged. Ajit moved his eyes, signaling Pulkit to come to his cabin. Kartik followed.

"I want your resignation in the next ten minutes," Ajit instructed Pulkit.

"But why, sir?" Pulkit said shaking.

"You dirt bag. You draw your salary from me. How dare could you forget your position before eyeing my daughter." Ajit's face was red in anger.

"I wasn't looking at her in a bad sense," Pulkit pleaded.

Ajit finally thumped his fist on the table, "I don't want your resignation. You are fired. I'm nice, and that doesn't mean you guys go out of control." Ajit snapped his finger and asked Pulkit to submit his I-card.

As Pulkit left, Ajit turned to Kartik. "Make sure he doesn't get any benefit out of the company. It will set an example for anyone who dares to do that again."

Kartik was thunderstruck and he stood motionless for quite some time. Eventually, he nodded and walked out.

"Kartik, please help me. I promise I'll never do that again," Pulkit pleaded. Everyone around stood up to see what the ruckus was about.

"I'm sorry man," Kartik still in shock, "but sir's word is the last one."

Pulkit sobbed for a long time before walking out of the door with heavy feet. Kartik stared at him with dry eyes.

"What happened?" Sahana asked standing next to Kartik.

Kartik panicked and moved two steps away from her, flustering!

A choice he made –
Beginning of the end?

Kartik was thoroughly disturbed ever since that incident. Sahana's smiles and gestures were making him more doleful. He avoided her and did not even make eye contact. Sahana was clueless about the sudden change in Kartik's behaviour, but he was doubtless about his choice.

Having failed to withstand his ignorance, she stormed into his cabin. "What is your problem?"

"I'm very busy right now, Sahana. Please leave."

"You can't talk to me like that."

"If you bug me, I would have no other option."

"What's wrong with you? Did I do something wrong again?"

"Even if you do, neither one of us can dare to point it out."

"Please Kartik, don't make it so difficult."

"Can we please talk later?"

"When?"

He sighed. "After office today."

She began to leave, "And Sahana...."

She turned back to listen.

"Your shirt's button is open, please take care; you're in office."

She stood fazed. Kartik didn't even raise his head to check her expression. He dived into his laptop, ignoring her completely.

After office, they went to a park nearby and talked on the bench.

"What's wrong Kartik?" she asked.

"There's nothing wrong, but you need to know it's an office. You have to behave in a certain way."

"I did behave myself after we talked. I should be complaining about you treating me like everyone else at the office."

"And that's my biggest mistake. You're far less important; I should keep my priorities right."

Sahana was offended. "That's insulting."

"I'm honest."

"To hell with your honesty," she spat out.

Kartik lowered his head and locked his fingers in his hair. Sahana slid closer, resting her hand on his shoulder. "What exactly is wrong with you? We need to talk."

He took a deep breath. "Tell me what do you want out of me?"

"As if you don't know? Why test my patience beyond the limit?"

Her eyes went moist.

"I gave you four years; you are three years elder...you're the guy. It's high time for you to make that move. I can't live on that letter deal forever; we need to take our bond forward."

Kartik's thoughts jolted with Sahana's on-the-face confrontation; there couldn't be any other blow to worsen the conflict between his mind and heart. He battled for long to give the answer sent forth by his mind.

"I'm sorry Sahana. But that's not happening."

Tears rolled down as claws of his merciless words nipped her delicate heart, "Please don't say that."

"Your father has made me what I am today. I'm sorry, but I can't fool around with his daughter."

"Fooling around? For heaven's sake, don't disgrace our relationship."

"We have no relationship. And we'll never have one. I don't plan to spend my entire life with a girl like you. We can't be anything more than friends." He seemed to be in no mood of mercy.

She still hoped to shield her bleeding heart. "Girl like me? What's wrong with me?"

"Sahana, we come from different worlds. I may be infatuated by your beauty, but surely there isn't any feeling beyond that."

"What are you trying to tell me here?" Sahana gushed.

"A clear message to please stop throwing yourself at me. You make me highly uncomfortable. I can live with you behaving like a mistress in the company, but bloody hell, stop behaving like my girlfriend. Stop ogling at me."

Sahana sat devastated; she pulled her hand back from his shoulder. What Kartik didn't know was that it was not her hand but his soul that was retreating.

Her tears also froze due to the setback her life had just suffered. A dream of years butchered in minutes, heartlessly. She pushed herself up and walked away, wordlessly.

Kartik burst out crying after she left. He had never felt that timid and helpless ever. He had achieved success due to his excellence; the only thing he wanted out of destiny had been refused to him for not being rich and high-class as Ajit would expect Sahana's partner to be. He opted not to compete for it either; he wanted much more out of Ajit than his daughter. *I can't afford any conflict with sir; he's very protective about her. He can go to an extent of firing me as well. And should I feel guilty? I didn't break any promise or breached her trust.*

He made a clear choice of basking in the glory of being one of the nation's youngest COOs. He wiped his tears and assumed it would settle in a few days.

It wasn't a break-up after all.

What worst would happen if one silly letter doesn't arrive in my mailbox daily?

The world would certainly not come to an end if I don't get to see the most beautiful face of the world.

I'd lived for myself exclusively and matters of heart have always been beyond me.

Kartik managed to make a mental note of the lines he needed to chant to himself daily to deal with the feeling of sudden emptiness.

Sahana didn't come to office the next day. She, however, called Garima and thanked her sincerely. She left for Nagpur a week later to complete her studies.

It wasn't only her dream for four years, but perhaps his too. But his dreams of a much wider span had ultimately taken over.

Kartik's life began losing all its colours gradually. He grew irritable and less social. It took him a long time to convince himself that no one on the planet was waiting to be a part of his life anymore. No emails, no messages, no calls to make him feel special.

The battle with the pillow at night continued, but no longer out of the tickling feeling, but heart-stabbing ones. He was dejected and so as to avoid addressing that emptiness, he dived even deeper into work and kept away from the country.

The Business-Intelligence Consulting attempts also kicked-off successfully. DataMagica grew even larger in just three months. A man once known as the debonair was now called arrogant, rude, and selfish in the office gossip circles. There circulated many rumours about his change of attitude – 'he had a break-up', 'he's unable to handle', and 'success has gone to his head'. None true, but neither false either.

His friends at work believed the last one to be true and were convinced that the only thing their COO cared about was his own growth.

◆

Childhood friends still managed to get hold of their dear buddy on his Amritsar visit. "What Happy, don't you miss us or home anymore?" Bobby said.

"Rajoo went so all interest in city dissolved?" Honey teased, and all laughed but Happy.

Bobby kept a hand on Happy's shoulder affectionately, "You okay bro?"

"Yes," Happy said briefly. "Just work."

"Happy is too busy printing notes," Jolly said jokingly.

Happy nodded agreeably, "Remember what rich guys at school used to call us? Poor pants."

"Hey," Honey said with a baffling smile, "It was their low thinking. Attempts to pull you down because you were way too bright." He patted Happy's shoulder, "Get over it."

"Pieces of dirt used to walk around intimidating us just because they jumped out of a car and us from a rickshaw." Happy gulped a big sip of his beer, "I'm far over it. But yes, I want to make big money," he opened his arms wide. "And now more so since I have already paid a price in a way. So big big money, big big dreams."

The other three looked at Kartik in confusion. He was perhaps high they thought, but being bullied at school by a few guys never faded from his memory. He bravely always answered them back, but the acrimony they threw at him, made him a maniac about earning huge bucks and repute.

Honey made an attempt to change the topic, "Leave money! Let's talk girls. How are the chics at your office?" Bobby encouraged the question. "We are counting on you to get us Delhi girls."

"Shut up guys!" Happy again did not seem amused, "They are my co-workers. I'm not supposed to look at them lustily."

"Outside office Happy, outside office. Just tell us how lucky a bastard are you these days," Jolly said grinning.

"He's a born lucky bastard," Honey added teasingly, hoping to cheer Happy up.

Happy looked at them listlessly for a while, "I need to go." He tried getting up with swaggering feet. "Talking about girls is such a waste of time. They've always been a waste. I don't need to get lucky there. I don't care if they hate me or dislike me. I need to make a grand life. So much work to do; I want to keep rising higher and higher." He finally managed to stand with shaky legs, "and if something tries to distract me, I will cut that portion out my life. But next time I meet those rich guys, they should look poor."

"Happy, do you think being in such tender age they meant what they were hurling at you? They were also stupid," Bobby said assertively.

"Whatever, I want to be rich and successful. And it's no crime," he said curtly.

"Don't lose your niceness, my friend. You won't need money when it comes to winning hearts," Honey chaffed his arm.

"I don't want anybody's heart." His eyes were bloodshot and gestures went cinematic, "They better keep it to themselves if they want its safety. I'm not responsible or answerable to anyone for damage. Did I ask for it? Did I offer mine? No, right? A big no! So why should I be guilty. Didn't they know my ambitions are my only religion? What were they thinking? If at all they were thinking." His senses were truly drowned; not in that moment under the influence of alcohol, but affected by ill-influence of few delusions of life. Carrying a grudge of being teased at school for being a poor-pant, brought him so far from the actual richness of survival. Giving justifications to oneself was not ceasing for Kartik.

Friends looked at him with worry as he walked with staggering feet on the path of life. Happy's life was conceivably full of ambitions, but his friends felt wonderful about themselves for being happy. Less money and more smiles made them look more worthy. More money and no satisfaction made Kartik looked merely worthy of pity.

◆

It was the four-year anniversary party of DataMagica. The same venue, same ambiance, same gathering and the same enthusiasm. No matter how much Kartik wished to have a glimpse of her one last time perhaps, to see her smiling evidence of her moving on, Sahana didn't turn-up for the celebration party.

Kartik sat alone in the bar, not even drinking, while the others were torturing the dance floor.

Alka came over coughing lightly; something had got stuck in her food pipe. Kartik sensed the urgency and got some water for her.

"Thank you Kartik," was the first thing she said as soon as she felt better.

"You should have some juice."

She smiled and accepted, "Why are you sitting alone? It's your hard work's celebration as much as Ajit's. He mentions your contributions very often."

"I'm not that great. He's too modest with his appreciations."

"Oh, please," Alka fluttered her palm. "He's anything but modest when it comes to sharing credit. He doesn't even lend a penny of appreciation easily." She smiled. "Ask me."

Kartik laughed lightly.

Alka's phone rang. "Hey, Shona...all well. We are missing you at the party." A pause. "Yah, everyone has come."

I know what that question meant.

"Everyone is having great fun." *I'm not. Hey please, correct yourself. I've been nice, no?*

"You know he's always super-thrilled for his company; DataMagica is almost his second child." A pause and clenching of teeth, "Shut up! He can't even dare to want a second wife." Kartik smiled interpreting the obvious remark darted from another side of the call.

Ajit walked over while Alka said goodbye, "Good night Shona."

"It's Sahana," Ajit said, "Don't behave like her silly friends."

"Shona sounds cute," Alka said.

"Anyways, is she alright?"

"Just alright. Hope she comes back home soon."

"And why are you here?" he asked Alka. She explained she had wanted some water.

"You were coughing and came running here instead of asking me. Both you ladies behave like I'm invisible even when I'm around. Thank you for not considering me as family anymore."

"You were talking to few people, and it wasn't a big deal," she tried to pacify her annoyed husband. "Family begins with you."

"Yah yah." Ajit tried rolling his eyes in Sahana's style.

"No, it goes like this." Alka corrected him rolling her eyeballs Sahana's way. They both laughed lightly. Kartik too smiled seeing her parents' fondness for her.

Ajit nodded, "Come let's go join the others." Alka nodded and started walking. "Kartik, come along," she said smiling. Alka smiling angelically reminded him of Sahana. It was the first time he noticed that apart from the blue eyes and excessively whitened skin, Sahana had inherited her facial features from her mother.

"Thanks for asking, ma'am. I'm fine here though," Kartik returned her smile.

Ajit asked, "Anything wrong, Kartik? You seem to be tense these last few months. No work suffers, but you appear very vexed," he gently chafed his shoulder. "Take a break for a few days."

Kartik smiled weakly, "Thanks for your concern, sir, but I'm alright."

"Take care, don't work too hard," Alka said smiling, reminding him of another otherworldly face of this world.

After they had walked away, Kartik rolled the eyes in Sahana's style. Closest of what all three of them could get.

Nagpur blues

It was late November 2006 when there was an email from a placement cell coordinator Sagar, requesting confirmation of the date for the guest lecture in their college; Sahana was cc-ed.

Kartik peeked into his calendar and replied instantly, confirming the Saturday after two weeks.

Kartik reached Sahana's college in Nagpur well-dressed to leave the right impression. He was escorted by Sagar, a few more students and the faculty members.

All he hoped out of the day was one glimpse of her.

It was a huge auditorium, accommodating over four hundred students. Though the speech was for Operations and Marketing students, others flocked in hearing that one of the country's youngest COOs had graced the college with his presence. Few girls scurried in, having learnt that the COO guy was drop-dead handsome too.

Kartik made his presentation highly interactive, summing up all his experience and expertise. He added an extra flavor of witty humour to enhance the stature of Ms Khurana.

His only disappointment was that the particular attendee was missing from such a huge attendance, to whom all his efforts were targeted. He darted his glances in all directions – near, far, far away. Sahana anyway wasn't hard to find; she shines out distinctly. Kartik still delivered his talk with an outstanding tenacity of spirit.

Later a few students flocked him with additional questions; it was obvious that Kartik eyes were searching for someone and he wanted to avoid any more queries.

"Are you looking for me?" Sagar asked humbly.

"No, I have something to hand over to Sahana Khurana," he replied.

"Oh!" Sagar made a quick call to Sahana and turned to Kartik. "You can give it to me, I'll pass it on."

"No, I need to do that in person."

"Come with me then, she must be in the girls' hostel."

Kartik was pleased to stroll around in college, remembering his young days seeing the students playing, chatting, a guitarist singing circled by fondly listening friends, and a young couple sitting on the bench and giggling.

They reached the girls' hostel. There was a basketball court just in front of the hostel. Kartik sat perpendicular to the hostel facing the court while waiting for her. Sagar walked back to him after talking to the watchman.

"Just wait for a few minutes," Sagar informed him.

Kartik nodded and pulled out the parcel from his trolley bag that Ajit had passed to him. Kartik waited a long while and Sagar continued attending to him very courteously.

"Thank you for coming over," Sagar said.

"My pleasure," Kartik replied.

"You know Sahana's miffed at me. She confirmed you'd be coming during her internship itself, so I didn't ask her before reaching out to you. Right after the mail, she came looking for me and didn't want to bother you with that silly request and asked me to rollback. And while we were talking, your confirmation arrived." Sagar said smiling, "Thank you, sir, for honouring our institute."

Kartik nodded.

Kartik's eyes were looking at the hostel expectantly. He, after about half an hour, saw a girl on the second floor coming to her balcony donning fluorescent orange pajamas. She pulled the bedsheet to cover the railing of the balcony as if using it as a curtain. She sat down on the floor to hide herself. After about ten minutes, she rose up and slid the bedsheet to the corner. She then picked up a freshener and sprayed it in every possible corner of the balcony. Kartik's neck straightened; most likely that was Sahana's room, he thought.

Kartik was proven right in another few minutes. Legs walking in the balcony wrapped in those fluorescent pajamas, marched up to him.

"Where's the parcel?" she asked Sagar in an unfriendly tone.

"It's for Sahana. Why did you bother?" Sagar replied in the same tone.

"I'm just returning a few of her favours," she smiled aslant, "Give it to me."

She extended a hand to Kartik.

"Well, isn't she in the hostel?" Kartik asked politely.

"Princess is unwell," she said sarcastically.

"Oh! Does she need a doctor?"

"Maybe, but you're MBA. We heard it today."

"Did she hear me too?" he asked.

"Not sure, and anyway, she's in the HR wing," she opened her fist. "Please. I'm not her spokesperson. Give it to me, I'll pass it on."

A boy spoke from behind Kartik, "Learn to be a little respectful, Fish Curry. You're getting very phlegmatic nowadays."

Kartik turned to see a tall, stout guy standing with both hands in his pocket. Sagar greeted him as Prez. An abbreviated form of President, of course only of the college.

"Keep out of it, Prez," she bellowed.

"Don't return anyone's favour, favour me and be paid," he extended a Marlboro packet to her, she passed a wry smile and picked one.

"Sorry for her misbehaviour, Mr COO," Prez said.

Kartik gave her the parcel.

"And this too, Fish Curry." Prez extended a roll of papers to her.

"Love letter?" she asked with a crooked smile, giving chills to Kartik.

"I'm not that stupid that I'll hand that over to you," Prez answered instantly. "This is our final skit."

"Why do I remember her saying that she isn't interested?"

"Fish Curry!" he extended the Marlboro pack again, "Just do what's asked, and keep out of the rest."

She pulled both rolls of paper and that of tobacco.

"Few guys are just so shameless," she said staring.

"And few girls are just you," Prez said staring harder, and then jerked his eyes funnily, asking her to leave.

Kartik returned to the bench after everyone had left. Sagar wanted to drop him till the gate but he wanted to spend some more time in the campus. He removed his coat and hung it on the bench.

Kartik again waited for a glimpse of Sahana. Finally, he texted her being impatient, *"can u plz come over to meet? I m waiting."*

He got no answer.

Prez and Sagar returned again after an hour with twelve more guys to play a basketball match. Kartik busied himself hearing the double-meaning slangs boys were throwing at each other. He smiled sparingly, recalling his college days; being six feet tall, he used to be a good player at the game back then.

It's been a while I've spoken to any of my friends; I don't even return their calls. I didn't even call Gobind on his birthday this year. I'm losing out so much on life chasing my ambition. It seems that is all I have with me now, he thought.

It was a close match; Prez had the ball close to the final minute. Another boy yelled at him clapping hard, "C'mmon Prez, get the goal."

"It should be a glorious win."

"Glorious enough to pull the second floor out of the blueszzzzzz."

Prez dunked the ball into the basket, making his team win. A loud cheer did pull many to the balcony, but not the one desired.

Prez continued bouncing the ball and aiming at the baskets even as the other boys started walking out of the court. He had been observing Kartik looking at Sahana's balcony and smiling watching their game. Prez spoke out loud, spinning ball on his index finger, "Mr COO! Match?"

Kartik looked up, expressionless for a while, and then smiled. He pulled out his tie and folded the sleeves of his shirt. As he walked into the court, Prez passed a crooked smile and bounced the ball towards him. All other guys gathered outside the court cage to watch; few more eyes peeped out of the girls' hostel, but not the blue ones yet.

Both Prez and Kartik played well. To everyone's surprise, Kartik played not only defensively but also made a few skillful attacks. Prez wasn't a fool either; he gave Kartik a good run to save his baskets.

Prez took advantage of Kartik's divided concentration between the game and the balcony. But despite his split attention, Kartik gave Prez a tough call.

Prez was soon flummoxed with the kind of game Kartik was playing. Not desperate to win but unwilling to lose; not breaking any rule yet pushing them to the extreme; neither for fun nor for a run; just venting out some frustration on the ball; Kartik's turmoil of his personal life stood barefaced during his game.

They stopped when both of them were dead tired, breathing heavy, holding their knees and sweating tremendously. "Well played, Mr COO."

"Kartik Brar," he said wiping sweat from his face using his shirt's sleeves. "I have a name."

Prez too cleared his sweat using his wristband, "I thought you'd prefer being addressed with your title."

Kartik stepped closer to him, "My achievement can't eclipse my actual identity. And thanks for today's match."

Prez smiled askew, "Another one?"

Kartik smiled, "Some other day."

Prez spoke abruptly while Kartik was walking away, "Mr Brar, you're wasting your precious time sitting on this iron bench." Kartik turned sharply, "She isn't in the hostel."

Kartik narrowed his eyes, walked closer to Prez and murmured, "None of your business."

"For sure. I was just trying to make it easy for you," Prez said humbly.

"Thank you," Kartik gazed hard at him, and turned to step out of the court. Everyone left the area after a few minutes.

Kartik kept sitting there for another one hour. He called her three times, and before he could for the fourth time, she switched off her mobile.

Kartik finally left losing all hopes of being forgiven or understood.

◆

Kartik shot a few emails from his BB to get hold of a phone number. He dialled that Swiss number the first thing when he reached home.

"Hello, Am I speaking to Ruchira Banerjee?" Kartik said.

"Yes, who is this?" she asked.

"Kartik Brar, we were at IIM."

After a little silence, "Yes, of course, I remember." An awkward silence again. "So, how's life?"

"Nothing great, you tell me. All settled?"

"Yes, I got married last year. We both work in Switzerland."

"Congratulations. Glad to hear that."

"Thank you. So, what made you call me?"

Kartik cleared his throat, "I called to say sorry."

"Sorry?" she was confused. "For what?"

"For being a jerk, for behaving emotionlessly, and behaving as though I have just one organ in my body," he choked. "I'm sorry, you were probably nice. It's just me who thought that life was all about achieving success, that being on top is the ultimate happiness. I never thought I'd end up being so shallow, so displaced, so lonely."

She thought through before answering, "Don't feel so bad about it. Even I never had any such feelings for you; it was when I met my husband that I discovered that it is love that is the most satisfying feeling in existence. Don't feel so guilty, we both behaved equally callously."

Kartik tried to calm himself, "It's so great to know there are men around who make their ladies feel proud of themselves. Do congratulate your husband from my side, for being truly successful in life."

Ruchira took a while to inform him, "You are in love, Kartik."

"Doesn't matter. I didn't know this in time. And now she doesn't even wanna see my face," he cleared his choked throat. "Thanks for your time, have a great life, I just thought I owed you an apology."

"It's alright Kartik, life is a vicious circle of making mistakes, learning new lessons and evolving. Life has to move on. And you never know which tragedy will turn into a blessing in disguise."

Troubled rings

It was late January of 2007. Kartik was late for office after picking his parents from the railway station. They had come to stay for a few days. Ajit walked over to his cabin when he arrived.

"Did your parents have a comfortable journey?" Ajit asked.

"Yes, they did. Thanks for asking."

Ajit's face was glowing that day. "I have come over with a request, and I hope it won't be refused."

"You don't have to request, just order."

Ajit laughed lightly. "I want to meet your parents Saturday night at our residence. Hope you all aren't busy."

Kartik smiled at a bleak ray of hope. "Anything in particular, sir?"

"Yes, it's a very special day." He smiled. "Sahana is getting engaged."

Kartik stood lifeless as Ajit handed him the invitation card. "Please be on time and I'm ordering you, bring your family." He smiled and took his leave.

Kartik sank in his chair staring the card that had 'Sahana & Rahul' printed in a calligraphic font.

Having committed his presence, Kartik did attend the occasion along with his parents. The Khuranas lived in South Delhi in a big two-storied bungalow. The house was illuminated with lights, flowers, and laughter. It was a grand celebration.

Sahana walked down along with her friends after a few minutes; probably giving two and not one heart a miss in the gathering. She wore a lavish baby pink lehenga and, as always, looked charismatic and desirable.

A tall, good looking fair man awaited her. As she approached the altar, the guy extended his hand to help Sahana climb up the three stairs to the platform.

Soon both sides popped up the rings to be exchanged. It was then that Kartik noticed Sahana's hesitant body language. She raised her eyes a little and moved them around in the crowd. Before her sight could reach Kartik, she was asked by her mother to extend her hand.

Sahana was quivering as she brought her left hand out. Rahul held it immediately, evident of being impatient to declare her as his. Kartik shut his eyes as Rahul's ring made way onto Sahana's finger. Everyone cheered loudly as Kartik's girl entered someone else's life. After another minute, he heard the people around cheering again as Sahana's ring adorned the finger of the second man of her life.

There were many rounds of congratulations, and everyone got themselves photographed with the couple. Kartik engaged himself with his family and colleagues. Samar couldn't attend the function, being down with viral fever. Soon after, people began to dance; Sahana refrained to get on the dance floor.

Kartik accidentally moved to where Sahana was standing at some distance ahead of them facing the other way. Rahul came over to ask Sahana to dance; she shook her head. He then held her waist and she was clearly uncomfortable. She gently pushed his hand down. Rahul returned to the floor after his failed persuasion. Kartik could comprehend that she wasn't very happy.

Sahana walked away to a less noisy place at the corner. Something flashed in front of Kartik, and he started walking towards her. Sahana's face paled noticeably as he stood in front to her.

"Hello," he said hesitatingly.

She smiled back bleakly.

"Congratulations."

She nodded her head lightly.

Kartik's parents came over as they thought it was time to leave. Coincidentally, Ajit and Alka also came looking for Sahana right then.

Ajit greeted Kartik's family warmly.

"This is my father Mr Arminder Brar and my mother, Mrs Gauri Brar."

Sahana and Alka also greeted them respectfully; so did they.

"Gauri ji! So now we know how Kartik has his name," Ajit joked.

"That's not all. My younger son is named Vinayak on the same lines," Arminder said smiling.

Everyone laughed. Sahana too smiled though she'd heard that family joke several times before.

"Well, legend says that Kartik was younger," Alka said in good humor.

"Vinayak was born seven years after Kartik; so there was no way we could pull back his name to set the order right," Gauri said. Everyone laughed. Sahana had heard that too.

"I'm so glad to meet you both. I always wanted to thank you for the wonders Kartik is doing. And I'm nothing but the devil of his life."

You actually are, unknowingly, Kartik thought.

"We hear great things about you all the while as well," Arminder said.

"And it seems he even listens to you more than us. I request you to insist that he thinks of getting married now," Gauri beamed.

"I'm so glad to hear that someone listens to me in office." Then he gave Sahana a hug. "It's the first time my daughter listened to me."

Sahana smiled weakly.

Kartik was disturbed at Sahana's unhappy face.

"Such a beautiful daughter you have," Gauri admired. "I'm sure someone can live all his life just looking at her."

Sahana just smiled.

Kartik couldn't contain his emotions any further.

"I think we should leave now," he turned to his parents. Everyone bid goodbye to each other warmly and Kartik left the party with his parents.

◆

The next day at the breakfast table at Kartik's apartment in Noida, his parents were still going on about the previous evening. Gauri couldn't stop admiring pretty Sahana. Arminder though found her a little arrogant.

Early in the afternoon, they went to Kartik's room where he was pretending to be busy replying to official emails, though he was reading stuff that brought back personal memories.

"We need to talk," Gauri said.

"Tell me, Maa," Kartik said keeping his laptop aside. They both sat down on his bed.

"You know each time I see a pretty bride like I did last night..."

Gauri was interrupted abruptly, "Maa, yesterday's party is over. Can we please talk about something else?"

Gauri was a little irritated, but was gestured by Arminder to deal with Happy calmly. "Yes, let's talk about something else," she paused. "You remember that girl Priya we met in Jalandhar during Navjot's wedding?"

Kartik narrowed his eyes for a while, and then nodded.

Gauri swiftly turned to her husband, "I told you he would remember. You don't pay any attention to your boys. I saw him following her for four days..."

"Maa, I was twenty-one then."

What Gauri didn't know was that Kartik had even managed to make out with her while the ceremonies were going on. They had never approached each other after that though.

"I know. But you do remember her. Isn't that amazing?"

"No, Maa. There's nothing amazing about it."

"Happy!" she said a little louder, but mellowed instantly. "She's also a computer engineer now. She works in Hyderabad; her company can transfer her to Gurgaon, or she can work in your company."

Kartik sighed, "Maa, ask her to send her resume. If there's suitable opening, she'll surely be considered."

Gauri sighed, "Happy, what's wrong with you? I'm not asking you to give her a job. Her parents sent over a marriage proposal."

"Hang on, Maa." Kartik stood up, "I'm tired of the same topic all the time."

Gauri finally lost it, "Even I'm tired of your weirdness. It's dragging on for a year, and we need to put an end to it now. And if you liked her at twenty-one, then why not at twenty-eight?"

Kartik fumed, "Is it just me or do other folks also go through the same? What I did at twenty-one or at twenty-four still keeps following me. I've grown up; I am a changed person now. And even if I'm not changed, I at least would want to change?"

Mother and son had an argument over his anti-matrimony stand. Arminder had to finally intervene.

"Gauri, can you please make some delicious lunch for us?" he said smiling. She left angrily. Arminder gently closed the door and asked Kartik to join him in the balcony of the room. He waited until Kartik calmed down.

"You paid the loan for this house, right?" he asked.

"Yes, last year itself."

"Car loan?"

"The car was never on loan."

"Oh yes, you told me. You mentioned an investment last month."

"I'm still thinking, Papa. It's a big amount."

Arminder nodded, "Happy, your mother is always worried about you. She wants to be with you to ensure your well being, but it's actually you who mostly runs away from us."

Kartik looked up at his father.

"We are standing at the threshold of a phase of life, where the kids have flown out of the nest and all we need out of them is that they call us warmly, exchange love when we meet and we should have a little say on how our grandchildren should be brought up." Arminder patted Kartik's back, "And this doesn't come as easy as it appears."

Kartik paid full attention.

"It takes a lot of understanding at all stages of life so that at the end we reap the benefits of successful personal life." He smiled. "I have done my bit, son; now it's time for you to start investing for the sunset years of your life, not just financially, but also emotionally."

Arminder held Kartik's shoulders, "Buying a house isn't good enough; carving a home out of it is what really matters."

His father's words moved Kartik. "Give me some time, Papa."

Arminder smiled, "Sure, but some means some. I want to hear about this from you next time."

Kartik nodded.

Arminder sighed, "Your Maa thinks I don't bother about my boy. What exactly went wrong, Happy? You weren't like this ever. I always thought you'd find a girl yourself. I never imagined we'd be discussing your marriage heatedly with you ever."

Kartik was quiet for a while, "It's just work Papa, nothing much."

"I hope that's really the case. But for some reason, I have a hunch there's another side to it."

Kartik shook his head. "Seek peace, my dear."

A thoughtful father ruffled his troubled son's hair and hugged him warmly, hoping his anigush would perish soon.

◆

Sahana went back to Nagpur to complete her studies; she returned in April and discovered her father's health was deteriorating. For the past few months, Ajit was complaining of constant headaches and blackouts. Alka had accompanied him for checkups, and he was being diagnosed thoroughly. Ajit, however, ignored the doctor's suggestions of refraining from stress and taking rest. He continued inflowing his company with his passion.

It had been just a week since Sahana returned. Ajit requested the groom's family visit to fix a wedding date and other details. He was chatting with the ladies in the living room when Kartik called up.

"Your flight landed?" Ajit asked.

"Yes, sir. Just arrived."

"Tell me something great. I just want to fly today."

"We cracked the deal, sir. They'll buy 2,500 licenses for their offices spread over three countries."

Ajit gushed with excitement, "Kartik, you rock!"

As he hung up, Ajit's gestures were exuding thrill. Both Alka and Sahana were seated on a sofa when Ajit started talking loudly. "For Sahana's wedding, I want movie stars to perform and the best chefs to cook; it should be the talk of the town."

He turned his back to them with his hands stretched out above his head. "The house will be decorated no less than a palace. Flowers, lights, diyas…"

Alka and Sahana smiled at each other watching Ajit's childlike enthusiasm.

Then all of a sudden, Ajit froze and then turned towards them, trembling. His face had turned red and his head was spinning. His body was shaking, and he fell on the floor with force. The ladies went running to him. Alka held him while he fumbled.

The driver took out the car, and he was rushed to the emergency ward. It took the doctors two hours to let the family know of his state.

Senior Dr Sharma was visibly irked. "I had warned him several times, insisting on rest and taking the medication seriously. Health should be above all; we need to ensure we live to chase our ambitions."

Sahana still managed to ask through her tears, "Is he alright, doctor?"

"I'm afraid he's not. We have no other option but brain surgery. And for that, we would suggest you take him to our Singapore hospital. We have a specialized panel of neurosurgeons there."

Dr Sharma sighed. "He'll be awake in another few hours. You guys decide and let me know."

"Doctor, there's nothing to decide. Please proceed with the formalities," Sahana said.

"You may think so, but your father doesn't. It would require him to be bedridden and away from his company for at least four months. I'm not sure he'll agree. Also, if he chooses to stress his mind along with the treatment, then I'm sorry but I can't allow my patient to kill himself right in front of my eyes."

"He'll abide by you, doctor. Take my word. Please proceed," Alka committed.

They waited for another three hours for Ajit to gain consciousness. Ajit gently raised his hand to hold the hand of his sobbing wife and moved his eyes to gesture that he'd do as she wished him to. He then moved his finger to make a rectangle in air and stammered at Alka, "F...F...File".

Alka wiped her tears and rushed home.

Ajit then gently put his hand on Sahana's head, and said, "K...K...Kartik." She nodded.

Sahana came out of room to make a phone call as her father had directed. Kartik was stunned to see Sahana's number flashing on his phone at 3.00 a.m.

"Dad...Dad is in the hospital; extremely unwell...wants to see you."

She hung up and texted him the address of the hospital. Kartik reached in his nightwear in less than thirty minutes.

Ajit was marginally better; Sahana was on her knees beside her father when Kartik arrived. Alka handed over the file to Ajit.

"I need to give up my life's biggest obsession for the time being to ensure I live to complete my unfinished tasks. I can't let Alka down at this point of my life," Ajit spoke, taking many breaks.

He extended the file to Sahana. "Until I return, DataMagica belongs to both of you. No decision can be taken unless you both sign together."

Sahana was astounded. "Me? Dad?"

He rested his hand on her face, "Kartik has watched me for five years...putting every ounce of my energy into my dream...and you're the one who grew up watching me chasing it." He grew weaker. "No one can better protect the body of DataMagica than him; no one better than you to defend its soul."

Tears flooded her eyes. "I'm good for nothing, Dad."

"I never said this, my child, but I'm very proud of you." Ajit said as his eyes filled with tears of affection.

"Your soul is very pure, and I'm sure with your accession, DataMagica's soul will also purify. You won't let anything go wrong morally."

He turned at Kartik, "Take care!" Saying that, he closed his eyes.

Sahana shouted, "Doctor!" Dr Sharma came running to Ajit and asked everyone to move out. Sahana and Alka sat holding each other and sobbing. Sahana had the file close to her heart. Kartik sat at some distance with wet eyes, cursing himself for not being able to pacify Sahana.

The doctor came out after a few minutes, "Please come with me. We need to make arrangements quickly."

They all followed the doctor. He elaborated on his plan and emphasized that they leave for Singapore in the next two days.

"Will you be fine alone, Sahana?" asked a concerned Alka.

Sahana nodded. "Take care of Dad. Bring him back hail and hearty."

They hugged.

At around 9.00 a.m. Rahul arrived at the hospital with his parents. They complained of not being called at night. Alka explained that they were too disturbed. Kartik sat in the corner.

The nurse asked them to collect the reports; Sahana said she'll get them. Kartik followed Sahana but stopped at the door of the doctor's room when he heard Rahul approaching with quick steps from behind. Rahul went into the room where Sahana was alone, looking at the reports.

"Are you okay?" Rahul asked. Sahana nodded.

"What is this file?"

"Nothing."

"Let me see."

"I said nothing."

He pulled it with a jerk and flipped the pages. "You know what it means?"

He paused. "It means you have the decision-making power for the company. Be wise and make the right choices."

She pulled the file back.

He gently touched her shoulder; she shrugged his hand away. "What's your problem Sahana?" He touched her again.

Sahana fumed. "How many times do I have to tell you to keep your hands off?"

"I'm just trying to console you."

"You can do that from a distance as well." She paused, "And I don't need your consoling."

"You really behave awkwardly. I have all the right."

"No, you don't."

"It can't work out this way."

"Go and tell your parents that."

"Phew, Sahana. You are getting on my nerves now."

"Then please leave and let me be."

Rahul walked out, realizing it was the only thing she wanted. Kartik heard the entire conversation and was crestfallen to see Sahana's refusal to accept him.

Rahul's family stayed for a few more minutes. Alka even asked Kartik to leave as Ajit was resting. As Kartik turned to leave, he heard Rahul asking Sahana, "Who's he?"

"He's DataMagica's COO."

Kartik's long withheld tears flooded his cheeks on hearing the only introduction Sahana had for him.

Sahana takes
charge and discovers...

The mother and daughter were soon alone.

"Mumma, Dad must be thinking at times...what if he had had a capable son instead of me," Sahana said hugging Alka. She realized after the words left her mouth of having touched her mother's aching nerve.

Until Sahana was eight, she kept badgering for a sibling. She childishly skipped dinner one night over that demand. Feeling terribly hungry in the middle of the night, she was quietly creeping to the kitchen when she heard her mother sobbing. She was medically incapable to fulfil Sahana's wish. Sahana never brought it up again, and it was when she was fourteen that she learned that when she was two, her mother had delivered a dead boy. And it was just Sahana who'd pulled her out of the acute depression unknowingly.

"I'm sorry, I didn't mean to..."

"It's alright dear; it's an old story. And then, cherishing what you have is more important than mourning over what you don't," she said as she rested a hand on her daughter's face. "You always made our world so perfect."

"You know Sahana, despite me feeling low occasionally over our incomplete family, you father never did. He makes a great husband even though he hardly has time." Alka's eyes filled with pride, "I'm very proud of him, and even more proud of him being such a thoughtful father always."

"He's the greatest dad," Sahana said.

"Dear, I just want to share a life's secret and that is all I want from you as a mother." Alka held Sahana's face between her hands, "A happy marriage yields to happy children. Kids learn what they watch. And when I look at you, I feel accomplished; you being wonderful evidence that our marriage is a success. You need to ensure the same for your child."

Sahana nodded emotionally as her mother continued, "Please dear, the rift between you and Rahul is very apparent. Try resolving issues amicably. Promise me so that I can travel light."

"I will, Mumma. I assure you."

Alka tenderly kissed Sahana's forehead.

Two days later, Alka escorted the ailing Ajit to Singapore and Sahana joined office.

◆

Sahana was visibly nervous standing in a big meeting room while addressing the top management. She spoke about her father's plan for the company in his absence.

"I'm sorry Sahana, but I won't report to Kartik," Samar made it very clear.

"Well, to the best of my knowledge, that's the laid down hierarchy," Sahana replied.

"I always reported to Ajit. And if he isn't around, I may report to you, but not Kartik."

"It will be a big insult to your experience and knowledge if I even dare to ask you to report to me. I'm sorry but if my dad decided that the company will run under Mr Brar's guidance, there's nothing I can do about it." She paused.

"All I can do is request you to be cooperative in our tough times and emerge as a pillar of support."

Samar nodded and took his leave followed by the others. Garima and Kartik were very impressed with Sahana's words. They stayed back on Sahana's request.

Sahana turned at Garima, "DataMagica makes financial contribution to the NGO Ahem Bhumika."

Garima replied, "Yes, Ajit sir's recommendation."

"I would like the company to do be more involved not just monetarily, but also actually visiting and spending time grooming the children."

Garima replied with little hesitation, "They may be reluctant."

"It's not an order, but you may send out an email stating that those who wish to join me are most welcome. I go there every other Saturday." Garima nodded with a smile and left.

Sahana turned at Kartik looking down, "Let's get started. What are we working on?"

Words clustered around Kartik's throat, begging for courage to climb a few inches to reach the lips, watching the sad eyes of the most chirpy girl he had ever known. He finally lugged his words to climb up to the throat to frame sentences about operational details.

Sahana chose to sit in his father's cabin to feel his presence. She spent three big days sitting in that office, struggling hard, but couldn't make any sense of company's know-how, leave alone making any contribution. It was the end of the fourth day, Friday when Garima almost forced her to join the hangout-party in the pub nearby.

The absence of the most popular guy made Sahana wonder. Everyone was very welcoming, however soon the official worries took over.

"Sahana, I have a question if you don't mind?" Raghav, the head of administration asked.

"No, tell me Raghav," Sahana said sweetly.

"Is Kartik going to be the only supreme authority in the office now? Do we have no one else to go to until sir returns?"

"Well, you have me. And I think you all are very fond of him."

"What?" all said in chorus.

"Let's not get there, Sahana," Aman Sinha, the chief technical officer said. "All we want is that there's someone to help shield us from his weirdness. We have faith in you. Samar could say that openly in the board meeting, but that doesn't mean he's the only one nursing that concern."

Sahana sat appalled for the rest of the time at the pub. Garima dropped her back to the office where from she would drive home.

"Sahana," Garima said smiling, "What are you thinking?"

Sahana closed her eyes and threw her head back on the car seat. "I don't even know what to think."

"Can I help?"

"Please do. Be my guest."

"At office, sir always very clearly knows the potential of each one of us. Being a father, he would have known yours well," Garima paused, and Sahana turned to her with eyes wide open. "Do you think we needed you to run our business? What does it mean to be a soul, Sahana? You should know pretty clearly about your expected role to mollify things around."

Sahana smiled as tears welled up in her eyes, "Thank you, dear. I'll be always be obliged to you for taking me along today."

◆

Sahana spent the next week talking to various associates at every level and understanding their issues. There was a lot of frustration with the company's policies and over the appraisal system. The HR team was expanded to look for resolutions. Sahana led the drive aiming for the attrition rate to attenuate.

She worked till very late in office and Kartik also stayed until she appeared online on the company's messenger. She restricted interaction with him to the minimum and mostly chose email as a medium of correpondence.

They received a blow in the middle of the coming week – agitation from the newly formed teams who were mandated to move to the new office. Sahana jumped in to hear their concerns on security which wasn't being addressed. They were all working in US time and had the noon to 9.00 p.m. shift.

Sahana turned to the group manager of the teams, "The reason is valid. Why didn't you bring it up?"

"I did, but top management was adamant that new projects were to be moved, irrespective of geographies, to a new location," he replied.

"Who is this 'top management'?"

The manager said in low voice, "Ajit sir and Kartik, of course."

Sahana gasped and walked hurriedly back to the seventh floor.

"I need to talk," Sahana stormed into the marketing team meeting that Kartik was addressing.

"Urgent?"

"Highly. More urgent and critical than winning new contracts."

The team walked out quickly, sensing the urgency, and waited outside.

"Did you ever happen to drive to the new office? Leaving that office at night is so highly unsafe. Has any human consideration gone into picking what needs to be moved there?"

"Well, all the new projects that are rolling out. Why disturb the already settled ones?"

"Apart from being new, did you happen to look into the other details of those projects? They are all twelve-nine shifts."

"Well, whatever. Some projects need to be moved there; anyone who'll be asked to move will make noise. You pick the Asian ones of the eight-five shift, they'll also have some problem. We are not the only company that has multiple offices. When hired, associates were not promised that they'd be working from one office. We have one-third of our people working at client locations. It's worthless to worry about it. And honestly, it is silly to walk around the office and ask who wants or doesn't want to move. As management, a few decisions lie in your hand and require diligent decision making," Kartik said in his true professional avatar.

"But their safety?"

"The office is highly secure; that shouldn't be a concern. Five other companies are already operational from the same location with similar working hours."

"After office security? Way back home?"

"Sahana, I was also apprehensive about that office in the beginning, but I think sir had a point as the area will develop very soon."

"But it isn't so developed as of now. How can we just disown their concerns? There are young girls in the team. One unfortunate incident and we'll be blaming our souls for the rest of our lives. For what? A few extra dollars?"

Kartik stood quietly with his soul bowing once again to Sahana. She took a chair being highly emotional and said thoughtfully, "Can we run a cab service?"

"Now, that's a great thought," Kartik said admiringly. Sahana cheered a bit as he called Raghav to join the meeting.

"We did run this idea for this office as well. But most of them chose the conveyance allowance over the office-provided cab service," Raghav said.

"Let's send out a communication about the conveyance for the new office. They can avail the guarded cab service in exchange for the conveyance allowance," Kartik said.

"I'll do that right away," Raghav said and left.

Sahana smiled a little with that 'good-for-all' solution. Kartik too smiled exactly the same width watching her relaxing, "Anything else, ma'am?"

Sahana shook her head, and as she walked out, an incident at Noida park, when she had walked out of his life, flashed in his mind. And like that day, she didn't turn back.

The marketing team started filling in again. Kartik stood still to collect himself.

◆

The next day, Sahana called in a meeting with Garima and Kartik.

"What the hell is happening?" Sahana said apprehensively, "Last night I was studying the attrition data. We fire employees so often. Why? And so casually! And at all levels!"

"Actually this attitude is being cascaded from the top. Since Kartik started it, the others drew encouragment. Honestly, I see it as a prime reason of the shrinking loyalty towards the company." Garima said boldly. She was a loyal employee and wanted the company to flourish.

"All terminations sans appropriate reasoning," Garima said looking at Kartik.

"I don't want low performers. That's it," he sounded snarky.

"It will be a little inhuman to expel in such haste."

"It's mentioned in the contract they sign that they can be expelled without prior notice."

Sahana was appalled. Until the previous year, Kartik had been helping to attune her little childish behaviour at work, but now he had turned into an epicenter of negative energy.

"I know that, still..."

"Garima, I have many urgent things to look into."

"But is termination the only option? You may consider demoting or issuing a warning letter. If you'll allow your mind to think, you'll surely be greeted with few fairer ideas."

"They'll not think of us when they get a better offer from a rival company. Fairer ideas will not cross their minds," Kartik said harshly.

Sahana finally interrupted his attempts to overhaul Garima. "I agree. But you're not on the same platform as them; you're an employer. You have greater responsibility.

And trust me, if you'll show generosity, you'll be also showered with the same."

He smiled sarcastically, "You really think so?"

"Yes, I do. And this termination spree needs to terminate now, and this has to start with you," Sahana was stern. "I want company's employee satisfaction data to appear better."

Kartik was bewildered at her adamancy. He never knew Sahana could be so assertive. "Wonderful, someone's data interpretion skills have remarkably improved." He said appreciatively rather.

"Yes, I finally know what 'looking from all angles' means." Sadly, it landed on her ears as a taunt. Sahana stood up. "Garima, from now on, every termination that isn't a harassment case of any kind shall not be entertained. And every means every. No matter who's giving the order. We need to make DataMagica a better place."

Kartik once again just sat immobile, watching Sahana walking out. He wondered why Ajit had chosen her to walk into the company.

◆

For the rest of the week, Sahana took care of other attitude issues, insisting on better camaraderie amongst the seniors. Garima was instructed to gather feedback from the teams. This instigated a sudden spark for all the managers to improvise their working behaviour and methods. Kartik had been silently admiring Sahana, literally shooing the evil out of company's soul. Sahana was satisfied to notice Kartik's cooperation. He implemented everything she had suggested, hoping it would make her smile.

On Friday evening, while walking out of office, Kartik bumped into Garima and said, "I was about to call you, I was wondering if we can have an offsite picnic this weekend; just a few of us. It's been so long since we have had any gathering."

"That's a great idea. But let's do that next week. Sahana isn't available this week."

"Oh! Is she traveling somewhere? Singapore?"

"No, it's her fiancé's birthday celebration. She'll be out for two days," she winked, "and a night."

Kartik's face paled. Garima bid him bye; he continued to stand as still as a statue.

♦

On Saturday night, Rahul hosted a big birthday bash at Sohna Resort. Alka had been speaking to Sahana and had advised her to strengthen her bond with Rahul. Sahana was a highly courteous host to all his friends, looking regal in a royal blue party dress.

Rahul held her waist and whispered, "Hey beautiful, stop being the host now. Please enjoy the party too."

She smiled back, "I'm having a great time."

"Great, want a drink?"

Sahana's smile shrank remembering the only boy she ever drank with. "No, I don't drink. A mocktail would do," she managed to say, and they walked to the bar area.

"So, any birthday resolutions?" she asked.

"Yah. Getting married this year," he replied gleefully.

She chuckled lightly, "Well apart from that, you may also want to start working."

"I work out daily."

"I meant going to the office regularly."

"I go there twice a week."

"And for just two hours. And you barely show any interest in the business. And since you're starting a family, you should be ready to take up more responsibilities."

"Hang on, Sahana," Rahul was irritated. "Not today at least. You have no such ambitions, well until very recently and just for the time being, perhaps."

"I'm not someone you should exemplify here. You're the only son of the family; you need to be sincere."

Rahul looked at her angrily, "Somehow I get a feeling that you're ashamed of me."

"I want to be proud of you."

"It's my birthday party and all my friends and family are here. I don't want any unpleasantness," he said firmly.

"I meant it for your good."

"Thank you but I don't want your freelance advices. My dad is a business tycoon, whatever he's doing is for me, exclusively. He just wants me to enjoy my life."

"Until a certain age, but you aren't a lad anymore. He may..."

"Just stop it," he said harshly. "Each time I meet you, I end up regretting having met you. You need to mend your ways. You're my fiancée, not my boss."

Sahana stood a little shaken. Some of Rahul's friends came to her rescue by pulling him to the dance floor. Sahana spent the rest of the evening mingling with his friends, and watching him literally drowning in alcohol.

Rahul had booked a single room for himself and Sahana, which invited another round of heated arguments. She didn't let Rahul inside as he was very drunk. The next morning, as

Sahana was strolling in the hotel's corridor, she saw Rahul coming out of a room buttoning his shirt. He froze to find Sahana standing in front of him.

"Good morning," she said a little surprised at his expression.

"G...G...Good morning, darling," he said stammering.

"You look nervous. Is everything alright?"

He was palpitating, "Oh yes, just a little hangover."

Sahana became suspicious and tried to look into the room he had stepped out from. "Hey, there are boys inside, you shouldn't peep," he held her hand firmly.

"I want to check," she pushed his hand away. She opened the door, and Rahul jumped right in front of her.

"Don't! Let's go and have some tea."

She bent over his shoulder to look inside. There was a girl sleeping on the bed, naked.

"Sahana listen, I slept on the floor. I was absolutely wasted. I didn't do anything."

He was sweating and trembling.

Sahana stood still for a while and then pointed a finger at the girl, "That's Minisha, I met her yesterday. She's your best friend Nipun's fiancée; they are getting married in three weeks."

"Exactly."

He wiped his sweat, "Nipun was in this room until early morning. He got an urgent call and had to leave. I was on the floor all this while, not in a position to even get up and say bye to him."

Sahana turned at him sharply, "You didn't see him going?"

"No way, I was too high."

She narrowed her eyes, "Then how do you know he left for an emergency, and why the bloody hell didn't he take his fiancé along?"

Rahul stammered, "Oh my...my bad memory. Nipun left from the party itself. Minisha was drunk, so he didn't consider it appropriate to take her along in that condition."

"So Nipun never came to this room?" She stared hard at him.

Rahul was stunned. Sahana was much smarter than he assumed. "Okay, you're right. But nothing happened between the two of us."

"Clothes shed, but nothing happened." Her face was red with anger.

He froze again, realizing nothing but a confession would work. "I beg, I truly beg for forgiveness. I was too high and confused. I thought it was you."

He tried reaching out to her hand.

She pulled her hand back rudely. "I'm five feet seven inches tall, she's no taller than five feet; I'm fair, she's dusky; I have long straight hair, hers are short and permed. Not even a blind man would confuse her with me."

She pushed Rahul hard and ran to her room to pack her stuff. He followed her running, pleading guilty, but Sahana treated him as though he was invisible and moved to the reception area. Many of his friends were standing there at checkout.

"Sahana wait," Rahul said, agitated in front of everyone, "I said I'm sorry."

Sahana took her engagement ring out and threw it on his face, "I'm sorry too."

◆

Kartik did notice that Sahana's ring was missing from her finger the next day at work. He mustered a lot of courage to ask a simple question, "Are you okay?" She nodded.

"You don't appear to be so."

"None of your business."

"We need to be more polite to each other."

"Rather than worrying about me, focus on yourself."

"You're making it very awkward."

Sahana thumped the table hard, "Please stay out of it."

She stormed out of his cabin.

After about an hour, Kartik walked to her office and ordered coffee. "Are you doing better now?"

Sahana was agape. "Excuse me?"

Some coffee arrived just then.

"Come, let's have coffee and try being friends."

"You aren't my friend," she said curtly.

"I know I'm not. Let's try at least."

"I don't see any need."

"That's the need of the hour."

Sahana stood still for a few moments. Kartik gestured to her to sit down for coffee; she sat but was still arrested in her thoughts. Suddenly she broke her silence. "I need to talk to you."

Kartik couldn't believe his ears for a while, "Tell me."

"Somewhere outside office today."

"Dinner?"

"No, maybe just another cup of coffee."

"Okay," he was happy with whatever was granted.

Sahana found Kartik standing in her office ten minutes earlier than the decided time. There was a twinkle of hope in his eyes.

Sahana cleared her throat many times at the coffee shop before speaking, "See there's lot of dissatisfaction over your dictatorial management style. You seriously need to consider toning it down. It's not favourable for anyone – the employees, the company's image and for you as well."

He looked at her with mixed emotions. First, disappointment since he had been hoping she would talk about them, second, pride for her talking about it so maturely, and third, shame that they were talking about this.

"I just meant to bring out the best in the others."

"But the approach also needs to be the best. Don't you think?"

He sat silent but soon realized all he wanted was to see her smile, "Tell me, what can I do for you?"

"Don't do it for me. Don't let what you built together with Dad from scratch fall apart so disgracefully."

He smiled to himself; the second feeling of pride defeating the others. "Will you help me?"

"Of course. But you need to start helping yourself first."

"No, tell me how to fix things? I'm too stressed. Will you be my friend and help me rectify my mistakes?"

She sat shocked. "No," she said without any expression. "I'm not here to resolve your stress. Or to even try guiding you about how to manage your life. I mean, I can't let you bring down the company like a house of cards."

"Trust me, I would never do any such thing."

"Mr Ratan Tata said that nothing eats iron away but its own rust."

She paused and continued, "You truly need to circumspect things."

Sahana stood up to leave. Unconsciously Kartik held her wrist. She freed it the very next moment.

"I'm sorry," he said hesitatingly. "Please sit. I need to talk about something."

Sahana sat down. Kartik struggled to find the words to touch upon the sensitive topic.

"Listen Sahana, about that evening."

She looked confused. "Which evening?"

He joined both his shaking hands on the table, "That evening in the park last year." Sahana sat stoic.

"I...I...I'm sorry."

"For what?" she snapped.

"I didn't mean to be so rude."

"Perhaps I deserved it for being hugely stupid. Don't be sorry."

"No..." he choked.

"I need to leave now."

"No, let me finish please," he stopped her again. "I didn't mean to...." He paused. "I don't even know what to say."

"Let me help you," Sahana said with dry eyes and a blank face.

"It is not your mistake. You never made any promises; there's no point blaming yourself for my lost years. Feel better."

Sahana stood up instantly, "You were right actually; life isn't an accidental vacation. I should have known that."

And before he could say anything, she added, "And never talk about this insignificant topic again. We have many burning issues to take care of. Like it or not, but yes, you are right – it's the need of the hour for us to be friends. At least we will pretend to be so."

She left taking the feeling of pride along, leaving him behind with disappointment and shame.

◆

The rest of the week was equally eventful as the previous one. Reforms kept circulating in the air.

Kartik came over to the NGO on Saturday; there were a few more colleagues helping Sahana sharing information on basic hygiene and first aid.

"Can I help?" Kartik stood right behind her and asked.

She turned over her shoulder, "Anyone can help."

He smiled and came forward. "Tell me, please."

She stared at him, "But why are you doing this?"

"You just said anyone can help."

She nodded.

He then helped her out, elaborating on the need of basic hygiene. They distributed soaps, band-aids, and antiseptic creams bought out of company's funds.

Kartik discovered Sahana's fan-following among the kids there. They treated her like she was a movie star or a model.

The staff left by evening. Sahana was also preparing to leave when Kartik approached her, "Aloo tikki?"

"Excuse me?"

She was a little surprised.

"Why the hell do people always ask for coffee in Delhi? For a change, one can ask for aloo tikki or goplgapa?"

"Thanks for asking, but I need to go home now."

"Roadside Chat Party is a little down-class, but yummy."

"I do that very often; there's nothing down-class about it."

"Amazing. Let's go then."

"Kartik, please. Let it be."

"Sahana, please. Let it go."

Sahana stood silently. Her eyes intensified his alien feeling; however, it wasn't alien anymore. Kartik knew it. Very very well.

They stood at the chat corner enjoying golgappas. He was really amazed to see her fondness for street food.

"How's sir's health now?" Kartik asked.

"The results of the tests are encouraging. He will undergo a surgery next week."

"Are you going there?"

"No, Dad wants me to be here," she said prudently.

"He really loves you. He wants the best out of life for you," Kartik said.

Sahana nodded.

"But don't you think you added to his troubles?" he said pointing at her left hand.

She smiled weakly.

"For twenty-four years of my life, I've heard my dad say that I have no aim in life. I don't want to screw all the other years to follow actually having none."

Kartik said very hesitatingly. "He appears to be a nice guy, Sahana. I repeat, sir will be really disheartened. He was very excited about your safe future with him."

She looked right in his eyes, "You really care a lot about Dad."

He nodded, "The kind of trust he invested in me did wonders to my career. He always stood by my side providing his unshakeable faith. I owe it to him to protect the interests of his family."

Sahana got an answer to Kartik's boorish attitude a year ago.

While Kartik pulled out a wallet from back pocket to pay, a folded pamphlet dropped out. Sahana picked and was astonished to see a meditation center details. He was visibly uneasy to see the pamphlet landing in Sahana's hands.

"You are attending this?" she asked being shocked.

"Well," Kartik struggled to answer, "I did attend it the last two weekends, but the guy's words aren't helping much. So I thought of helping at the NGO. After all, doing good deeds is more soothing than merely hearing good words."

Sahana's eyes caught Kartik's weariness, "Everything okay?"

"No," he blurted out. "I mean yes, all is fine. Just a little overworked."

"You sure? All good at home?"

"Yes, absolutely," he turned to the other side. "Let's go."

◆

Kartik visited Amritsar over the weekend and rested his head on his mother's lap. "Mumma, please massage my aching head."

Gauri gently started massaging his head; he lay silent as she said, "You really need a companion in life now."

"What will she do?"

"She'll love you unconditionally. And take away all your pain."

"Why are you so hellbent to bring pain to someone's life? I can't keep anyone happy. "

"Find love and spread love, my boy," Gauri said. "Find out what will make you happy. If we don't get what our heart truly desires, even winning the world won't matter."

"I know Mumma," he said with a heavy heart, "I know."

Oops

The next Monday began with distinguished media coverage of the company's COO in a leading business magazine. What triggered giggles in office was the selection of the editor's words for a caption below Kartik's picture on the cover-page: 'Most Eligible IT Bachelor.'

Congratulations flowed in. Sahana, however, made no comment and smoldered in fury.

In the late afternoon, she was seated in Kartik's office. At the end of the discussion, she rose up to walk while he was standing, slightly leaning on the table, turning the pages of the contract they had just signed. Her eyes fell on that magazine lying on his table.

She moved her eyes around his cabin that was already rather full with such accolades. "So where does this one go?" she asked without warning.

He looked up, "Well," he answered after deliberating, "I guess nowhere. I will keep a copy in my drawer."

"Are you kidding me? It's the most flashing compliment possible."

Her words were bleeding of satire.

"No, ma'am. I have no such misconceptions about myself," he said humbly, closing the file.

She smiled askew, "Go fool somebody else, Kartik," she said and spun quickly to walk out. He caught her wrist.

She turned slowly, still fuming, and burning eyes darted at his grip. "Next time you do this, I'm going to gift you a tight slap."

He released her wrist, "Go ahead with your slap."

"I have better things to do. And anyway, I just wanted to congratulate that someone matched your own personal thoughts about yourself."

He smirked, "No ma'am, my view about me is nothing like this headline, because someone showed me the mirror."

He looked straight into her eyes. "I don't even deserve to be looked back at and am easy to erase from one's memory."

"Right. Good for her," she said curtly.

"I thought the same, but it ended up being good for no one."

"No, no!" she spurted in anger, "It was good for her!"

And she stormed out.

Kartik gazed at the magazine savagely for a while and then tore it into pieces. The air from the fan caused the pieces to fly all over the room. It was a reflection of what his life was – disarranged into an unmanageable mess.

◆

Later that week there was a burning issue reported by a client in Florida on the performance of the tool. The technical team had worked extremely well to fix the issue in less than two days, but the top management of the client company wanted to reconsider their association. It could be a huge loss financially and more so, affect the reputation for DataMagica, so both Kartik and Sahana flew to soothe the customer.

At the airport, Sahana arrived ahead of Kartik. He saw her heading towards immigration when he arrived at check-in baggage. He buzzed her asking her to wait. Sahana took her phone out of her purse, neither answered nor disconnected it, and kept it back. Kartik's face hung at Sahana's merciless indifference.

Post security check, he saw Sahana entering a bookshop. This time he shamelessly waited outside. There's no way she could avoid spotting him this time.

"I called you," he said with mild anger.

"Did you?" She took her phone out. "Sorry, I missed it."

"No, you did not. You didn't answer on purpose. I saw you taking the phone out," he said agitatedly.

Sahana rolled her lips.

"I wanted you to wait for me," he said hastily.

"What?" she smirked.

"I mean, we could have discussed how to tackle the issues."

"See, I'm just moral support. Do however you want to."

She was quick on her steps as soon her sentence finished.

◆

Kartik's strategies and deep knowledge of the tool helped win the client confidence back. Sahana also assured them of better after delivery services. They both were relieved to close the issue amicably.

"Can we go to the beach today?" Kartik asked Sahana on Saturday morning.

"No, thanks. I need to shop before our flight tomorrow afternoon."

"You can't shop for two full days," he said smiling.

"I can do anything."

"Come let's go," he urged again and she reluctantly agreed.

Kartik hired a car, and they drove to Keywest beach. It was a breezy and adventurous drive with the sea brimming on both sides of the road. However, the conversation was not flowing. The weather, the ocean took their thoughts momentarily back to where it all started, but Sahana was firm to stick to the present.

On their way back, they made a quick stop at the 7-Eleven store to grab some juice. Kartik walked out to get the car fuelled while Sahana was still inside.

A big convertible jeep came speedily, and six goons rushed inside the store and locked it. Kartik's heart came to his mouth. He swept closer and tried breaking its glass-door to get inside. The goons pulled out guns and asked everyone in the store to kneel down. Sahana also did that out of fear.

One of the goons looted the cash counter. Bystanders had called 911 already. Several cop cars arrived in less than two minutes and took positions outside the store. The goons tried to create a hostage situation to evade arrest. Kartik's heart was pumping fast; he was nagging at the cops to get inside the store. The cops noticed a way inside from the top through the AC outlet. A cop had already started making his way in. A goon heard the sound of some movement over the AC and fired in the air.

"Next time you guys try to act smart, it will fire on someone's head here," the leader shouted through a mike.

Kartik's face reddened with fear; his biggest worry was that he couldn't see Sahana from outside. She was in the last aisle away from the glass pane doors.

The hostage situation had dragged for an hour; before a commando managed to reach inside through the washroom's window. He knocked two goons down using a silencer, but the other four got attentive. They all held one hostage each and walked out pointing a gun at their heads. The leader held Sahana.

"Leave the innocent people. We'll let you go," the cop said.

"And you want me to believe you?" the leader pressed his gun harder at Sahana's head.

"Don't do that. I beg, don't," Kartik pleaded. Kartik continued. "Consider exchanging your hostage; let her go."

Sahana's eyes opened wide in stupefaction.

"Shut up! She's easier to handle. And when we are out of here; she'll be more advantageous than you."

The goon moved the gun down from her head to her cleavage.

"Don't you dare!" Kartik jumped at the goon.

"Attack," shouted the lieutenant.

Kartik managed to pull Sahana out of his lock. But the goon stood five steps away, still pointing his gun at Sahana's back. Kartik held her close facing the goon.

The rest of the hostages had been freed due to the panic caused by Kartik's sudden action. It was only the leader who hadn't given up.

Kartik and Sahana froze at gunpoint. The cops' team stood behind Kartik some steps away.

"You idiot," shouted the goon. "You jumped in to ensure no one can have the fun you had."

He mocked. "You silly emotional Indians."

Kartik tried to move back; his only hope was to get closer to the cops. "You dare do that and I'll make sure that your fun toy doesn't exist anymore."

The goon aimed a gun at Sahana's back wrathfully.

Sahana was shivering out of fear; Kartik was frightened too, but still stepped back dragging Sahana along too.

Then there was a gunshot that changed it all. Sahana screamed and jerked her back.

"Sahana!" shouted Kartik falling on his knees resting her head on his arm.

Sahana tried to say something, but he interrupted, "Don't worry. Medical help is here. Nothing will happen. Keep your eyes open."

Kartik sobbed and held Sahana's face, "You can't go away. There's a mount of sorrow on my heart, and you can't go killing my soul forever."

Sahana's eyes filled with tears, Kartik rested his head over hers and murmured, "I love you."

Kartik heard a moaning noise and the sound of the cops' footsteps approaching the goon leader. He looked at the goon to see him lying bleeding on the ground. But all he had heard was a single gunshot.

He raised his head from Sahana's and scrutinized his hand that was on her back. There was no stain of blood. Sahana shrugged a little to free herself from his arms, stood straight and walked away.

Kartik sat there on his knees looking at the sky murmuring.

After some medical treatment on a minor wound on her hand, they drove back to the hotel. Kartik couldn't even dare to look at Sahana. He drove like a racehorse wearing blinkers.

It was 1.00 a.m. when there was a knock on Kartik's door. He wasn't surprised to find Sahana standing there. She scampered into the room and headed straight to the balcony. Kartik followed her landing his feet exactly where she stepped.

"Sorry to bother you so late in the night, but I wanted to see clearly a face of love that isn't jealous," Sahana said sarcastically.

Kartik closed his eyes hard. "I was helpless; I still am."

"Helpless about?"

Despite knowing it's wrong, his emotional surge eroded his rationality finally, and he pulled her closer. She put her arms around his neck.

"Sahana, you're a Delhi girl. You're supposed to be the smartest lot of our country when it comes to boys. I should be hated by you, rather than being loved. You are three years, four months and five days younger; I should have behaved myself on the trip; you were a little girl, I should have acted like a man rather than a boy. You should be disgusted with me for forcing physical intimacy on you. You can't be so dumb not to make out my intentions. The inspector, who raided the party, accidentally saved you. I could have damaged your soul severely that night."

Sahana's tears were rolling down uncontrollably, "Are you trying to tell me what you said a few hours back was an accident?"

"No, my dear. But that is an outcome of what you caused me to feel each time we met the last few years."

"When I heard your and Dad's conversation at the station, it was the first time ever I wanted to see DataMagica's organizational chart. I learned then about whom I had spent my five days and one night with. And trust me, Kartik, I would have been really disgusted had you approached me. Your never calling made me realize that you're worth waiting for." Her voice wailed with grief.

"I'm not worthy of you. You're too pure, Sahana. I'm a below average human. I've lived the last one year of my life realizing how shallow and timid a person I am."

"Are you trying to tell me you didn't mean a word of the promise you gave me about being your first girlfriend?"

"Sahana, I have had girlfriends. I'm not a virgin."

"Being a virgin..." Sahana interrupted. "Don't..."

"Hear me out, virgin..."

She interrupted again, "I say don't! Whether you are or not...keep that piece of information to yourself."

"I could have died today, Kartik."

He loosened the hug and put his finger on her lips, "Don't say that."

"I'm not very alive otherwise also," Sahana cried. "I actually have an aimless life. You're the only aim I have ever had for years."

Kartik embraced her again, "Sahana, you dad answered my question on what draws me towards you so madly," he said. "It's your soul. It can't be anything less than the purity of your soul and the innocence of your feelings."

She sobbed harder, "Still you chucked me out of your life so easily."

"You'll always remain my unfilled desire. You have a very special place in my life, in my heart. But you belong to someone else now. And sir would have expected this out of me. To show you the right way in his absence. Let me try to do some good to you."

Sahana tried to unclasp the hug to which he objected. "No. Let it stay for a while. You have no idea how soothing it is. I haven't felt this great since four years nine months and three days."

"Do you have someone in your life, Kartik?"

He smirked, "Your silly questions again. Do you think I'm the kind of man who can keep anyone happy? Look what I did to a girl who dared to foster feelings for me." He choked with guilt.

"Can we be friends Sahana?"

She nodded.

"So that means you'll pick my calls?" he asked, and she smirked in response.

She again tried to free herself, "Leave me, Kartik, it's wrong."

"I've never been a right guy anyway," he was not willing to let the moment go.

They embraced each other a long time, then sat on the floor of the balcony resting their backs on the wall. She rested her head on his shoulder. He gently rested his head on hers, and they both slept soundly that night after a very long time.

Yet another
Rustic Charmer

Sahana and Kartik finally made peace. She assured him that she'd move on. He assured her that he'd mend all his ways and bring back the real Kartik.

"I have a request to make," Sahana said humbly as she took a seat opposite him in his cabin on Tuesday.

"Please tell me."

"I want to help a friend and would like his resume to be considered for the marketing team."

"Which college?"

"Mine."

"Didn't he get through in campus placements?"

"He didn't go for the interviews. He didn't need a job then, but now he does. And I'm not asking to issue him an appointment letter; just an interview which I'm sure he will be able to pull off."

A streak of jealousy flashed across his face and he looked down. He nodded.

"Thanks."

Kartik, unable to hold on to his query, questioned her further "But why didn't he need a job then?"

"Well, he belongs to an industrial family of Meerut, so he joined his family business. But for some reason he has been expelled from the family. He needs a job now."

Kartik's eyeballs widened, "Expelled from the family?"

"It is a long story. His girlfriend is Hindu whereas he's a Muslim. So when he told his family about his choice, they refused furiously. He was asked to choose between his family and the girl. He waited sometime for the situation to mollify; but in vain. Finally, his father disowned him saying that since he had the guts to have an affair against his will, he should also have the guts to build his career too. And that's what he's figuring out."

"And why are you taking so much trouble?" Kartik asked annoyingly.

She passed a rueful smile, "There's no trouble. And then the company will also benefit from smart associates."

"Oh!" he said sarcastically, "Your friend is smart too?"

"Certainly. And, by the way, you've met him too."

"Me? When?"

"In Nagpur."

"Sagar?"

"No, the one you played basketball with. Pervez, Prez for short – serving a dual purpose."

Kartik sat quietly and passed an unfriendly smile.

"Any problem?" she asked.

"You knew I had come to honour your words to your college. You should have shown some courtesy to come over to meet me, provided I tried reaching you so many times."

"We decided that we wouldn't talk about the past."

"You're so kind otherwise. Bloody hell, you should have shown some kindness to me as well in Nagpur."

"Aren't you being silly?" She was stunned.

"You knew that I had come all the way just for you," he said looking into her eyes angrily.

"You're too selfish, Kartik. In that case, you should also know why I was in that MBA institution in the first place," she said choking mildly.

Kartik's expression mellowed; Sahana stood up to leave his room.

Just when she reached near the door, Kartik said, "I waited there for more than three hours. What if I had been sitting there for three days?"

She turned and smiled sarcastically, "You're a busy COO. Even three hours was astonishing; three days would definitely have been out of the question."

She walked out leaving Kartik feeling belittled.

Prez's interview was scheduled three days later. He indeed cleared it on his own capabilities and was offered the job. He joined on the fifth day itself.

◆

The duo went out for chat-party on Friday evening. Kartik was delighted to see Sahana smiling in full colours. His world also blossomed with her smiles, and the vivacity returned in their conversations.

The next Monday in office, Garima invited everyone to her engagement the coming Sunday. Kartik's mother arrived on Tuesday as Arminder was traveling to Jalandhar for ten days for official work. On Wednesday, he saw Sahana weeping in her cabin as it was Ajit's birthday. She was missing her family terribly. On Thursday he asked her out for dinner on Friday night.

While briefing the new marketing team's associates on Friday, his eye caught a familiar face sitting in the audience. Sahana did the HR part, and the briefing ended in less than forty minutes.

While all others walked out of the conference room, a familiar face stayed back to greet his college mate.

"Hey, Bluess," Prez said smiling.

"Hi, Prez. All settled in the city?" Sahana asked in a friendly tone.

"Thank you so much for the job."

"All your own effort. It's the least I could do."

Prez turned to Kartik, "Hello Mr Brar. Pleasure meeting you again."

Kartik gave a half smile, "Good luck. Hope your personal matter doesn't affect your performance."

"How's she?" Sahana said instantly.

Prez turned to Sahana with confusion yet answered, "Very well, thanks."

"You're so brave, Prez. It takes so much courage to choose love over gelt," Sahana said appreciatively.

Prez smiled sweetly, "Not that much courage and even if it's about courage, I draw it from her."

"I'm so proud of you, my friend." Sahana patted his shoulder gently.

"I have another meeting to attend," Kartik said and left, not being able to withstand the scene anymore.

Prez's eyes followed Kartik until outside the door; he then darted his eyes to Sahana, "What was that?"

"Leave it," she said pressing her lips.

"At least let me know what courage I just talked about."

"You're a very good actor, Prez. I'm so impressed you didn't screw it up." Sahana narrated to him the entire fiction she had scripted.

"What?" Prez freaked out. "But why?"

"You wanted to be close to Meerut. You have it. Be happy."

"Blues! What's cooking between you and the COO? First you keep him waiting outside the hostel and don't even care to turn up despite his long wait. And then back here you're setting a trap for him?"

"We have a long story and be happy you get to play a cameo. Offer your help to me whenever I need it."

"My absolute pleasure," he sighed, "but I pity him."

"He doesn't deserve any pity."

Her eyebrows rose, "It's time for him to learn a few important lessons of life the hard way."

"Phew," he smiled, "Somebody is in blue trouble."

Sahana rolled her eyes, "Whatever."

◆

Sahana was so lost in talking to Kartik in his car as they headed out for dinner on Friday, that she didn't even realize which place they had reached. It was his apartment.

Kartik pressed the doorbell; Gauri opened the door. It was then that Sahana returned to her senses. She paid respectful regards to Gauri.

Gauri ushered them inside warmly and took leave to make tea.

"You shouldn't have bothered you mother for dinner," Sahana said.

"She loves cooking and you don't eat much anyway," he said beaming.

"By the way, thank you," she said.

Kartik offered her a seat and moved to the kitchen to speak to Gauri. "Mom please don't mention her engagement to her."

"Why so? Did it go sour?"

He nodded.

"Oh God! How can someone leave such a pretty girl? The guy must be blind."

"Whatever Maa. Just don't put her mood off. She's our guest."

She smiled and assured him she would not.

They had a delightful conversation over the tea; just the change Sahana needed. Gauri went to the kitchen for finishing the dinner preparations; Sahana walked along to help, despite Gauri's insistence that she did not want any help. Kartik walked to his room to change.

The doorbell rang, and it kept ringing unceasingly. Gauri paid no heed, which triggered Sahana's curiosity. She stepped out and spotted Kartik running out of his room to open the door.

A young man stormed inside and threw his backpack on the ground. Bearing a striking resemblance to Kartik, Sahana guessed it had to be his younger brother Vinayak.

"What the hell! This is last time I'm coming to Noida. I don't care even if Papa is out of town. I prefer staying in my hostel than coming here," said the final year student of an engineering college in Patiala.

"Take it easy Vinny, you're blowing it out of proportion," Kartik said while closing the door behind him.

"Coming from Patiala to Delhi is easier than reaching Noida from Delhi. What's wrong with the auto drivers? Why can't a Delhi auto come to Noida?"

"They are different states."

"And why the hell don't autos run on meters? It's a full gang of cheats," Vinayak fumed. He pulled out two bills from his pocket.

"A hundred and sixty-five rupees!"

"You need to reimburse this. I'm not paying for autos out of my pocket money."

"What crap, Vinny? You could have just told me the amount."

"Like you'd pay my bills otherwise."

"I would love to pay your shopping bills," Kartik said smiling. This agitated him further, and almost dancing with fury cinematically.

"I'm not a princess that I need a wardrobe of lavish dresses and closet of fancy footwears!"

He pointed to his backpack. "This would suffice for a year."

Sahana rolled her lips between her jaws to suppress laughter.

"You should consider paying some other bills of mine."

Vinny raised his hand above his head with fingers rolled and thumb pointing out to his mouth.

"No way; as soon as I start doing that, you'll go unchecked. I have strict instructions from Papa. You get that from your pocket money like I always did," Kartik spoke like a concerned elder brother.

Vinny appeared flabbergasted, "I should get some perks in life for having a rich elder brother."

"I'm not rich, Vinny."

"You'll never be." He stared at Kartik. "Because only those people are rich who have a philanthropist's heart." Vinny broadened his chest and pointed a finger to himself. "And charity begins at home!"

Sahana finally burst out laughing. Vinny's eye sparkled seeing a beautiful guest at home.

He turned at Kartik with his back at Sahana and mutely said, "Wow!"

He brought the tips of fingers together of both hands and joined them to confirm with Kartik if she was his interest. Kartik waived his head gently to signal no. Vinny winked at his elder brother and walked towards Sahana.

"Hi, I'm Vinayak Brar."

"Sahana Khurana. Nice to meet you."

Gauri sauntered out of kitchen finally. "Is it settled?" Kartik nodded.

Gauri sighed. "Good. Vinny, go and freshen up, we need to get dinner started."

"I'll be back soon," Vinny smiled at Sahana and returned in less than five minutes.

As they sat down for dinner, Vinny pulled a chair for Sahana.

Gauri went to the kitchen to get water.

"You surely are from Delhi," said Vinny.

"Yes, Vinayak."

"Vinny. My friends call me Vinny," Kartik scratched his nose to Vinny's useless attempts. "Have you ever been to Amritsar?"

"When I was very young. I remember it very vaguely."

"I must have been very young too. I also don't remember seeing you around in the city."

Sahana contained her laughter.

"You should come again and see it from the eyes of a true admirer," Vinny said smiling. Sahana nodded smiling.

Gauri returned. "Yes, you must come over someday."

"Surely, aunty."

"Maybe on Kartik's wedding day," Vinny said unanticipated. Sahana's smiled vanished for a while, but she kept herself strong.

"Is that happening soon?"

"No." Gauri sighed. "I'm tired of bringing it up with him?"

Sahana looked at Kartik sitting right in front of her, "Why so Kartik? You're getting old now."

Kartik grew uncomfortable.

Vinny laughed, "Mom, you have another son too. You can put that question across to him at times."

Gauri passed a wry smile, "Finish your studies first."

"They are getting over in ten months."

"For sure the order of printing the wedding invites will be Vinayak followed by Kartik in my family to set the order right," Gauri said shaking her head.

Everyone laughed.

"You know Sahana, I don't even know what kind of girl Kartik would like," Gauri said.

"Oh, that's simple. Everyone is always looking for their type. So in simple words, she should be intelligent, agile, straight-forward and head-before-heart kind."

Vinny turned to Sahana for the first time with a serious expression. "You know him pretty well."

Gauri smiled, "Well, I'm not surprised, even I guessed so."

"No," Vinny interrupted, "the last one you'd never believe."

He looked at Sahana again, "It requires very keen observation to make that comment. Because from what he projects, it appears he's a hearty being which is…trickery of sorts."

Sahana sat bewildered. It also revived a few disturbing memories of her being tricked mercilessly by Kartik a few years ago.

"So, what kind of girl are you looking for, Vinny?" Sahana attempted to change the topic.

"I'm so glad someone finally asked me this question," he smiled and gave a side look to his mother. "Do you have a younger sister, Sahana?"

Sahana's eyebrows rose. "Vinny," Gauri said a little louder. "Sorry Sahana, he's a little childish."

"No, that's okay." Sahana turned at Vinny. "You remind me of somebody."

"Somebody special?" Vinny teased.

"Not really," Sahana said keeping her expressions straight; Kartik dropped his smile though.

"Sahana, I insist you must come," Gauri said.

"You know coincidentally, my friend's cousin is getting married after two weeks there. She has to attend the wedding but she isn't very thrilled about it, so she was also asking me to tag along," Sahana said.

"That sounds like a good plan," Kartik said.

"Not really, when she isn't thrilled about her cousin's marriage, I should be the last one to be."

"But you'll have someone to travel with," Kartik said.

"Yes," Vinny interrupted. "Leave the rest to me. I'll make sure you see around every beautiful corner of the city in two days."

He paused. "You'll love my city, ma'am."

Kartik shook his head at Vinny's useless interjection. Sahana smiled broadly at his innocent flirting.

Gauri made a trip to the kitchen; and signalled Vinny to come along to savour a little dose.

"Vinny has this habit of silly jokes. Don't mind that please," Kartik said.

Her broad smile turned into a giggle, "Rustic charm seems to be running in the blood of the family."

Kartik giggled along.

After dinner, she insisted on driving home in her car parked in the office's premises.

"No way! You're *our* guest," Vinny rang in again. "We'll drop you back home in *our* Honda City."

Kartik wordlessly stared at Vinny, who paid no heed as he was more excited about the ride.

Sahana was offered the front seat to help with directions. Vinny kept his charm flowing from the back seat.

"Do you like Delhi, Sahana?" Vinny asked.

"For sure, it's my home. And you?"

"I like the city, but I don't like the people."

She turned her neck to him, "What's wrong with Delhiites?"

"They are very rude and always in a hurry. They are kind of always irked."

Sahana narrowed her eyes, "I don't disagree with you, and big cities do have such issues. It has more to do with the busy lifestyle than the people themselves."

Vinny nodded. "I particularly don't like Delhi girls."

"What's wrong with them?"

Vinny sighed, "They are not kind!"

Kartik slapped his head, and Sahana bit her finger to curb her laughter. 'Not being kind' was well comprehended.

While getting down Sahana parted genially. "Thanks, Vinny, I don't even remember the last time I smiled all evening."

"My pleasure. Visit my city soon; there are many more smiles coming your way." They shook hands and bid adieu.

Kartik castigated Vinny on the way back home, "Do you even realize what you keep saying? She was my friend."

"Not your girlfriend, for sure. And if she enjoyed my company why are you mad?"

"She was just being nice..."

"Nah! She was nice for sure. Cute girl." Vinny said. "By the way, bro, what about my demand? "

"No way, you don't need a bike till you complete your studies. Why do you need it, by the way?"

Vinny didn't like it. "To drop girls back home like you." Kartik gave him a rueful smile.

"Okay !" Vinny sighed, "After my engineering. Pakka?"

"Pakka!" Kartik assured him.

"Black Bullet! Nothing less." Vinny made it clear.

Kartik nodded. "Great! Then let's celebrate."

"Celebrate what?"

"I dropped a girl back home for the first time in my life." Vinny smiled.

"Vinny, I repeat she's a good friend, so please check yourself."

"You're too much, bro, can't you pay my beer bill at least once in a lifetime. I had such a troubled ride today." Vinny emotionally blackmailed him and had his way finally.

Plan B

"Hey, Shona," said Sahana's childhood best friend Anusha when she opened her door.

They were soon lolling in Anusha's bed in her room.

Sahana abruptly picked Anusha's phone and threw it at her, "Can you please call Sweety Aunty in Amritsar that I'll be coming over two weeks later and will be staying over on Saturday night. She'd be okay?"

"More than okay. But why are you going there?" Anusha asked.

"Because her daughter is getting married two weeks later. You also need to go but you aren't very keen. So you want me to join you for company," Sahana said flipping the pages of Anusha's holiday album.

Anusha dropped her jaw and sat on her knees, "Wait a minute! First, that cousin of mine is a sweetheart. Second, it will be unlawful to even think of her marriage for the next three years, she's just fifteen. And third, I certainly have no plans to go there."

"Relax," Sahana said, calmly flipping the pages. "If you'll think with a cool head, you'll get all your answers."

Anusha narrowed her eyes, "Oh! I see."

She came back to the original position. "Amritsar! Mission COO."

The friends laughed out aloud. "That's a great plan, Shona, why did we never think of it before?"

"I swear! The idea struck me when his younger brother invited me to the city yesterday; your Sweety Aunty flashed into my mind as a devi."

"Oh, Shona!" Anusha held her hands, "It's so great to see you laughing again!"

"You need to thank an unknown American goon for it."

The girls rolled in laughter, lying on their backs facing the ceiling.

"But dear, do you really have to do all this? I mean, now since all you need to tell him is the little truth about you and Rahul." Anusha said.

"No, Anusha. I can't even afford to do that."

"But what's the harm? Since you know he loves you."

"Because I know he loved me then too." Sahana sat up, "And love alone is never enough. I want my due respect too. And he's a kind of species who doesn't value what they haven't struggled for."

Anusha sighed, "Okay dear, I believe you. All I want is for you to be happy always."

Sahana smiled, "Me too. Very happy, with him, always. But this time, I can't afford to present myself so easy to get."

"Bang on," Anusha chimed along, "So when is that HR's engagement?"

"Tomorrow."

"You know what you need to do. Plan B should hit the right target," Anusha winked.

"You bet!"

"And then, I have a plan C ready to convince Ajit Uncle."

"What's that?" Sahana asked with curiosity.

"Click some semi-nude pics of you both and send them over to Ajit uncle."

"You seem to be watching a lot of B-grade Hindi movies these days."

"Plan D is even wilder," Anusha said with pride.

"Please go ahead."

"Ensuring that you get pregnant."

Sahana hit her playfully with the album, and the friends peeled in laughter. "Not plan D, but maybe plan Z!"

◆

Sahana and Kartik arrived nearly at the same time to Garima's engagement in Karnal. The exchanging of rings was cheerfully applauded by the guests.

"Garima is wonderful; this is how a girl should behave on her engagement," Sahana said abruptly, standing right next to Kartik.

He turned to her with confusion, as she continued. "I really screwed that evening and mood of many close ones. I shouldn't have done that. You know, Rahul's mother was too mad at me; she teased my mom that it seemed she was forcing her daughter to get hitched."

They moved to sit down. "What happened?"

"I've been thinking about your suggestions since a few days now. Rahul is truly a nice guy," Sahana said looking at the just-engaged couple.

Kartik sat numb for a while before he spoke cautiously, "But you weren't very happy about his advances."

"Wasn't that also very stupid on my part?" Sahana turned at him, "Wasn't that an obvious thing for him to expect out of his fiancée?"

Kartik's eyes opened wide as she kept going, "And as someone told me a few years ago; it's as natural as nature wants you to be." She sighed, "I should call and apologize for my churlish behaviour."

"Don't jump to any decision rashly," Kartik said quickly, "Think thoroughly this time."

"Anyway, dad will get us back together when he returns; at least that would cover my blunder."

"But his parents will tell sir anyway."

"Maybe they will. But at least if I patch up with him, it won't appear very messy?" she paused. "What say?"

Kartik said while scratching his nose, "Take some more days to think."

"I've already decided…" Sahana said but was cut short.

"I said take some more days; it's pertaining to your entire life. Don't decide in haste."

She nodded and smiled innocently.

The rest of the party was fun; Kartik, however, was very perplexed throughout. He drove back home in the same mood and reached home even more annoyed.

"How was the party?" Vinny asked as he opened the door.

"Okay," Kartik answered with a dejected expression.

"What happened, Happy?" Gauri asked as she walked out of the room.

"Nothing. I just want to catch some sleep."

"Your mood swings are becoming a big concern for me now," Gauri added.

"Please, guys," Kartik exploded. "What's wrong with you both? I just came in and want some sleep."

"Why are you so upset?" Gauri prodded.

"I don't get this, Maa." Kartik vented all his frustration on his mother. "All the words you're left with for me on this planet are 'upset', 'over-worked', 'irritated' and 'angered'."

"Take it easy, bro." Vinny patted his shoulder.

"I'm fine." He shrugged his shoulder and stormed into his room.

Vinny and Gauri looked at each other conveying their worry over Kartik's dolefulness.

◆

As always, Kartik realized he had been unreasonably mad at his mother the first thing in the morning. Gauri was sitting in the living room, biting her nails in worry.

"I'm sorry Maa," Kartik said kneeling down, resting his hands on her knees.

"We can sort that later," Gauri's attention homed to the noise from inside the room. She turned to Kartik sharply, "Can you do me a favour?"

"Order me, Maa."

"Just ignore Vinny if he says something absurd."

She rested her hand on his shoulder, "Behave like the elder one. Ignore him."

She emphasized on the word 'ignore'.

Vinny stormed out of the room in his signature style. "I'm leaving, Maa."

"Where are you going? You were to leave on Thursday night with Maa," Kartik stood up, glaring at Vinny.

"I stayed last night on Maa's insistence. I can't stay here for a minute now."

"What happened?"

"I'm not talking to you," he said to the air between him and Kartik and jerked his neck to Gauri, "Bye, Maa."

"Hey wait, what is all this about?" Kartik walked up to Vinny, followed by Gauri, but she bypassed him to stand in the middle of her boys.

"Vinny, don't be theatrical," Gauri said.

"Maybe you can live with this, I can't," Vinny said angrily.

Kartik covered his face with both his hands. He remembered that Vinny never tolerated anyone being rude to Gauri, not even Arminder.

"Hey see, I said sorry to Maa just now," Kartik clarified.

"Don't you get it? I'm not talking to you. Honestly speaking, I don't even consider you worth talking to."

"Hang on, it's between me and Maa. You don't have to sound like Papa."

"I'm not surprised if I sound like Papa to you; we both love this lady."

"I too. And..."

"No way," Vinny scowled. "You don't have it in you to love this or any other lady for that matter. The root cause of all your frustration in life. Maybe only a few can see it. It's not the head before the heart; it's just head and head, heartlessly."

Kartik stiffened as Vinny continued, "All your life as far as I remember, was all about your grades. And I've overheard parents worrying about 'from-where'," he said snarling, "and the only thing I wonder looking at your pitiable state is 'to-where!' "

Vinny turned to his mother again, "I'm leaving Maa. See you home on Friday. And that's the only place we both will ever meet."

He stormed out, and Gauri called his name once, but her focus diverted to Kartik attentively. Kartik stood there pallid like a zombie. "You ignored what he said, right? You did what I asked you to?" Gauri touched his shoulder and lifted his hung face. Red sore eyes looked up.

She held his face, "He's your baby brother. You need to forgive him. We all know he's an idiot."

Kartik's condition remained unchanged and Gauri repeated her lines several times. After a while, Kartik held both her hands over his face and moved his neck a little to kiss her palm. "He's not an idiot. He's your good son."

He slid her hand gently away from his face and went into the bathroom, where he finally let the water from his eyes flow along with water pouring from the shower over his head. That from the eyes being more saline.

◆

At the office, the next three days also continued in the same fashion, Sahana treating Kartik as a colleague. Kartik unable to contain his building frustration asked Sahana out for dinner. She accepted smiling and sent out an SMS for a cameo actor to be ready with a smart script.

While the duo was walking outside the office, they 'coincidentally' bumped into Prez.

"Hey, Prez. Still in office?" Sahana asked.

"Yes, but leaving now." He replied.

"Why don't you join us for dinner?" Sahana said, even without consulting Kartik.

Prez looked at Kartik though, who in turn passed a weak smile. Sahana said again, "Come, Prez. Three friends better than two."

Prez joined them to display his other talent. Prez's phone beeped with an SMS while they seated for dinner. It was a bank alert message.

He said beaming, "She always wishes me good night in her sweet way."

"It's just 8.00 p.m." Kartik japed.

"Well, we start saying good night from eight, and it carries on till ten-thirty until we fall asleep," Prez replied cleverly.

"How sweet," Sahana said joining her hands under her right cheek.

"So we can expect your phone to be beeping throughout dinner," Kartik said a little unpleasantly.

"Let me write to her that I'm out with friends."

"Things any better, Prez? Did you try speaking to your father?" Sahana came to the agenda.

"I tried, but in vain. They are very adamant."

"Isn't it a little rude on your part to walk out on your family?" Kartik said harshly.

Sahana turned towards Kartik, expressing displeasure over his tone. But Kartik didn't bother.

"I didn't leave them; they disowned me."

"But you know this girl for just a few years maybe; they caused your existence," Kartik continued.

"I completely agree with you, sir, but then Ayesha is also my life. When I came to know she's Ayesha Tomar, I was also jolted. But then I couldn't abandon her at that stage of our relationship," he choked cinematically, and Sahana extended a glass of water. "Her name was confusing, mine wasn't. She loved me truly and didn't bother about petty issues, belittling me, whose mind even for a minute had sheltered such thoughts."

Sahana heaved artificially. Kartik turned to her and was disturbed seeing her so emotional.

"Ayesha's such a lucky girl," Sahana said, wiping her crocodile tears.

The rest of the dinner, Prez kept bragging about his sacrifices for his true love. Prez took leave for his PG, while the other two opted for ice cream.

"How's sir doing now?" He asked on being caught watching her clean ice-cream that had fallen on her shirt.

"Much better, he even speaks to me every two-three days now. Docs don't allow more than that as of now."

"That's wonderful. He'll be back soon in that case."

"Yet another six to eight weeks to go as per the docs."

"Sir is really spirited. His courage is outstanding," Kartik said admiringly.

"Oh yes. My dad is my hero."

Kartik smiled along, "Mine too."

She nodded, "I'm very proud of my mother too. She's my father's backbone. My dad doesn't say that very often, or maybe he does say, but I'm unaware, but he truly loves my mom." She crossed her arms around her.

Kartik smiled, "For sure. You miss them a lot."

"Yes. And I promise I won't trouble them ever again in my life."

Kartik's smile shrank as Sahana dropped a tear from her eye, "I understand what you must be going through."

"You can't," she wiped her tear, "Let's go. I don't understand why we slip into such discussions each time. You were very right, we both come from different worlds, but that difference has more to do with the heart than the mind."

Kartik was muddled, "What happened? My heart can relate to your feelings."

Sahana was pestered; she wasn't faking or enacting; she was actually pissed off with Kartik.

"Really? That's news that you have a heart," she said with venomous sarcasm. She did realize she was being harsh; but didn't back off. She drove away in her car.

Kartik sat still for a while, struggling with his turbulent thoughts.

◆

Sahana avoided him on Thursday. At his mother's insistence, he attended his cousin's engagement in Amritsar on Friday afternoon, taking a day off. Happy was dragged by his old friends for a get-together on his terrace. Bobby was engaged by then, while rest of the three friends were still bachelors.

"Razoo," said an artificially sad Honey.

"Here he goes again," Bobby said and patted Honey's back, consoling.

"My mom told me she's coming next week." Jolly hiccupped.

"Really? I'll get to see my Razoo," Honey said romantically.

"Yah! It's her baby shower," Jolly said, and huge laughter followed.

"Tell me the truth, you scoundrels. Whose baby is it?" Honey stood up wavering.

"Not yours for sure," teased Happy. Everyone guffawed.

"Happy!" Honey broadened his chest cinematically. "You're laughing at my true love. You'll know how it feels when someone else will take your girl away."

Happy, who was a little high himself, couldn't manage to take it as a joke this time. He threw his bottle hard and pieces of glass flew all over. Vinny's room was right below; he came up running alarmingly.

Happy held Honey's collar hard and punched him on his face. Jolly defended Honey, while Bobby was trying to bring Happy down. Vinny came and stood right in the middle of the two groups. "Hey big bros, what's happening? You'll wake the entire mohalla up."

"I'm going to kill Honey today," Happy was clearly agitated. "Bloody hell! For that chic Razoo, you cursed me last time too."

"What curse?" Bobby tried to pacify him, "He's drunk, Happy. You know he's joking."

"Scoundrel boozer." Happy screamed as he tried to reach Honey. "Was I produced to stand clapping in the audience?"

"Clapping in the audience?" Vinny was still unsure what had made Kartik so furious.

"I always knew he wanted to play for team India," Honey said swaying.

Only Bobby was in his senses. "Happy relax. He was joking. How can someone take your girl away?"

"Someone did. I always knew he loved Razoo," Honey continued blabbering. "So now we know whose baby it is."

Happy threw off Vinny and Bobby to reach Honey and hit him hard again. Both came up quickly and held him back while he still kept kicking at Honey.

"What's the matter, bro?" Honey said while being helped by Jolly to stand up.

"Evil tongues should keep their mouths shut," Happy pointed his finger right between Honey's eyes. "Even if someone dares to take her away this time; I'm going to crush his bones to make tooth powder."

Vinny stood stunned, trying hard to connect the dots. Everyone around looked at him dumbstruck.

Jolly's hiccups broke the silence. "Is tooth powder made of bones?"

"Could be, both are white," Honey said thoughtfully.

"Then how about red tooth powder?" Jolly asked with a serious expression.

"Maybe bones are not cleaned, so some bloodstains remain," Honey answered scratching his head.

"Are you sure?" Jolly asked.

Honey bent his head shaking hard, "Happy is M wala B.A; if he's saying so, then it must be so."

They both nodded together, convinced.

Vinny pulled Kartik downstairs to his room while he was still throwing slangs at Honey. Vinny gestured to him to quieten, so their parents would not wake up. Kartik continued murmuring even when put to bed.

Vinny chose to sleep next to him to avoid any other scene at night. Kartik's confession caused Vinny to have a sleepless night, *"I do have a heart, I do. And bloody hell, it even beats for you."*

◆

Next morning, Kartik was a little embarrassed at the breakfast table when his mother questioned him about the broken bottle on the terrace.

Vinny was lost in his thoughts. Who could she be?

Gauri abruptly spoke, "Is that Sahana coming next week?" Kartik nodded.

"Who's Sahana?" Arminder asked.

"Happy's boss, Mr Khurana's daughter."

"Whose engagement we attended?" Arminder asked.

"Sahana's engaged?" asked a surprised Vinny.

"Yes, we told you that we attended Happy's boss's daughter's engagement," Gauri replied.

"But there was no ring on her finger when she came over; I thought she has an elder sister."

"Wait a minute." Arminder intervened. "First, why is she coming here?"

"Anyone can go anywhere in India under the law. We are a free nation," Kartik replied with mild irritation.

"Yes, though our house isn't a public place." Arminder asked. "And it's far below their standard. You should think wisely before inviting her."

Kartik sat quietly.

"It's okay, she isn't staying here. We may invite her just for dinner. The boys will take her around the city and drop her to her relative's house," Gauri elaborated the plan.

"And what the hell is this standard issue, Dad? Sahana appeared to be a very warm person," Vinny said.

"On the face, all the rich are nice, but not for very long. They soon get irritated. And what went wrong with her engagement?"

"What's your business?" asked an ireful Kartik.

"Just asking," Arminder said.

"But why? Is that a big deal?"

"Well maybe not for them, but we in a small town do consider that a big deal."

"It has nothing to do with the grandness of a town; all it has to do with is the grandness of the mind. I don't think it's anything that even calls for a discussion," Kartik's anger grew.

"What's wrong, Happy? " Gauri's concern filled her face. "Your papa asked a very simple question."

"My point is why is he even asking," Kartik thumped hard on the table and swiftly walked away.

Gauri and Arminder were stumped; Vinny finally smiled, having found his answer. He hoped to be of some help.

◆

Late at night Vinny walked up to a place where Kartik could be found ever since their childhood whenever he was in a bad mood. Vinny walked up to the terrace and then climbed a wooden ladder to reach the parapet constructed for keeping water tanks; the highest point in the neighbourhood.

"I knew you would be here," Vinny said breaking Kartik's thoughts. Kartik, however, turned his face away, avoiding eye contact with Vinny.

"What are you doing sitting here?" Vinny asked smiling.

"Hiding from you," Kartik said curtly.

"Bro," Vinny said with sincerity, "I wanted to say sorry for my behaviour last week. I should have checked my words."

"No, you're fine. Any good son would have done what you did. I'm proud of you, actually."

"I'm sorry, bro."

"Don't be," he cleared his choking throat. "You know, a few days back Sahana said something beautiful. I was furious at our major vendor and was on the verge of blasting them, but Sahana intervened and gracefully handled the situation. She said, her mother taught her that even when you're extremely mad at someone, never forget who that someone is."

He choked again, "And I bleakly remembered that our mother had also taught me something similar in childhood, but I never cared to learn or to even register it. I just wanted to break some jaws by making it big in life."

"You're right, I should have remembered."

"No, I meant my behaviour. Your reaction was more than justified."

"So, are we going to continue or you'll sort it out saying you've forgiven me."

"I'm no one to forgive..."

"Oh! So we are continuing."

Kartik smirked, "You'll always be my darling."

"Better be," Vinny smiled broadly. He pulled out few beer cans from a paper bag he had brought along.

"Here, treat on me." Kartik shook his head. They both started talking looking around the neighbourhood. Kartik though was still sullen.

"You know, when I was nine, I thought you like this spot because you could see Razoo on her roof from here," Vinny said.

Kartik smiled askew, "You were right."

"Things didn't work out or what?"

"They did work out, but a few months later Jolly found out that she was working multiple shifts."

Vinny laughed out loud.

"Now you can laugh, we all also do. But it was anything but funny at that time."

He turned a little to Vinny, "It wasn't entirely my fault to think about girls that way. It didn't end with Razoo. I always only met girls of that feather. My bad luck or whatever."

"No relationship?"

Kartik waived his head, "Just meaningless sleeping around. Disgusted I feel about myself at times now," he heaved. "But for some reason I was convinced it's an era of shrinking emotions. I never felt guilty."

"Until very recently," Vinny said halting on every word.

Kartik's face turned grave. "No, it's been a while. Being proved wrong too innocently, too beautifully, and too magically," he said quietly.

Vinny took a while before resuming probing, "What dad said this morning about standards, is the way the world thought in his time; it may not still hold good."

"But what he said is inspired by his rich experience of life; it can't be overlooked. I too think the same. Ajit sir too."

"And how long have you been thinking about this standard issue?"

"About three years."

"And do you have an answer?"

Kartik turned towards Vinny with amazement. "Then certainly something is much superior to this petty issue that is causing such emotional turbulence within you," Vinny smirked, "You almost killed Honey yesterday."

Kartik lowered his head, "I'm tired of thinking. I've reached a point where I have to decide and live up to it, no matter what it takes."

"Now that sounds like my spirited brother," Vinny beamed. "Keep aside all the issues of standards, the connection you share with her and any other stupid reason possible."

He jumped and sat right in front of Kartik, "What do you really want deep in your heart?"

Kartik closed his eyes. He remembered many faces of his unfulfilled wish: her innocence, her charm, her smile, her possessiveness, her anger and her oceanic eyes full of love. He then remembered the day of her engagement when she was standing at a podium and searching through the guests for him. He imagined her eyes falling on him that day; she called his name mutely. Kartik started moving towards her, and she too walked down. They were walking towards each other, much to the bewilderment of everyone around them. They walked faster so as to cover the distance between them forever. They stood quietly as soon they reached two steps apart; looking into each other's eyes and expressing their torment. Just when Sahana raised her foot to swing in his arms, a hand held her wrist firm and started pulling her back.

Kartik unconsciously raised his hand as if stopping someone from moving away; his face filled with ardor. Vinny held his shoulder gently, "What do you want to do?"

"I want to be with her till eternity."

It took a while to bring his emotion down and be in a position to talk. Vinny came back and sat next to him.

Kartik opened his eyes slowly and smiled feeling relieved. "You did pull it out of me finally?"

"You left me with no other option," Vinny teased.

"Don't tell Maa."

"She'll want to hear from you."

"I have nothing to tell Maa right now."

"Of course, you need to tell somebody else before you tell Maa. It's already been three years."

"I said I'm thinking over issues for the last three years; it's actually been five."

Vinny shook his head in disbelief, "Five years!"

"We've known each other since five years, and since three years my thoughts are oscillating between to-be and not-to-be. *Mujhe laga meri life ki lag jayegi.*"

"*Veere, teri life ki toh waise bhi lagi hi padi hai. Kam se kam ladki toh milegi.*"

"Sir would have thrashed me; my career would have ended, or at least won't have been this successful. And then, I'm also not classy rich."

"We are rich too. Very very rich in love, family values and the spirit of life. Avarice that makes life grand! " Vinny broadened his chest. Kartik smiled broadly.

"By the way, bro," Vinny winked flirtatiously, "Good pick!"

Kartik pulled his ear and the brothers shared warm light moments over the beer Vinny had got.

"By the way, I have another thing to make you feel lighter."

"What?"

"Finally a bill of mine that you can pay without any guilt."

Happy Amritsar

Monday morning was surely a new dawn for Kartik; he pledged to give all the happiness she ever wanted out of him. And more importantly how she wanted it; the rustic way.

A little later in the morning, he walked inside Sahana's cabin.

"How was your weekend back home?" Sahana asked smiling.

"Heavenly."

His rediscovered spirit was apparent on his face.

"It really appears so."

"All set for the weekend?"

"It's just Monday yet."

He moved closer to Sahana, "By the way, nice hair style."

"Thank you," she replied in confusion.

"And orange suits you the best."

"Thank you again."

His appreciation appreciated her confusion.

"And I truly wonder how you manage to look so fabulous always."

Sahana's eyes widened.

"You missed saying thank you?"

She blinked animatedly, "I can't believe this."

"Seems it's been a while someone reminded you of your beauty."

"Not exactly," Sahana said. "But I can't believe you're being so upfront."

And before Sahana's confusion could reach apogee, an alarm rang for the board meeting.

◆

Kartik reached Amritsar on Friday night and Sahana on Saturday afternoon by the Shatabdi Express. Sweety Aunty picked her up from the station.

When Kartik was preparing to leave from home, Vinny refused to join him.

"She asked me to get you along," Kartik insisted.

"How old is Sahana?" Vinny asked abruptly.

Kartik gave him a weird look, "Twenty-five."

"So I stand no chance, why the hell should I spoil my weekend?"

Gauri passed a pressing smile to Vinny, "Go along. It's not always about chances."

"I'll be home with Maa to help prepare dinner."

"An elephant isn't coming for dinner that Maa needs to cook all day," Kartik said. Gauri also insisted again.

"Maa, Amritsar is a welcoming city; our first aim towards our guest is to help solve the purpose of the visit."

Kartik read between the lines and smiled. Gauri was confused though. "What purpose?"

"Shopping," Kartik said abruptly. "And we know Vinny hates it."

Vinny smiled stupidly.

Kartik left home and picked up Sahana in his dad's WagonR.

"Are you sure you won't be irritated helping me shop?" Sahana asked the same question again that she'd asked him fifty times already.

"You'll end up paying double the price if you go alone," he paused. "You may not mind paying, but it's not a good practice."

"Why won't I mind that? It will be foolish to pay even a paisa more than what a thing is worth."

"Good. So let me negotiate."

Sahana was delighted to visit the cramped and flashy shopping street. "Wow, this looks so much like Chandni Chowk; I'm sure prices will be even lower."

Kartik was addled, "I never knew you like street shopping?"

"You always judge me per your assumptions," Sahana said offended. Kartik smiled back.

First, they went to a dupatta shop. Sahana picked a beautiful green *phulkari* dupatta.

"How much for this?" Sahana asked.

"Rupees 950," the shopkeeper replied.

And before Sahana could say anything, Kartik spoke, "Not more than 800 and that's it."

Sahana turned at Kartik with a dirty look, "You should consult me before speaking," she whispered.

"I told you to choose and sit back," he whispered back, "I've been brought up here; I know how much what should cost."

"It could be your native place, but for sure, shopping isn't your skill."

"That is fine," the shopkeeper replied.

"No," Sahana said firmly. "Not more than 650 rupees."

Kartik blinked hard to believe it.

"Not a paisa more."

"He said 800," the vendor pointed at Kartik.

"He was joking, ignore what he said. That is my final price."

Kartik struggled to curb his laughter as Sahana bargained assertively in her broken and funny Punjabi. She felt victorious after buying it on her quoted price.

Alternatively, Kartik chose to sit back as she shopped with her typical Delhi-accent-stricken Punjabi.

"*Aae* yellow *wala,* how much?" Sahana assaulted the Punjabi language.

"*Aae pilla wala kinne da?*" Kartik corrected her whispering.

She smiled foolishly, and finally got it right after two attempts.

"I always thought Khuranas are also Punjabi," he teased.

"Oh yes they are, but we Delhi brought-ups with no roots left behind in Punjab and are only living on Daler Mehndi songs!"

He smiled.

"How cute it could be to jump on a song, a word of which you don't follow."

Sahana narrowed his eyes, "You seem to be back to your original self. Meditation has definitely worked some magic."

"Crappy philosophical lectures can never help. They at least never helped me. I finally found what would inject life in me again."

"That's cool. Self-discovery is the best. So what's it?"

He looked straight into her eyes, "Follow my heart."

She pretended to be confused and turned back to the shopkeeper.

Kartik had a fun ride but he also felt hugely sympathetic towards the shopkeepers.

He helped her carry shopping bags; they were sixteen already. "Do you have space in your luggage to carry it back?"

"Oh yes, my big bag has just three sets of clothes presently," Sahana smiled childishly.

Kartik bumped into Honey, who still had a bruise below his eye. Honey passed elfish expressions seeing him with a pretty girl. "I didn't know you were coming this weekend too?"

"It was a last minute plan," Kartik replied. "I'll catch you later."

"Oh yes. Tonight at my terrace." Honey said, still staring at Sahana, making her a little uneasy.

"Hello ji." He smiled.

Sahana smiled back.

"Today not possible," Kartik said and moved his eyes to ask Honey to get going.

"Why not? Are you doing something else tonight?" Honey's double-meaning question irked Kartik.

He took him to a distance, asking Sahana to stay. "Why are you creating a scene?"

"What scene? At least introduce me to bhabhi ji."

"What bhabhi ji? She's my guest."

"You should carry some weapon along today to protect your guest."

"Honey, please behave, you're making her uneasy." Kartik fumed in a low voice, "Else I'll smash your other eye too."

Honey got offended and swore to settle for the insult in the evening.

Next, Kartik took Sahana to the Wagah border. They had a good time spending a few moments feeling patriotic watching the flag ceremony.

He then disclosed about the dinner plan at his residence. "No please, why do you keep bothering Aunty each time," Sahana said.

"We all have dinner at night, and you anyway don't eat much," Kartik winked.

Before Kartik could reach home, news had reached his entire neighbourhood that Kartik was roaming around with a chic from Delhi. When he parked his car on his street, all the aunties, uncles, youngsters, kids, pets and stray animals were staring at the Brars' residence. Kartik was visibly irritated at the kind of show being put up by his people. He knew whom to thank and swore to bruise his other eye before he went back to Delhi.

Sahana was very warmly greeted by the Brar family. She was particularly delighted to meet Vinayak again. She asked directions to the washroom that Gauri escorted her to.

"Maa, what's the entire lane doing standing at their gates and balconies for?" Kartik asked in a low voice.

"They've all almost tagged her as my elder daughter-in-law," Gauri rolled her eyes.

"Not a bad idea," Vinny said smiling.

"Please behave, Vinny," Arminder said. "Relax, Happy. By tomorrow, they'll find some other business to gossip about."

The door bell rang, and Jolly, Bobby, and Honey walked in.

"What are you guys doing here?" Happy asked pushing them to the corner.

"I wanted to see under what conditions bones get crushed to tooth powder," Bobby teased. Rest giggled.

"Please leave buddies, don't make it awkward for me," Kartik pleaded. Sahana walked out just then, and her eyes fell on Kartik's friends. Bobby walked up to her, the rest followed.

"Hello ji, Welcome to our city," Bobby said grinning. "We are Happy's childhood friends,"

Sahana narrowed her eyes, "Who's Happy?"

Bobby pointed at the man in question, "Kartik?" Sahana asked.

"Who's Kartik?" Bobby asked confused. Sahana smiled to herself. *Aha! Happy since birth!*

Kartik exhaled a deep breath upwards and shunted his friends out of the house. Vinny stood next to Sahana while he was busy doing so. "We met this bruised-eyed guy in the market today," Sahana said to Vinny lowly.

"Did he tell you how he got it?"

Sahana shook her head.

"Bro hit him last week."

"Kartik?" Sahana's eyes opened wide, "He gets into brawls too?"

"No." Vinny smiled. "Not always. Only when he gets too high."

"He gets so high that he starts beating people?"

Vinny smiled naughtily, "You should know him better." Sahana smiled back.

Kartik returned after almost throwing his friends outside the house, "I'm sorry, they are nice, just slightly mannerless."

Gauri and Arminder also walked out of their room where they had been attending a call from a relative.

◆

"How's your father doing now?" Arminder asked the first question on the dinner table.

"He's almost perfectly fine; will be back in a few more weeks," Sahana replied smiling.

"How did you like the city?" Gauri asked.

"The shopping was amazing. You should have come too."

"Kartik doesn't take me shopping," Gauri said.

"Ideally you should not take him; he was a disaster today," Sahana narrated the 950-800-650 incident. Everyone laughed.

Kartik gave a look sideways to Sahana who was sitting next to him, "You should be thankful rather."

Sahana replied almost whispering, "Forget it."

"How mean."

"I almost had a loss of 150 rupees because of you."

"Almost a fortune!" they giggled.

Gauri noticed their special bond for the first time then. She too hadn't thought about the connection they shared. Credit most belong to the gossipmongers around that Gauri observed Kartik was actually 'Happy' when he was with her. Kartik refused to meet any girl; there was no sign of any girl in his life otherwise. But with Sahana, he was not only comfortable, but treating her very specially too.

"You're quite friendly; last time I met you I thought you were very reserved."

Kartik's smile vanished at Arminder's out of place comment. Gauri preferred silently observing their countenance.

"Try the *chhole*. It's Mumma's specialty," Vinny said to change the topic. Sahana continued to smile, not taking Arminder's remark negatively.

The boys took Sahana to their favourite place in the house, the terrace, to have the dessert. It was a beautiful, breezy, partially cloudy night. They were standing in a semi-circle with Sahana in the middle. Moonlight fell on them when the moon emerged from behind the clouds for a flash, grabbing their attention.

"Aim for the moon..." Sahana and Kartik said in a chorus. Kartik smiled and gestured for her to complete, "you'll at least land on a beautiful star."

"Wow, that's a lovely thought," Vinny said appreciatively.

"That's one of Dad's favourite quotes," she said with moist eyes.

"Sir uses that often in the office too," Kartik added.

"The first time he said that to me, I was nine. He was putting me to sleep and his eyes fell on the moon outside the window." Sahana said wiping the droplet that ran down her cheek.

"I was half asleep and woke up alarmed. I said, 'No Dad, let it be. The moon is shining so bright and isn't bothering you, then why do you want to aim an arrow at it? Make friends with the moon instead.'"

Vinny chuckled. Sahana turned at him smiling. "You can laugh. I know that's stupid."

Vinny said, "But that was so sweet."

"No, it's just stupid. And the worst is, I think the same even today."

"That means you're equally sweet today too."

"A correction. Equally stupid," she rolled her eyes. "And I know scholars consider 'my kind of girls' good for nothing."

"Because most scholars don't have the ability to look at life as a whole. Their aims are monetary or momentary; it's only someone like you who can comprehend the beauty and true merit of life," Kartik said, smiling almost like a saint.

The two turned to Kartik. Vinny silently stepped back and disappeared from the scene taking the empty bowls of *kheer;* after all he had to give some excuse to head downstairs. But it was of no use, Gauri didn't give an ear to Vinny's well-intended untruth.

"It doesn't suit today's world. Everyone is very busy trying to conquer the moon. The only thing I hope for the one who does, that he doesn't miss the earth someday," she replied.

"That's doomed to happen. The moon can be gratifying for a few moments, but the earth is the ultimate truth. Even that conqueror will fall back into her lap finally."

"And is it an assumption that the earth will always be there to accept him back?"

"Not sure. Some decisions have to be pronounced by someone who created the moon, the earth, the conqueror, you and me."

Sahana stood expressionless purposefully. Not able to find anything else to say, she uttered, "Where's Vinny?"

"He slid away before you expressed your disappointment about a conqueror choosing the moon over you."

She narrowed her eyes, "I was talking very generally, rather hypothetically. I'm nobody's earth."

"Very true. Someone like you should be a cosmic completeness – the earth, moon, sun, stars, venus included."

"Are you trying to flirt with me?"

"Yes."

"Why?"

"Why not?"

"Stop it. I'm not liking it."

"I know you love it."

"Are you out of your mind these days?"

"Yes. Help me out."

"Even God helps those who help themselves."

"Be my God. Help me."

"Behave yourself, Kartik. It's your home."

"Safest place for both of us."

"Safest for what?" Sahana fumed.

And even before Kartik could explain, Sahana gestured him to stop talking. "You need to learn to behave while talking to someone else's fiancé."

Kartik eyebrows rose, "Really? Then his fiancé should be with him. Why did you bother to come all the way here?"

"Vinny invited me."

"Who's Vinny to you?"

Sahana stood still like a six year old caught putting on her mummy's makeup, "Are you trying to tell me that it's troublesome for you taking me around the city?"

"It's my absolute delight and honour."

"Then please tolerate me for one more day."

Kartik looked into her eyes, "You're very angry with me?"

"No," came the quick reply. "Why should I be? Everyone has right to decide their lives."

Kartik was interrupted again.

"It's getting late, can you please drop me back? If it's not a problem."

Kartik nodded, and they walked downstairs. Gauri gave them a sweet smile, and her glance at Sahana had a different emotion altogether.

While Sahana was getting ready to leave, Gauri gave her a special gift. Sahana was reluctant, but Gauri insisted; they shared a warm hug. Both the boys dropped her back to Sweety Aunty's place. Sahana made an excuse that the marriage was a low-key affair hence they hadn't decorated the house.

◆

When the boys returned home, they saw their parents sitting in the living room. Arminder was switching channels while Gauri was lost in her thoughts.

"What happened Maa?" Vinny sat beside her, giving her a hug.

"Isn't it strange, you struggle so long to find some answers while they are right in front you? All you need is to look from a different perspective." Gauri gave a highly convoluted philosophical answer.

Arminder turned the TV off. Kartik also sank deeper into the chair. All the three men looked at each other, hoping that it wasn't anything related to them.

Gauri stared at Kartik, "You want to talk about something?"

Kartik closed his eyes slowly. He shook his head, scratched his nose and rose to walk away.

"Kartik!"

His mother calling him by that name was indicative of her grave temper. "If you've been away from home for twelve years that doesn't mean you don't have a family or they like you, have learned to live without you."

Kartik turned sharply at those harsh words, "Maa, please don't say that."

"Do I have to ask directly? Or can I hope that my son will talk to me?" Gauri said angrily.

Kartik stared at Vinny, suspecting him of having leaked the news; Vinny mouthed a "no" instantly. Gauri's anger aggravated watching them, and she started to walk away. Kartik held her by her shoulder when she was passing by him. "I have nothing to say, Maa. I would have loved to talk about it otherwise." Gauri turned to him.

"You need to trust me here, Maa."

The honesty in his eyes mellowed Gauri a little. She sat down and he kneeled in front of her. "Why are you fighting yourself so hard?" she asked.

"Because I can't fight the situation."

"You should avoid her in that case."

"I did that for a year, and that had been the most difficult of all. Do you have any idea, how painful it is to deal with a feeling...knowing that eyes like hers don't want to see your face?"

His eyes damped.

"Wait a minute," Arminder took off his glasses. "What are we talking about here?"

"Of course Sahana Khurana, Papa," Vinny answered.

Arminder turned to Kartik with confusion, "Are you mad, Happy? She's your boss's daughter, and on top of it, she was almost someone else's wife."

"You've got to stop saying that, Papa," Kartik fumed.

"Are you the reason she broke her engagement?" Gauri asked narrowing her eyes.

Kartik turned his face; Gauri held it and turned it back to her. "I'm not sure. I hope yes," he answered hesitatingly.

"How could you encourage her?" asked a stunned Arminder.

"I didn't," Kartik replied. "But I'm glad she did that."

"Isn't that strange, you attended her engagement..." Arminder was instantly cut short.

"...hoping that seeing her celebrating would also help me move on." Kartik rose up, "But what I saw couldn't have been more devastating."

He closed his eyes in pain, "You were right, Papa, anyone meeting her for the first time that day would have considered her reserved and arrogant. But she isn't the one to be blamed."

He moved two steps backwards, "And one thing I'm really done with is thinking. I can handle a company of 11,000 employees, 110 clients of eleven countries, but I failed so miserably to handle myself when it came to one girl."

His eyes were soaked with longing emotions, "All I know is that it took me a long time to put that smile back on her face and all I care about is that it should stay there, no matter what it takes."

His voice shook as he continued, "At the same time, I understand that we can't be together and I've accepted this stalemate situation. And I'm grateful for being her friend at least. I can live with this; and it's far better than the last one year. And anyway, no one really wants to be with me. No one wants to be with the company I run; no one wants to..."

"Listen listen, the feeling may not be mutual. You could be troubling yourself over nothing." Arminder tried to pacify him.

"What do you know about us?" Kartik rubbed his nose with his sleeves, "It was me who turned my face away and chose my career over our mutual feelings. My fate was smiling until then, but now it's always mocking at me for choosing a suffocating cabin over a spirited life. My fate could have been beautiful, but I'm that blind man as Maa said who let her go." He choked, "I'm damn selfish. I deserve all the pain I'm suffering. I deserve every bit of this bloody hell."

He stepped a few more steps backwards and turned to move up to his room, leaving the rest dumbfounded.

Kartik had his eyes open almost all night; they finally closed on their own as he was dead tired. He slept until very late; and was woken up by Sahana's call. Kartik freshened up quickly and went downstairs .

"Where are you going, Happy?" Gauri asked. "We've been waiting for you for so long for breakfast."

"Please carry on. I need to go."

"But where?"

Kartik heaved a deep breath, "I need to take Sahana to the golden temple, and then drop her to the railway station to catch the Shatabdi early in the evening."

Gauri smiled, "That's a good plan."

She walked up to him and chaffed his forearm affectionately.

"Gauri, what did you gift her yesterday?" Arminder asked peeking out of the newspaper.

"A Ganesh idol made of silver."

"Why me?" Vinny said abruptly raising his hands and making double-quotes in the air. "She's Kartik's friend, you should have gifted a silver Kartik."

Gauri's smile broadened, "She doesn't need that, and she already has Kartik and one of gold."

Kartik knitted his eyebrows at the confusing conversation. "Never heard of a silver idol of Kartik," he said looking at Vinny.

"Anything can be made to order. You want a silver Pamela Anderson?" Vinny's answer triggered a grin.

"You look so good grinning; you should always be happy," Gauri said affectionately. Kartik nodded and prepared to leave again.

"Happy, wait," Arminder stopped him in his tracks. "I'm highly disappointed with you."

Kartik sighed and turned, "I know and trust me, I won't bring any shame to you."

"You have already brought enough shame that I had to lower my head last night."

He folded the newspaper aside and stood up.

"I'm sorry for having caused you pain."

"You'd better," Arminder moved closer to his son. "You're born Punjabi, bloody hell! Behave like one."

He smiled.

"Now what does the entire community have to do with this?" asked an annoyed Kartik.

"Because if I tell them about your choice, they might disown you," Arminder stretched his palm as if he was about to slap Kartik. Gauri came running to hold his hand, *"Ki kar rahe ho tussi, jawan puttar teh koi hath uthanda hai?"*

Kartik was clueless; Gauri spoke to bail him out.

"He has worked hard for years to be successful. People hardly get their BA degrees in our area; my Happy stands out distinctly. He deserves our understanding. He should be pardoned."

"Who are we to pardon him, Gauri?" Arminder clasped Kartik's shoulder. "Make me proud now, go win back your love. I want her in the family by the end of this year." Arminder's words lifted the spirits of the entire family.

"And stop troubling my wife now, I have had enough. Get your own and trouble her for all I care."

Kartik's eyes dampened as his father continued, "If you want I'll speak to Mr Khurana when he returns, there's no reason for him to think of your intentions otherwise. Don't burden your young shoulders with stress beyond that is required."

Kartik's face sparkled, witnessing the generosity of his family. Arminder embraced Kartik, who in turn held his father tight. Arminder lovingly stroked his back, "You could have talked to me years ago, my child. There was no sense for both of you to go through so much pain."

"I have been thinking since years and always deduced it as a bad idea. But it wasn't a matter of mind actually."

"And you'd better think good about yourself. It doesn't appear even a bit that someone special doesn't want to be with you. She could be a little angry. She has a right to be; you need to set it right."

"She won't listen. I tried talking to her, she's too mad."

Arminder came closest possible to Kartik's ear and whispered, "They all are actually mad, and illogical too. And these two features of women makes love the loveliest feeling of the universe; generation after generation, age after age."

Arminder relaxed his hug, "And I think you both look fabulous together."

He turned to Gauri, "What say, Happy's mother?"

Gauri smiled angelically. "I had said earlier that she's the kind of girl a guy can live all his life with by just looking at her. I didn't know then that this good luck would fall into my boy's lap."

"I knew from day one," Vinny pitched in.

"Really?" Kartik said ironically.

"How come?" Gauri asked.

"Experience, Maa, experience," Vinny hugged his mother from behind.

Kartik's phone rang; he didn't even check whose it was. "I need to push off now; I'm running late. I promised her street-food for lunch today."

"Pick up the phone at least," Arminder said.

"I know who it is. I'll get her home again this evening."

"We'll be waiting," his father said waiving bye.

"Thank you, Arminder ji," Gauri gave him a light hug as Kartik left.

"Anytime dear."

He shook his head.

"What happened?" she asked.

"Why does this boy never aim for easily attainable goals?"

◆

After drooling over Amritsari naans, Kartik took Sahana to the Golden Temple. After the darshan, they sat beside the holy pond facing the temple, watching the colorful fishes. Though it was the last week of July, it was pleasant as the early morning rain had oozed some heat off the scorching summer day. Sahana looked pretty in a turquoise salwar kameez with her head covered with a dupatta.

After watching her fairylike face for some time, Kartik spoke abruptly, "So did you call your ex-fiancé up?"

Sahana turned sharply to him at this weird question, "Not yet."

"When do you plan to do that?"

"Maybe tonight," she gave a wry smile.

"You'll reach late at night, won't it be too late to call someone?"

Sahana was irked, "He'll be more than pleased to receive my call, irrespective of the time."

He narrowed his eyes, "Oh Lord! All the guys on the planet are dying to receive one call from Ms Sahana Khurana."

"What?"

"Why don't you call him right away?"

Sahana was dazed, "I'll decide when to call him."

"I insist," he said and snatched the phone from her hand and started scrolling down the contact list.

"What do you think you're doing Kartik?"

They engaged in a good tussle for about a minute until she got her phone back.

"Why do you say things you don't mean?" Kartik said.

"Whatever."

"I'm really finding it very hard to read you these days," he said staring at her.

"You should consider reading something else in that case."

"I've considered everything I could, Sahana," he sighed. "I even fail to want to read anything else."

Sahana contained her angry expression and slowly raised her eyes to meet his. He continued, "And you really think after screwing my life so royally, you can walk over and reunite with him?"

Sahana stiffened with anger, "You got me into trouble and were super delighted congratulating me. And now you're trying to tell me I screwed your life. Hope you enjoyed the party? Did you dance too?"

"Why the hell could you not smile that day? Holy smokes! Even an artificial one would have done."

"My wish! I only smile when I feel like smiling."

"Watch your attitude," he growled. "You sucked the golden years of my life. I was one firm believer of hedonism. Thanks to you, however, from the age of twenty-four to that of twenty-nine, there was no girl, and no fun."

Sahana sat on her knees, "The golden years are actually twenty to twenty-five, and you should know whose actually sucked."

"Bloody hell! Mine was the only car you could find in this entire universe to escape in?"

"And bloody hell! Even if I ran away, who in the universe asked you to flirt with me?"

"It was no less than religion for me being optimistic with every pretty girl I came across. And you were the sexiest I had ever bumped into."

He balled his fist, "Why did you drop those tears on my shoulders; I still feel the burden."

"So are you trying to tell me just because I'm sexy, you're buzzing around?"

Kartik eyes widened, "I'm around because I care."

"Not your job. I can really manage on my own."

"Sure you can. It's me I'm more worried about."

Sahana sat still. All she wanted to hear was for him to declare his love. Not contemplating its rightness, but just surrendering to the ultimate truth of their hearts. Not fearing the consequences anymore, just a determination to fight the world if need be.

Kartik held Sahana's hand and his eyes revealed his true feelings.

"Sahana, you set my world right. All I know now is that you are an inseparable part of my life."

Sahana's heart beat faster. She looked at him for about sixty ticks of the second-hands of the watch before standing up hastily. Kartik also stood up straight as a reaction to the unexpected-yet-expected reaction from Sahana.

"So now you want to fool around with me?" she asked.

"I will be twenty-nine in three weeks; it's not my age to fool around."

"Oh! Because your biological clock is ticking."

"I said twenty-nine, not thirty-nine."

Sahana crossed her arms, "And you really think I'm the kind of girl whom you think you can manipulate anytime?"

"I don't intend to."

"You were the one who accused me a year back of throwing myself at you," she was furious.

"It was a bad remark."

"Bad?"

"Nasty."

"That's a better word," she said sternly.

Kartik stepped towards her; she raised her hand to signal him to stop. "I'm getting late. Can you please drop me to the railway station?"

"Sure, but please hear me out."

"You should know where you are. There's no way you should try to beguile me here."

He stepped closer, not heeding to her request. "I can't beguile you standing anywhere in this world; not in this place especially as this city is sacred for me."

"I've been fooled mercilessly by you," she fumbled. "I don't want any discussion about that. You're a closed chapter of my life."

"Please don't be too harsh."

"You taught me that, Kartik."

"You're always nice to everyone. Even to homeless people, parentless kids...worthless passouts."

Sahana jaws dropped at the last two words.

"I should get some of your greatness as well."

"No, you don't deserve it. None of those people have ever hurt me."

"At least as a friend, hear me out."

"Will you hear me out for a minute?" she asked. He nodded.

"You have a wonderful family, make them smile. Get married."

"Find me a girl Sahana, as amazing as you."

"I'm nothing but a stupid girl."

"A girl as stupid as you," he said looking right into her eyes, "Perhaps the world's biggest fool to shower so much love on me."

"As if you care, Kartik?" Sahana choked.

"Don't I care? I could be selfish, but I'm not heartless. Had I been, I would have managed without you. Will you now please stop punishing me?

I am tired. I want to live now. And the only way I see that happening is to have you back."

"Back? We never had a relationship. How could you forget your own words?"

"Please dear, stop being so hard on me. I realized it late, but..."

"But? But what Kartik? Nothing has really changed; you may still lose being the COO; top of it I'm someone's fiancé. And well, if it's about the making out then..."

"I beg, don't make me feel so shallow. You know what you mean to me."

She asked him again to drop her to the station. He did so. Her luggage was heavy, and the train scheduled to leave at five hadn't arrived. Kartik wanted to wait to help her board the train comfortably. Sahana, however, was adamant.

"Now, you need to give me a break here. Answer my one question. Help me have sound sleep at least."

Kartik was agitated, "If I was being insane or cunning, wasn't it your job to rectify me? How could you also like me, just get up and leave...so casually."

"What was I supposed to do? Beg?"

"Set me right for heaven's sake."

"I would have gone to the extent of slapping you hard to bring you back to your senses, had I had any right on you."

"You should have slapped me. I would have been indebted. I would have saved myself the most painful year of my life."

"You should call it the most glorious year of your life," Sahana said shaking with anger. "A COO at your age is the coolest thing to happen. You were right in your thinking; nobody other than Dad would have done that for you. You both reached the perfect harmony of filling each other's pocket."

She looked into his eyes tearfully.

"Right. But you're different, Sahana. Even though I was chasing a dream, you loved me for years selflessly, and if for a short spell, I lost my senses, what did you do? Like me, you too turned selfish and cared only about how I hurt you. You also never cared to turn back to find out how I was doing. End of all the chapters indeed. In a flash."

Sahana sobbed and urged him to leave. Kartik finally gave in to her wish and left.

Kartik returned to the Golden Temple and spent the next couple of hours recalling the day's events. He went home to pick his bag and didn't answer any of his family's questions. Gauri packed dinner when he refused to eat with them.

Kartik returned to the station four hours later, and was already on-board when he received a call from Sahana.

"Where have you reached?" he asked.

"Nowhere. I missed my train."

"What?" Kartik flabbergasted. "And you're telling this to me now! It's so unsafe. Why do you do things like this?"

"I'm at your platform, what's your coach number?"

Kartik almost panicked when he heard the siren of the train. He said loudly, "B2, make it fast!"

Kartik ran to the door but was squashed by people and their luggage trying to get in. He did manage to get out and just like in the movies, extended his hand out of the door.

But the twist was that Sahana was hurrying up from the other door. The coolie passed her luggage quickly.

Kartik started walking towards the other end of the boggy; Sahana maneuvering the same. Their eyes espied each other from a distance.

Sahana was struggling to make her way through the crowd. She tried pushing a few women to make way. Kartik was a little faster and ruthless in clearing his way to her. Finally they met at a point and stood right in front of each other.

Sahana appeared still mildly angry, and mildly embarrassed.

"How did you miss the train?" Kartik asked lowly.

"I boarded the train but in the Shatabdi, the luggage has to be kept on the rack above. My luggage was heavy. I couldn't do it, so I stepped down."

Kartik smiled at her white lie. "You should have asked someone."

"There was a guy next to my assigned seat. I thought of asking him, but then I was afraid he might start flirting. That's all guys can think of doing with sexy co-passengers."

Kartik held her close, "Good you missed your train; I get this opportunity instead of him."

Sahana held him lightly by the shoulders, "You need to say 'sorry'."

"I'm sorry," he removed a strand of hair from her face.

"You need to mean it. That appeared very superficial."

"It was superficial. Can I say something I mean more than a useless 'sorry'?"

Sahana smiled coyly and nodded. "Our youth sucked for sure, and there's nothing we can do about it. Do you want to consider growing old with me?"

She blushed, "Growing old fooling around?"

"Yes. Won't that be fun?"

Sahana narrowed her eyes, "You really think I'm the kind of girl..."

"...on whom I would throw myself every day and every night."

She stood slack-jawed. He raised her chin with his index finger to close her mouth. He dragged her luggage up to his seat and helped her climb to the upper berth.

"This seems to be your favourite seat," Sahana asked.

"Yes, it's kind of more private and then the others need the lower berth more than I do," he replied.

Kartik suddenly realized, "Do you have a ticket?"

She nodded.

The ticket checker arrived soon and had objections over the sharing of seats. Kartik managed to persuade him. Unlike the train in Mumbai where everyone slept early and were busy, everyone here seemed to be looking at them.

They shared the rice packed by Gauri for dinner.

After dinner, people were still stealing glances at them, not very glad about being deprived of some live action. They started giving up gradually.

It was 1.00 a.m. again when Kartik blew air into the ear of the half-asleep Sahana. She woke up with a start.

"Did you miss your train to sleep?" he whispered.

"I thought you'd grown up enough to behave decently in a public place," she replied smiling.

"I'll behave, don't worry."

He pulled her closer, next to him, "Can I ask for a favour?"

"Tell me," she said.

"Please slap me. I deserve it for being such an ass."

She smiled angelically, "I have a better way to bring you back to your senses."

She opened her arms a little; Kartik rested his head on her shoulder. His pain began to mollify.

"Life at its best," he whispered.

"I'm sorry, but now your thoughts won't be permitted to vacillate."

"They won't, they can't dare. My thoughts, my feelings have no courage to go through that useless test of fire again."

"Why didn't you tell me? All this time I've been thinking that you're still pondering. Even in the US you chose to confess about the past rather than talk about the future."

"I thought that it is ethically the right thing to do. But being morally right may not not always be rightly fitted too."

She stroked his head, "You're wonderful Kartik, and you've always been. Why did you malign yourself for materialistic possessions?"

"Help me Sahana; rather save me. I want to live, and for the first time in life I want to love a lady."

She smiled shyly. "On that note, Mr Brar you appear to be quite a tough job."

He smiled too, "Don't worry, Ms Khurana, I'll make it very simple for you. Just for you."

"And what if Dad finds out?" she teased.

"Let him come back, that will be the first thing he'll get to know. And straight from my mouth."

She loosened the hug and looked at him, "You sure?"

"Wait and watch, ma'am," he snuggled into her arms again.

"But what will you tell Dad?" she said.

"That we really like each other."

"So we should be allowed to fool around?"

"Yes, precisely," he jested. "And that he shouldn't stop his daughter when she throws herself on me."

She slapped his head lightly, "You should meet Rahul someday to know what throwing yourself on someone really means?"

"That's nothing." He said and his smile turned elfish, "To learn that the best, you should meet Razoo someday."

"Who's Razoo?"

Love pays a visit

Sahana's world changed magically; she felt she was twenty years old again. She called up Anusha and shared the news of the success of all their plans. But they both acknowledged that true feelings can never be schemed; love can never be wangled.

It was Tuesday when Samar walked into Kartik's room to discuss late payment from a few clients.

"I happened to overhear Sahana and Garima in the hallway last evening; Sahana had a great time in Amritsar this weekend," Samar said with a cunning smile.

Kartik just nodded.

Samar folded his arms and scowled. "You're much smarter than I assumed."

"I take it as a compliment."

Samar raised his eyes in disrespect, "Small city and big dreams have always been a lethal combination."

Kartik didn't want the discussion to get sour. "I think we're done with our discussion, is there's anything else?"

"No," Samar smiled sarcastically. "I'll leave now so that you can continue focusing on your strategy to own this company someday."

"I don't want to own it; I'm more than pleased with my position."

"Your actions should match your words, young man. We all here aren't eye-less or brain-less. Have a good day," he said with a fake smile on his face.

Kartik was disturbed by that conversation for a few hours, but then shrugged it off.

Sahana never bothered Kartik in the office; no over-possessiveness or weird expressions like the year before. She was mature and professional and was appeased with her relationship status and her stature in his life. She had left insecurity, jealousy or any other similar feeling far behind.

That weekend, they went on a movie date. Kartik refrained from doing anything naughty until Ajit was back and held her hand decorously.

At dinner Sahana preferred Kartik's favourite eating joint and she was very cautious about correcting the impression he had of her being a spendthrift. They talked long about their growing up years.

On Sunday, Arminder visited Kartik at his request. Kartik sealed the thought he had been pondering over for months. He had booked a lavish penthouse in Noida. It was due to be delivered two years later. It had swallowed all his savings of the last two years, and he could foresee it gobbling the savings of the next few years as well. However, he did keep aside money for Vinny's bike, Sahana's ring and the D-day.

◆

In the middle of the following week, Kartik had a heated argument with Samar in a board meeting.

"I'll send out a monthly financial report to you, Sahana, and you may disseminate it after your review," Samar said.

"Seriously, Samar. We've talked this out," Sahana said with mild annoyance.

"But..." Samar had just begun when he was interrupted by Kartik.

"...But you are adamant on making it more difficult with each passing day," Kartik thumped his fist on the table. "And for sure I have had enough."

"You're not the CEO," Samar pointed his finger at him.

"We don't have a CEO right now. And being the COO, I would appreciate if you help me run operations smoothly."

"Whatever! I'm not taking instructions from you."

"Garima," Kartik turned to her, "Please issue a warning letter to Mr Samar Gahlot. His conduct is unmanageable and is not performing his duties."

"Mind your limits, Mr Kartik Brar," Samar said gritting his teeth.

"You left me with no other option. Half of my time goes in managing you exclusively. I can't deal with it any further. Either you amend your ways or walk out," Kartik made it very clear.

"I'll talk about these options to Ajit when he returns."

"I have the authority to act on his behalf, so either I'm receiving the monthly financial report in the next two hours or HR's letter is on your way," Kartik eye-locked him.

After a few seconds, Samar turned to look at Sahana, "Do you agree with him?" Sahana nodded in agreement.

In the next hour, Kartik received the report with a CC to Sahana.

"Now you must be happy?" Sahana said walking inside Kartik's cabin, "And don't you dare give me the 'happy since birth' answer. I've solved that riddle."

He laughed lightly.

"No, jokes apart, that was rude. He's the senior-most around if nothing else."

"You don't know him well enough. He's highly annoying."

"I agree, but you should have kept a cooler head. C'mon, a threat to fire him?"

"But then you supported?" he narrowed eyes.

"I'm not supposed to express my disagreement openly. Now, go and speak to him. Take him for coffee and talk it out."

Kartik smiled at Sahana's mature approach. "I'll go and speak to him but no coffee. That time is for you exclusively."

She smiled and nodded.

Kartik's changing demeanour brought him back the goodwill he had lost. None of his friends were happy without him. They truly liked him, but he had been so brutish for the last few months that they had parted. Kartik delegated responsibility to the next level to reflect faith in their potential. All his niceness was not going unnoticed.

It was Friday where everyone had gathered to sum up the week.

Aman, Garima, and Raghav intentionally cracked jokes to lighten up the environment after the heated meeting earlier in the week. Kartik was very friendly and pulled their legs just like the old days.

"Such a nice Friday," Garima said smiling.

Aman cleared his throat, "Kartik, we haven't had the hang-out party since a year. Do you think we all should hang out in the evening?"

Sahana sat quietly, not interrupting to disclose the fact that parties had been taking place, but Kartik had been left out. And Kartik didn't need Sahana or anyone to tell him that; he knew that very well. He sat quietly, giving no answer.

"Please join us, Kartik," Raghav said supportively. "We truly missed having the brat around."

Kartik smiled a little, "Missed you guys too. I'm sorry if I'd been too out of my mind."

"We forgive you," Garima said jokingly. All of them laughed together.

The day ended on a happy note. Kartik caught up with what he had missed. His life was a stalemate on records and whatever action was happening off records was not to be disclosed yet.

◆

Sunday was a perfect date day. After a movie in the evening, Kartik took Sahana home to spend time together in private rather than sweating it outside sitting in parks or talking over costly coffees unnecessarily. It was also the eve of Kartik's birthday, and Sahana got a cake packed.

"What would you like to have for dinner?" Kartik pulled out some home delivery pamphlets from the eating joints nearby.

"How do you manage dinner otherwise?" Sahana asked.

"A cook comes in but only if I manage to reach by 8.30, or else I order in. No time to cook anymore."

"Hmm. That's not very healthy."

He smiled sweetly, "That's why Maa keeps insisting that I get married."

A sweet smile spread conjunctively, "That's a good idea indeed."

He ran his fingers through her hair, "Do you know of some good homely girl?"

"You looking for a housewife?"

"Nah," he said. "Homely doesn't imply a housewife."

"As far as most Indians are concerned, a girl who works isn't considered a homemaker."

"Things are changing; mindsets will change as well."

"I hope so," she said. "So what does your definition of homely imply?"

His smile widened, "Someone who has a heart full of love and can take care of the home in the time provided... is a good companion and can cook occasionally." He sighed. "That would suffice."

She blushed, "I'm afraid I don't know anyone like that, but I'll keep looking."

"That will be a big help," he grinned.

"My pleasure," she said. "And that strikes me. I should cook tonight."

"Bad idea, you're my guest."

"Great idea."

Kartik insisted on ordering to save her the trouble, but she was determined to have her way. She was quick enough to rustle up tasty food in less than thirty minutes with the limited ingredients available. He freshened up in the meantime.

Sahana did whatever she could to set up the right ambience at the dinner table, but the resources at the bachelor's pad restricted her.

Kartik was really impressed with her culinary skills. Everything was delicious, and he wasn't saying it just to flatter her. It was 11.00 p.m. by the time they were done.

He put his arms around her waist from behind, "Let's dance."

Soft music played for the next hour, and love filled the air. The clock struck twelve soon. God never slows the clock for anybody, No matter what!

He cut the cake she had brought in a romantic celebration. They sat on the floor.

"I think I should leave now. It's a working day tomorrow."

Kartik was unwilling to let her go. He rubbed his nose next to her ear and whispered, "I have a better idea. Stay here until dawn."

Sahana was tickled and shook her head in refusal. He held her closer, "You're the safest with me."

"I sure am, but I need to go home."

"It's my birthday, you can't refuse me."

Sahana called some Kauveri aunty to inform her that she was staying over at Anusha's place.

She put her arms around him. Kartik played with her hair for a while.

She blushed, "You know I have an aim these days in life to write a book on our story."

"Wow. But we still need to know the end."

"A happy ending for sure," she smiled sweetly.

"Do you even know the beginning?"

"Of course, the gate of the hotel in Goa. What else?"

Kartik shook his head in no. "A young man standing at the reception of the hotel gawking at a beautiful girl walking beside the bride."

Sahana was stunned. She had heard that for the first time, "You saw me at the wedding?"

"For a very long time from the hotel's lobby. Since then, I have not been able to take my eyes off you," he gently touched his head with hers.

Sahana put her two fingers on his lips and kissed them. She nestled her head on his heart again and closed her eyes.

"This is the most beautiful evening I have ever had. Love paid the first visit to my house finally," he said clasping her close.

"We should consider celebrating your birthday every weekend," she said snuggling in his arms.

"Sahana, what will be the title of your book?"

"Let me think." Sahana said smiling, "Snowwhite and the Rustic Charmer."

Blossoming romance
spreading smiles

Sahana drove as soon as sunbeams rose from the horizon of the sky. She reached office a little late. She wore her first shopping memento with Kartik – the green dupatta over the springy green salwar suit. She looked like a cute Punjaban for sure.

The entire floor wished Kartik and insisted on a party. Pizza was ordered for lunch for all the close colleagues in the boardroom. Samar joined them too. Kartik, however, reserved the evening coffee only for her.

Dinner was a private affair. And before Sahana decided to head to the kitchen, he drove her to her favourite restaurant in the area. Kartik had already texted her when she had left in the morning to bring on her nightwear along, as sleeping in her day clothes the night before was visibly troublesome.

That night was the time of his favourite pose; wallowing in her lap and getting his hair ruffled.

"This is so relaxing," he held her other hand. "I'm just so tired."

"Life has just begun."

"It's a very ruthless world. Everyone's always trying to pull you down."

"Think of it this way. Just like you, they are also trying to push themselves up."

"You know at times I feel, you understand the value of life much better than I do," he said.

"At times? You should feel that at all times."

They laughed lightly. "You know, you should find some time for your hobbies. You've transformed into a Japanese robot."

"Right. But the glitch is that I don't even remember my hobbies."

"Come on!" She pulled his hair, "Photography. Make use of your SLR."

"Hey," Kartik rose instantly, "Let me show you the photos I took in Goa."

Kartik pulled out his favourite holiday's album from his closet. They revisited every place and moment as the pages turned. Suddenly she spotted a missing pic from the album, "Why is this blank?"

He smiled sheepishly. She contracted her left eye, "Tell me, what are you hiding?"

"Hiding? Me? No way!" he cried.

She folded her arms and pretended to be angry.

"Okay, okay, but no teasing."

He took out a book from his side table, and Sahana snatched it before he could show it to her. He tried pulling back the book, but they ended up in another tussle. Finally, Sahana pinched his fingers with her long nails to win.

She sat crossed legs and opened the book; she was surprised to see a photo of her he had taken on the beach. He sat next to her, "Pretty, no?"

"Nah."

"Huh! She's very pretty. You're just jealous."

"I have longer hair. I look more Punjabi. Why the hell should I be jealous?" she smiled shyly.

"Yeah right," he opened up her hair, "Long hair is even better."

"Can I have the photo back?"

"Why is it kept separately from the rest of album?"

"You want to dig into everything!" he didn't want to give her an answer.

"C'mon...a simple question."

"I look at it every night before going to bed," he said blushing.

"Ever since when?" she jerked her eyebrows.

"Your MBA lunch. When I realized that you still believed that I'd call you up someday to ask you out."

"Was I a fool to believe so?"

"Of course yes," he lay down in her lap again. "I was merely a beginner then. But anyway, it's my fate that is beautiful. It's my responsibility to be brave to fight it out. And then we've come a long way."

"Did you even look at it after that evening at Noida Park last year?"

He was quiet for a while, and then nodded gently. "I really missed you. I never thought I would, and so madly. I read our emails every day; I know them by heart. "

She bent down and kissed his eyes, "I missed you too."

"Sahana, promise me if sir throws me out of the company, you'll come along with me."

"Nothing like that will happen, Kartik."

"In case it does, you'll be on my side."

She put her finger on his lips. "Go to sleep now. It's a working day tomorrow."

She nestled her head on his heart. They slept nestled in the warmth of love. Stupefying the night at being deprived of any intimacy beyond pure, intangible emotions.

The Brars insisted that Kartik would have to come over during the weekend to celebrate his birthday. Kartik liked the plan but didn't want to leave Sahana alone. He asked her to join him, but she had Anusha's birthday party to go to.

◆

Kartik's three buddies insisted on a party for Happy on Saturday night. After dinner at an expensive eatery, they climbed up to Happy's terrace. It was to be the bar. Honey was particularly excited and said it was a party in honour of Razoo who had delivered a baby boy a week ago.

"Bloody hell! Beer again," Honey yelled. "I was expecting some whisky today."

"Bloody hell, go look at you face in the mirror first before asking for whisky," Jolly said.

"It's not about my face, but the face of our little nephew that's worth this grand celebration. Happy is a father now." Honey's remark triggered a riot of laughter.

"You dog," Happy pretended to be angry.

"The day I'll be a father, Blue Scotch will await you."

Bobby and Jolly whistled in appreciation.

"Let's go down and speak to aunty. I can't wait too long for Scotch," Jolly rose and started to walk. Happy gripped his wrist. "Take it easy; my marriage is her top priority."

"No, no." Honey interrupted and rose to walk, "To hell with marriage. A scotch party doesn't say he needs to be a husband; all it says is he needs to be a father."

Happy kept his bottle down to grip Honey with his other hand, "Let me correct myself, the party will be for me when I'm a legitimate father."

Bobby looked into Happy's eyes. "So you agree you're already an illegitimate father." Honey and Jolly plopped down and rolled on the floor in laughter.

"By God what friends I have. Anything for liquor," Happy shook his head dramatically.

Honey put his arm across Happy's shoulder, "I needed to ask you something."

"Bark."

Jolly held Happy's hands tight, "What are you doing?" Happy asked.

"You have developed violent tendencies, we are ensuring our safety," Bobby gripped Happy's legs. He tried to free himself, but the two Sardar friends locked him real hard.

"Shall I bark now?" Honey confirmed with Jolly and Bobby. They beckoned. Happy smiled aslant.

"Jokes apart, what's cooking on the legitimate side?" Honey eluded.

"You'll know for sure when things get finalized," Happy decoded his childhood friend's convoluted query.

Honey moved his eyes to ask the other the two to hold Happy firmly; they firmed the grip. "That almost white, blue-eyed Delhi *mem* is our to-be-bhabhi ji, right?"

"Oyeee!" Happy shook his body to free himself, but Bobby rolled Happy holding his legs to push him to the ground on his stomach.

Jolly also took Happy's arms and tucked them behind his back. "C'mon, time for you to bark the truth."

"You bastards! Are you asking or toruring me?"

"We are speaking the language you understand," Honey also lay down on his stomach in front of Happy, looking right into his eyes and rotating an empty beer bottle between them in a filmy way.

Jolly twisted Happy's wrist harder, "Don't waste our precious time," Jolly said.

"Precious time! As if you have mills running," said an irritated Happy.

Honey pulled Happy's hair, "Bark quick. Bhabhi ji, right?"

Happy's smile gave them the answer.

They all rejoiced in delight loudly freeing Happy and hugging him tight.

"You should have introduced us," Bobby complained.

"I still need to talk to her father," Happy said.

"Why the delay?" Honey asked.

"He's unwell and out of the country. He'll return next month."

Jolly's eyebrows rose, "Foreign treatment! Must be a solid party."

Happy's smile dropped, "Now that's the reason I never discussed it with you. I was so sure of being hit with such remarks."

Bobby chaffed his arm in a warm, friendly way. "You know we speak rubbish. We love blabbering."

"I know you all don't mean a word, but then, a few things are very personal."

"Okay, sorry for the comment," Jolly said to cheer Happy up. "But tell us more." Happy told them the whole story.

"Don't worry. Her father will grant his approval," Jolly said.

"And in case he doesn't..." Bobby broadened his chest, "...we'll kidnap and bring her here."

Happy slapped Bobby's head, "That's all you can think of."

"Of course."

They said in chorus, "It's a matter of Scotch!"

◆

The next afternoon Kartik was sitting in his parents' room looking at photographs of his childhood when Gauri walked in.

"Cute pic, right? You were seven then; Vinny was just a few days old here," she said sitting next to him.

"I'm also wondering since yesterday, why is my boy not asking me for a head massage."

"Oh!" Kartik managed to hide the fact that there was now someone else to give those to him. "It was just that we didn't happen to talk," he said and lay his head on his mother's lap.

"How's Sahana?" she asked.

"Doing well. "

"Still angry?"

"Nah. Honey sweet as always," he replied smiling.

Vinny and Arminder walked in.

"What's going on between mother and son?" Arminder asked.

"Well, my boys will come only to me when they want to understand a woman better."

"Is this service only exclusive for the elder son?" Vinny asked.

"No, it's exclusively for you, I don't need it," Kartik said.

"Why?" Gauri was amazed.

"Maa, my philosophy says: don't try to understand women, simply appreciate them," Kartik said raising his hands saint-style. Gauri slapped his head lightly.

"Let's do that, Maa, " Vinny said to pull his mother's leg. "I'll give you the kind of questions girls throw at boys, and you tell me the best-suited answers that a girl would want to hear."

"Great idea! Let's do that," Kartik said excitedly while Arminder sat smiling as usual; all these years he only pitched in when it was absolutely necessary.

Vinny laid rules, "And don't give away answers for the sake of it. Think hard and tell me an answer that would be a turn on."

Kartik opened his mouth wide hearing the last two words. His parents shook their heads smiling.

"First one; you think I'm stupid na?"

Gauri blushed realizing she was in trouble now; she looked up at her husband, "Say something. Your boys are getting out of control."

"Well, you wanted to help your sons. Now go ahead and answer Vinny."

Kartik cajoled her. "C'mon darling, be a sport."

After some thought Gauri answered, "It's not being stupid, it's being innocent. And love should always be so, and so should you."

The boys whistled at her answer. Arminder also raised his brows in appreciation.

"Second, I've become fat na?"

"No," all three said in chorus. Gauri added, "No, you always look great next to me. Flawlessly perfect always."

"Third, these days you get bored of me na?"

"No way, I can spend my entire life just looking at you."

"Maa," Kartik intervened, "This is a cliché and is highly annoying. You should consider saying something credible and practical."

"Arre, what's wrong with this? It's such a nice compliment."

"No, Maa," Vinny said, "It's just so deceiving,"

"I don't get it; it's just so true. Ask your papa?"

"Maa," Vinny said, "We are no second-graders sitting here that we need to confirm that with papa. If he could spend his life merely looking at you, we would have never been here."

Kartik and Vinny high-fived laughing aloud. Gauri tried to reach out to pull Vinny's ear.

"Arminder ji, say something."

"What can I say? You were telling the same thing to Sahana too when you first met her."

"You were so dramatic, Maa. 'Such good luck will fall into my Happy's lap,'" Vinny teased, "How can it be a good luck to get married to a girl like Sahana and end up living your life just looking at her?" As they all chuckled, Arminder did pull Vinny's ear.

"Let's pass this one to Happy. Let's check how well he's doing," Arminder said smiling.

"Hmmm," Happy thought, "Yes, I get truly bored when you're sitting in front of me and talking about anything other than us." His answer was much appreciated.

"Fourth; what do you feel for me that you have never felt before na?"

"Maa," Kartik said before Gauri could answer, "Did you notice something?"

"What?"

"Too many 'na na's'." he said raising his eyes still relaxing his head on her lap.

"So?"

Kartik winked, "South Indian."

Vinny face's paled. He gritted at Kartik hard, "I'll kill you, bro."

Kartik blew a kiss at him, "Come baby, kill me."

Vinny threw a pillow at Kartik's face. Kartik yelled, *"Teri toh."* He ran chasing Vinny outside the room.

Gauri felt wonderful and knew which romance to thank for this bromance.

◆

In the middle of the following week during the weekly board meeting, Samar invited everybody to his anniversary party on Saturday.

Sahana walked to Kartik's room after the meeting. "You won't be coming to the party?"

"I will, of course," he smiled. "Free food, Free drinks. Didn't he eat pizza at my birthday party?"

Sahana was amused, "So it's a revenge?"

"Not to forget, one more evening to dance with you at someone else's expense."

He winked.

Sahana laughed lightly, "It won't be free; you may have to buy a gift for him."

"Nah," he passed a wary smile. "Just add my name to whatever you're taking."

She rolled her lips and nodded.

"So it's free for me, see?" Kartik said as she giggled.

◆

Sahana was sitting with Garima when Kartik walked into the party.

"I don't believe this," Garima exclaimed. Sahana laughed out too.

"Hello, ladies. What's the joke?" Kartik asked as he took a chair to the same table.

Sahana gently hit his arm, "Your arrival of course."

"You're too daring," Garima said. Her phone rang just then to which she blushed. "Excuse me, guys."

"No, no, please stay." Sahana pulled her leg. Garima smiled and walked away to attend her fiancé's call.

Sahana turned to Kartik beaming, "Where are you coming from?"

"Home."

"Who else was at home?"

"My desires." He winked.

"For sure." Sahana lowered her eyes to bring his attention to his opened chest button.

"By the way sweetheart, if someone's chest button is open what could it mean?" He buttoned it asking her innocently.

Sahana rolled her lips realizing what he's referring to, "How could I know?"

Kartik pinched her waist from below the table, "You know there was this MBA intern last year, her top button was always open in my cabin and only in my cabin."

"Maybe she wanted to distract you?"

"Distractor or an attractor?"

"Were you distracted or attracted?" she asked smiling shyly.

"Both." He nano-winked.

A waiter arrived with drinks; Kartik picked one up. "You really have this serious drinking problem, right?" Sahana said.

"Excuse me?" Kartik was jolted.

"Five years back you used to drink beer like fruit juice or perhaps water."

"Sweetheart, I was on a vacation."

"Still you drank like a fish. And also I've heard you beat up people when you get high."

"What crap?" Kartik gently thumped his glass on the table. "Whom did I beat?"

"That friend of yours at Amritsar had a bruised eye because you hit him."

"Who the hell told you that?"

"Somebody who would have no reason to defame you."

He shrank his right eye, "Vinny?"

She passed a wry smile, and his naughty smile returned. "Good you got to know that sooner than later."

He gulped the drink in a single sip. "And I was wondering we should leave together after the party and go to my place," he hiccupped artificially. "It's been a long while since I have hit someone after boozing."

She narrowed her eyes, "And you think I'll let you bruise my eye?"

"Your bruise won't be on the eyes. It won't even be visible to the others."

She covered her open mouth with the hand again and whispered, "For some reason I think that's the only thing running on your mind."

"You bet."

"And that would be the first thing to happen as soon as we have dad's approval."

"You bet!"

"And you've assumed that I will have no say."

He shook his head. "I want to ensure you have a say..."

He too covered his mouth with a hand, "to say 'ahhhhhh'."

Sahana's hand unintentionally moved to her forehead, flashing the expression she was hiding. Kartik also removed his hand from his mouth, and they shared an extremely arduous smile.

Garima had finished her call and was walking back towards them. She halted in her tracks and considered it inappropriate to interrupt the budding romance. The two continued to grace the evening with their blossoming romance.

Return of the Boss

Kartik dropped Sahana home. Sahana bid him goodbye as she closed the main iron gate. She reached the entrance door, and strangely the lights of the living room were lit. Usually, Kauveri switched them off before going to her room. Sahana also discovered that the house was latched from the inside whereas she had asked Kauveri to use only the key-lock so that she could use her set of keys to let herself in. She rang the doorbell.

Her eyes filled with immense joy when her mother opened the door. She embraced her joyfully and was a thrilled child. She saw Ajit trying to get up from the sofa; she ran towards him and was choked with emotion to see him physically weaker than before. She gently hugged him "I'm so glad to see you, dad. I missed you both terribly," she sobbed.

Ajit gently patted her head, "I missed you too, my child. So we came a week early. The rest can be taken care of here."

"Where were you out this late?" Alka asked. "And you should have asked Rahul to come inside."

"It was Kartik, mumma."

"Kartik?" Ajit was stunned.

"It was Samar's anniversary party. It went on late so he dropped me back," she replied.

Ajit felt easy. "Let me call him, he won't have gone far."

Ajit stopped her as she was about to dial his number, "Let it be, I'll meet him after a few days. Not that important."

Sahana's smile shrank with that statement, but she convinced herself that he perhaps wanted to meet the family first.

Alka and Ajit shifted downstairs. They sat together and chatted for some more time. "Where's your engagement ring, Sahana?" Ajit asked.

"It was loose, so I left it at home so that I don't drop it while dancing," Sahana stammered.

"You shouldn't take it off; it isn't only yours for it is the pride of two families," Ajit said as he lay down on the bed. Sahana nodded hesitatingly. She took their leave so that they could rest and to avoid any further discussion on the topic.

She called up Kartik from her room, informing him about her father's arrival. Kartik was overjoyed and wanted to come over the next day. She asked him to wait.

The next day, Rahul's family was the first people Ajit called up. Mr Chhabra withheld speaking about the incident considering Ajit's health. When Rahul's parents visited Ajit, Sahana chose to be away from home. Ajit and Alka were miffed with Sahana's behaviour towards her future in-laws. Alka took it as her responsibility to speak to her daughter about her concerns.

♦

Kartik finally paid him a visit in the middle of the week after office.

"So good to see you, sir. We miss you terribly," Kartik said warmly.

"Just one more week, then I can get started at least for a few hours," Ajit smiled. "I'm so proud, you've done a swell job. I had been asking Sahana secretively over the phone."

"Not at all sir; I could have done much better had you been around."

"Did Sahana trouble you?" Ajit said smiling.

"She was great support, in fact. Her connection with the staff is amazing; the best amongst us. The attrition rate dropped significantly and we are more satisfied employees, all kudos to her," said an appreciative COO.

Ajit chuckled a little, "So finally DataMagica has a soul to talk about."

Kartik nodded gladly. After spending a few more minutes with Ajit over tea, Kartik walked out and bumped into Sahana in the living room.

"I was hoping you'd come to meet me," Sahana teased.

"Unlike mine, your home hasn't too much privacy."

"My room is upstairs. Come over for privacy." Sahana winked.

"Not now. I'll come over at night, up a pipe, and into your balcony."

They guffawed aloud.

Alka stepped out of the kitchen to see who it was. "Oh Kartik, how are you?"

"Good ma'am. Thanks."

"The way Sahana was giggling, for a minute I hoped it was Rahul."

Their smiles disappeared. Sahana in particular was very uneasy.

"Stay over for dinner," Alka said to Kartik.

"Thanks for asking; but I would request your leave."

"No, stay! Or else you'll eat that unhealthy packed food," Sahana said lightly holding Kartik's arm. Alka lifted her brows. Sahana soon realized what she was doing and released his arm.

Kartik bid goodbye to Alka and left. Mother turned to her daughter, "Sahana, you know that was unacceptable. No matter how good a friend he must be; he isn't your fiancé."

Sahana turned to leave. "Wait. I need to talk. Where's your engagement ring?"

Sahana took a deep breath, "I've given it back to Rahul; I don't want to marry him."

Alka was crestfallen. She turned sharply to check whether Ajit had heard them. "Sahana, do you want to kill your father?"

"He's fine, Mom. He needs to understand that I can't be happy with someone like Rahul."

"What's wrong with him?" Alka whispered angrily.

"He's nothing more than a rich man's son. Just an inefficient successor."

"Shut up, Sahana. You must show some respect. And if someone gets to bask in the luxury of their father's reputation, it's a great thing to happen."

"I don't think so. Even if you earn five thousand, it should be your hard work. A person should be known by his qualities and not his parent's wealth. He should use his father's reputation to build on, but all I see him doing is demolishing it."

Alka folded her arms, "Sahana, Can I have the exact reason? This wealth theory seems to be just a part of it."

"Perhaps you're right, but this is all I have to say as of now. Please speak to dad at a suitable time and let him know my final stand."

Sahana again started to walk away.

"Wait Sahana. You're not twenty years old now that you can just run away to have it your way."

"You're right, mom. I'm not twenty. I have all the courage to face the burns of my actions. Running away is out of the question; it's a matter of my life, and I stand strong by my decision."

Sahana hurried to her room upstairs; Alka sank in the chair rubbing her lines of worry.

On Friday night at the dinner table, Ajit said, "I think I'm good enough to get started at the office from Monday."

"The doctor insisted the work hours should increase gradually," Alka emphasized.

"Yes, my dear." Ajit smiled sweetly. "I'll take care of your husband."

"But before that, I need to address another unfinished task," he smiled. "Let's call the Chhabra family on Sunday for lunch and finalize the wedding date."

Sahana's face chalked; she turned to her mother.

"Yes, you must. That should be our top priority," Alka said smiling at Ajit, completely ignoring Sahana's expressions.

Womanhood behind fashionable clothes

Sahana left home on Sunday morning when Rahul's parents were scheduled to visit and kept her phone switched off. She went to meet Kartik.

"When are you planning to talk to dad?" she came straight to the point.

"Very soon. Let him at least join office."

"Give me a deadline."

"Deadline? It isn't a project," Kartik joked.

"I'm in no mood for jokes. You know the situation."

"I did get an inkling on Wednesday," he said, pulling her closer.

"By the way, what do you plan to talk to dad?"

Kartik gave her a look, "Can I have one more holiday with you?"

"I'm serious." She indeed was.

"So am I." He pretended to be.

She passed a wan smile. He cleared the strands of hair from her face, "On a serious note Sahana, shall I speak to sir tomorrow?"

"No, give it some time. Let the Rahul issue settle. I don't want Dad to view the two things as being connected," she realized she was panicky.

He looked at her thoughtfully. "That's wise thinking."

He paused, "They want you to patch-up?"

She nodded.

"The reason for him not being sincere isn't working?"

She heaved a deep sigh, "Well Kartik, there's more to it than just that."

"I know, you didn't like his advances."

"No, something even more disastrous," Sahana then narrated to him Rahul birthday's incident.

"What? And why are you not disclosing that to your parents?"

"Firstly because that Minisha and Nipun are a married couple now. And I don't want anyone to try and reach out to them to validate what I saw. Second, Chhabra uncle is very close to dad and I don't want him to get hurt."

Kartik looked at her in astonishment, realizing how considerate she was about everyone. She could disclose the incident and all her parents' anger for her would dissipate. But she was choosing silence for the sake of a couple she had met just once.

"And why didn't you tell me?" he asked.

"Ah well!" she smiled, "because I didn't want you to acknowledge your feelings for me just because I have no plan to reunite with him."

"But Sahana, had I known I would have proposed a long time back. At least after the US incident."

"I know what you were trying to do then. You were still trying to be morally correct by suggesting a patch-up."

"Precisely. I didn't know..."

"I didn't even want you to know. You love me and and that must stand tall independently. Even if we have to fight for it. Pity is the last thing I would want out of you."

He pulled her closer with one hand and kissed her forehead. Sahana thought it was the perfect time to disclose the truth about a few other incidents as well.

"I wanted to confess something," she said hesitatingly, playing with his collar.

Kartik smiled mischievously, being pretty certain of what was coming.

"Go on," he said staring sheepishly. *"Tu yeda banke bahut peda kha rahi hai."*

"Some other time." She turned to leave. He pulled her back and clasped her close. She bit her lower lip and it answered a lot of his questions. "Sorry."

"Why Sahana? There was no need."

"Of course it was needed. You were being so difficult. You're emotionally too cagey. I had to...to make you speak."

"No. Again, if you'd told me about the Sohna incident..."

"Again, what if that incident hadn't happened? If Rahul was actually a nice guy, and just that we weren't getting along? We both love each other. What does that have anything to do with any other factor? Did I ever bring up your past?"

"You're getting me wrong. All I'm trying to say is that we would have been together without so much emotional turbulence."

"Oh, you mean if you'd known I was so called 'available.' I know I had been little off-limits. But it's all because I loved you and wanted you to want me as much as I want you. Period."

He smiled. "Sahana, you hide your womanhood behind your fashionable clothes."

She said quietly, "It was very dark in the train that night, you perhaps missed to see closely. "

"My eyes are always X-rays when it comes to you."

She embraced him.

He said, "So? I know there was no wedding in Amritsar. What else?"

She giggled a little, "That Prez has no Hindu girlfriend, and he goes to Meerut every weekend."

"Thanks for this one. I can now chuck him out without any guilt."

She slapped his arm playfully, "You aren't chucking anyone out!"

"He'll be the last one, I promise."

"No."

"Please."

"I said 'no'."

"I say 'please'."

◆

She returned home, but Rahul's parents hadn't left as yet.

"There she is," said Mrs Chhabra faking delight. She hugged Sahana.

"You know," she turned to Sahana's parents, "We were after Rahul from a long time to get serious. Thanks to Sahana, he finally goes to office regularly now and has developed an interest."

She hugged Sahana again and whispered in her ears, "Don't make too big a deal out of what happened; men make such mistakes under the influence of alcohol. Take it as your shortcoming rather."

Sahana hugged her tighter, "Are women of the family also excused for mistaken sleepovers? I always wondered how the great Chhabra uncle can have a son like Rahul."

"Shut up my darling. I'm sure you can see that your parents are keen about this alliance."

"That's because I haven't told them that your son isn't only good-for-nothing, but also characterless." Sahana loosened the hug and said grinning, "Your son after all."

Mrs Chhabra gently put her hand on Sahana's cheek and said aloud, "Call him up and sort it out. You guys will be married soon."

She again said lowly, "Learn to manage your man."

Sahana also said with the same volume, "I'm managing my man very well."

"Definitely, bhabhi ji," Alka replied the question they all heard loud. "It's just that she had a tough time without us around."

"Please don't embarrass her, bhabhi ji," Mrs Chhabra said. "She is family now."

"Thank you," Ajit said. "I'm so glad you understand."

They left after few minutes. Sahana turned sharply towards her father, "Dad you need to hear me out."

"Shut up, Sahana."

"It's my life."

"I said shut up," Ajit raised his voice. Sahana chose silence as she didn't want him to get worked up.

After dinner Ajit asked Sahana to see him in his study room.

"Come here, dear," he stretched his arm. Sahana approached smiling and gave him a bear hug. "I'm sorry for being rude in the evening."

"It's alright, Dad."

"I need to talk to you, and it has to begin with sorry," he said. "Sorry, I threw you into my official mess without asking you. I know it must have been an emotional challenge as much as laborious."

He kissed her forehead, "But you know, you were the only name I could think of who could stand up tough and set things right."

"Bygones are bygones, Dad, but from Tuesday when you join office, make sure that you do nothing to disturb the harmony that has been finally reinstated."

He smiled. "And I assure you I won't even let anyone else do that."

"Perfect," she smiled wholly. "That's all I want from you and Kartik."

His smile shrank, "My dear, I have another thing to talk. See about Rahul..."

"Dad, please let me be quiet over that. I don't want to disgrace your best friend."

Ajit tried to bring up the discussion, but Sahana humbly refused to say a word.

Office-Office

Monday evening Kartik, Sahana and Garima were chatting in the office cafeteria when they spotted Ankur Bansal whom Kartik had almost fired two months ago.

"We've been using Ankur for a few in-house programmes, but marketing is his area after all. So in case you want to give him another chance..." Garima said hesitatingly.

Kartik asked. "Do you even have the full details of the so-called 'mess-up'? He opened the competitor's proposal instead during the live presentation." Kartik turned to Sahana, "And you thought I was being mean."

Sahana said nothing but decided to fix it in the evening.

Kartik turned to Garima, "Let me think about it. But it's nice for someone to let me know what my friends think of me."

"I'm sorry Kartik," Garima said. "But it could have been just this one case where you were right. Ever since Pulkit's resignation last year, our company has become a pink-slip company."

"Well, all I can tell you is that Pulkit's expulsion was justified; it's just that sir didn't want to disclose the reason."

He smiled, "And the rest should have been dealt with better, but maybe I was greyed. And I particularly didn't want to deal with my old friends."

"Never mind," she smiled. "Welcome back."

"And I would like to be treated as a friend if you consider me one," Garima said folding her arms.

"I always do," he said.

"You sure?" Garima asked narrowing her eyes.

"Well," he scratched his head. "I don't know what you're talking about?"

Garima turned to Sahana. "Would you agree?"

Sahana just smiled shyly. Garima smiled broadly. "That helps."

"See, I'm leaving." Sahana stood up, "I guess I should leave two friends alone."

Garima laughed lightly, "Yes, you're right. I need to hear it from the one who claims to be a friend."

"See dear. It's a little complicated," Kartik said cautiously.

"And perilous!" Garima added. "But I'm sure you must have thought it through."

"How do you know by the way?" Sahana asked.

"Well, you sat next to me last year. It wasn't difficult to read you then. And though mostly in his cabin, it's still far easier to read him this year," Garima said beaming.

"Wish us luck," Sahana said blushing.

"Goes without saying. My best wishes always."

That evening, Sahana insisted on dinner at Kartik's residence.

"So, why exactly was Pulkit fired?" she asked.

"None of your business."

Her mouth agape, "Just a simple question."

"You have anything else to talk about?"

"Oh yes," she put her arms around his neck. He blushed.

"I wanted to tell you something for quite some time now," she said smiling. "You look very cute in love. This smile, the expressions, look of possessiveness – it all suits you."

His face glowed, "So you mean I look like you being in love."

"I said, you look cute. I didn't say you look hot and sexy."

He burst out laughing and gave her a hug.

"By the way, do you know when you look super cute?" he asked amorously.

She shook her head.

"When you say 'bloody hell'."

Her face appeared over his shoulder. Her teeth were biting her lower lip. "It's always accidental. I swear it's always unconscious," she said shyly.

"And that's the best part." He winked. Love blew in the wind all evening.

On Tuesday, Ajit joined office after lunch and discovered that most of the seventh floor was empty. Garima and Samar greeted him. He enquired about the others.

"Well sir, they are on floor-walk," Garima said.

"What's that?"

"Every Tuesday afternoon they walk through one floor and address the team. It's to connect the employees with top management, know their issues, general discussion, etc."

"But where's Kartik?"

"He is there as well, sir."

"What!"

"Yes, sir. Kartik, Sahana, Raghav from Admin, Arijit from Technical squad, Nikita from T&D, and the Group Lead of that floor."

Ajit's eyes widened.

"Waste of precious office time in short," Samar said.

"No," Ajit disagreed. "A good idea indeed."

The rest of the week also Ajit kept noticing many such changes. An entire paradigm shift in Kartik's attitude. He had been spending most of his time with his team brainstorming, unlike earlier when he kept everyone under his strict control. Ajit was pleased to see Kartik helping others to grow and create the next line of leaders for the company. He was also smiling, sharing light moments with his colleagues, taking other's mistakes lightly, and was approachable.

At the Friday board meeting, Kartik came late as he was supervising the marketing call being handled by his subordinate.

"Can I ask you something?" Ajit said smiling to Kartik.

"Yes, sir."

"What's right with you?"

Kartik gave him a confused look, "Excuse me, sir?"

"Well you never answered what's wrong with you, maybe you want to share what's right with you?"

Everyone laughed a little; Sahana threw him an eye-kiss.

"Yes please." Garima cajoled. "Sir must know."

Sahana pressed Garima's foot with hers.

"Just learning to be nice again, and finding ways to ennoble my soul under your directives," Kartik answered sweetly.

The bumpy ride of love

There was a huge list of potential clients with whom negotiations were on. For Ajit that was the top priority. Kartik was to travel to three American cities.

Kartik asked Sahana to send him her shopping list. And before he had even landed, Sahana's list had arrived in his mailbox.

1. Love   2. Hug   3. Kiss   4. Condoms

◆

Ajit took it easy at the office for the second week too, not staying for more than three hours a day. On Saturday, his medical report was very encouraging.

He visited the Chhabra family along with Alka on Sunday. Mrs Chabbra guessed that Sahana would not disclose Rahul's act to her family. So she just informed Khurana family that kids had a fight on Rahul's birthday party and Sahana returned the ring.

Ajit was superlatively furious at Sahana when he returned home. "Give me one good reason Sahana, why did you insult me like that?"

"Dad, please understand. I know you're my well-wisher. But..."

"But..." she was interrupted.

"You aren't mine for sure. Did you think that throwing the ring at his face will get you a Padama Shri?"

Sahana stood quiet as he continued, "Now it's your job to call Rahul up and apologize."

"No way, Dad."

"Shut up, Sahana," Ajit screamed. "By the end of the week, I want this done."

Sahana was nonplussed; all she knew was that she needed to buy some more time. "Give me fifteen days, please."

Ajit gazed hard at her, "Alright."

◆

It was the middle of the week; Ajit requested Sahana and Samar's presence in his cabin.

"This amount is too high for the staff welfare and L&D," Ajit pointed.

"Well, that's Sahana's initiative 'Climbing Together,'" Samar replied.

"Why do we need to train staff in anything other than their current job profile?"

Sahana tried explaining. "They should be provided an opportunity to explore aspirational roles."

"Not at this expense."

"We should be a platform for growth," Sahana replied.

"You're always too philosophical." Ajit turned to Samar, "You could have at least explained the kind of financial impact such programmes could have. Bringing the attrition rate down shouldn't be at the expense of downsizing profit."

Samar shook his head almost a hundred and eighty degrees, "I had been trying my life to voice my concern over this drive, but I was completely disregarded. You have no idea Ajit, how I've suffered here in your absence. An on the face insult in the board meeting where I'm provided with two choices: that either I send the report to our COO or I quit."

Ajit eyes opened wide, and he stared hard at Sahana. She lowered her eyes.

Samar continued, "Whatever Kartik does Sahana supports, and whatever Sahana thinks Kartik implements," he sighed. "In fact, I did consider quitting for once."

"No, Samar." Ajit's eyes pleaded him. "Sahana's a beginner; she deserves your forgiveness."

"I pardoned her a long time back. It was visible that she was being manipulated by someone to settle a personal score with me."

"Excuse me?" Sahana said with irritation. "I have a mind of my own. And even if I chose to depend on someone's advice it's because he's considered the most capable by my father too."

Samar was offended, Ajit read his face. "Samar, please excuse her." Samar walked out of the cabin fuelling Ajit's irritation further.

He thumped his fist on the table, "I appreciate what you're doing, but you cannot waste finances like this. Samar's right."

"You're too driven by profits."

"Yes, I am. And when you invest twenty-seven years of life to a dream, that's the only time you can ever realize how careful you need to be about every move."

"Just like you, the others too have a dream. And only if you'll help them accomplish theirs, they'll help you achieve yours."

"Philosophy again."

"If you're in a position to help someone, then you should feel blessed."

"Sahana!" he almost screamed, "For heaven's sake, grow up."

He angrily picked up his desk phone and called Garima in. He instructed her to discontinue the drive and cancel all bookings of external faculties. "Drop a confidential mail to all the top executives about it, but handle it diplomatically with the other associates."

Sahana's face turned red as her father scrapped her altruistic drive for his surplus revenue.

Kartik also received that communication and was unpleased with the decision. He chose to talk to Ajit when he returned.

◆

On Sunday, Kartik was sitting lazily in his hotel room in the US. He thought of doing what Sahana would have wanted him to in his free time. Do something that interested him. He opened his personal laptop to do what he had loved doing during Sahana's first year of MBA.

But then he decided to make it more special. He pulled out a notepad instead, to write a letter to her in his handwriting. He posted it the next day with air mail. Sahana had a hard time waiting till evening to read the letter that arrived in the office. Each word, each sentence filled her heart, her eyes. The rustic charm floored her yet again and she drowned in the high tide of his emotions.

Dear Sahana...no...Maybe Dearest Sahana...even better...just... Sahana...Bingo...

My Sahana,

My boarding pass suggests I've reached a city called Charlotte today on Sunday afternoon. As I sit alone in this luxurious hotel room, oceans apart, miles away from you, it might be a highly romantic thing to say that I feel you're always around but I'm afraid that is not the case.

I finally conclude my love for you isn't platonic; it should have been as they say, but rustic I am, as you know. And then, why do I really need to change, after all what do I ask for more than few power-hugs, eyekisses 'as of now'.

There's something I wanted to tell you from very long now; I could never get the courage to in person. I feared your reaction, I feared a cross-question and chiefly I feared messing it up.

You've grown up Sahana. With you around, it doesn't feel like I am hanging out with a girl anymore; it's a phenomenal feeling of being with a woman. A woman who can hold a man as confused and enclosed as me. You've unfastened my clasped emotions. I engulf revived energy daily, and life appears easy once again and challenges timid. I in my restored self am cherishing my existence as the world seems nicer cozying with you.

You've redefined the word 'passion' for me, and alas, you'll have to face the outcome of the ardor I have for my passions like no one ever did. You'll pay a big price for making me so restless and finding comfort when with you.

The more I know you, the more I love you. And it has nothing to do with your blue eyes and fair skin; it's all about your red pumping organ that embellishes my achromatic life.

Work might keep me on my toes and boarding passes will keep flooding, but remember, I'm always a word away, a call away. And I pray that for most of my life, I'm your umbra.

Yours, Kartik.

P.S: - Was mine the only car in the whole universe you could get hold of to run away in?

Kartik returned to office a week later. Sahana was thrilled to bits seeing him but had to contain her excitement. Many colleagues were catching up with him. She waited for everyone to finish.

She walked up smiling then, "Welcome back."

"That was a very bleak welcome," he said lowly.

She blushed, "You got my gifts?"

"No," he said, "they got seized at customs."

Sahana covered her mouth again to veil her laughter. Ajit walked out of his cabin and caught the moment; Sahana's pink cheeks and shining eyes gave away her joyous state.

Ajit wasn't very pleased for several reasons. First, Sahana had been acting exclusively on Kartik's advice without looking at the larger picture. Secondly, her immature plans had been supported by Kartik, and he did not look at the larger picture as well. The third was that Sahana should be comfortable with Rahul, not with of Kartik.

And while the third reason also like the other two was peacefully retreating away from his mind, it got anchored by Samar's interjection.

"Hello, Ajit," Samar said as he stood by Ajit, who was preoccupied watching the jovial scene.

Samar smiled cunningly as he made his move. "Sahana is beautiful, but innocent."

Ajit turned to Samar, who smartly switched emotion of his smile from cunningness to kindliness.

Ajit nodded, "You know what, at Garima's engagement when my wife first met Sahana, she confused her to be Kartik's wife or girlfriend."

Ajit's eyes grew wider as Samar continued, "I gave her a piece of my mind for not being professional. We share such warm camaraderie but she's too orthodox to understand such ties."

Ajit read between the lines, and he then also noticed a few other associates including Garima passing pressing smiles at the scene. Ajit registered that the rumour was doing the rounds in the office.

◆

During dinner time, when Ajit was seated at the head of the table, he spoke with an agenda. "You went to Garima's engagement, right?"

"Yes, Dad."

"What does her fiancé do?"

"He's working in some bank."

"I see," he laughed lightly, "You know until few months ago, many at the office thought Garima and Kartik would get married."

Sahana's smile dropped noticeably. "I never heard any such thing."

"You joined four months back; what do you know about gossip circles."

"This is ridiculous."

"Hang on Sahana," Ajit said irascibly. "What do you really know about Kartik? I have seen him around and he has that impact on many females, not just Garima. There has to be a reason why he's still single."

"It's his personal life, Ajit," Alka said.

"Of course it's not my concern. As long as his charms are helping my business grow, I'm least interested in whom he's with."

"Dad, you're being disrespectful here," Sahana expressed her distaste.

"I'm not paid to respect him; he's paid to respect me. And this is my personal opinion of him, which for sure has nothing to do with his professional capabilities."

"I'm really getting sick of your attitude these days, Dad."

"Whatever my dear. I've seen the world and for sure know men better than you do."

◆

Two days later, Kartik texted Sahana to come over to Ajit's cabin where he was already present.

"Anything urgent?" Ajit asked Sahana as she entered.

"I called her over, sir. We have something to say."

Sahana's face turned ash white with fear. It was not the right time.

Ajit noticed Sahana's jitteriness.

Kartik spoke immediately to mollify her expressions, "Sir this 'Climbing Together' drive is worth a thought."

Sahana came back to life gradually. However, her sweating in AC chilled room didn't go down well with her father.

"Sir, we have to see it as an investment rather than a useless expense," Kartik made his point. Sahana managed to resume a little normalcy and took a chair next to him.

"I've seen the financial figures of that so-called-investment," Ajit said a little harshly.

"You must also give a detailed plan a look," Kartik said. "And I do see the potential benefits including monetary as well."

Ajit raised his eyebrow, "Give me one good reason in that case."

"Attrition rate is not healthy for our reputation, as well as for business continuity. An employee resigns and then we invest again in bringing a new one to the same speed; we anyway lose out billing as soon as we lose an existing employee." Kartik said moving pen in his signature style, "So if we allow them to learn their aspirational skills, we surely are developing them for their next role."

"Impressive," Ajit said sarcastically. "But I hope you did look at the funds it was projected to consume."

"I have a suggestion there," Kartik said. "Why not implement it in batches to keep a check on finances as well. Let's just target the experience bracket where maximum resignations happen and gradually move outwards."

"That's a great idea," Sahana exclaimed.

Ajit wore his 'pro-hat' for a while and could make sense of Kartik's suggestion. "In that case, let me know the new cost post modifications."

Sahana nodded gleefully, "Yes. By the end of day tomorrow positively."

Kartik also smiled at her.

Ajit's 'pro-hat' dissolved and the 'father-of-the-bride' turban emerged again. "Sahana, you may leave now. I have something to say to Kartik." Sahana did so.

"Kartik, I know I shouldn't be bothering with my personal matter, but Sahana's childhood friends are useless. You're far more sensible and for sure her good friend too," he said humbly. "Please convince her to patch up with Rahul."

Kartik slipped into a blue funk. Ajit continued mercilessly, "Am I asking too much?"

Kartik sat dumbfounded; his state confirmed Ajit's inkling. Kartik merely nodded and requested to leave.

When he walked out, Sahana passed him a sweet smile, but he smiled back half-heartedly.

◆

Over the dinner table at the Khurana house, Ajit continued pressurizing her. Sahana ate her meal quickly and walked up angrily.

"She's getting too difficult these days," said the worried mother. Though she didn't mention it, Alka was not happy about Kartik being discussed almost daily on the dinner table.

Ajit sighed, "You're also noticing that."

"Of course," she gently held Ajit's hand. "I was thinking that if she isn't very happy being with Rahul now, then there are chances that the marriage will be full of uncalled challenges. Let it go."

Ajit scratched the lines of worry on his forehead with the thumb of his other hand.

"Don't stress yourself; there will be many good guys wanting to marry her," Alka added.

Ajit heaved a deep breath," Alka, I'm too scared for that thought to even cross my mind, but it seems inevitable."

"Let's talk to her clearly and ask her what she wants."

"No," he said panicking. "I can't prepare my ears to hear anything disastrously absurd from her."

"What exactly is your concern?"

"It's not whom she doesn't want to be with; it's whom she wants to be with that's the prime cause of my worry."

Alka narrowed her eyes. She sank in her chair. "Is she mad? Can't she interpret the character of the man?"

Ajit turned at her rolling in his lips, "There's nothing wrong with his character."

Alka's eyes opened wide, "But you... "

"You should be able to understand why I did that." Ajit interrupted. "He's very nice rather. Remarkably grounded. It's obvious for him to be popular amongst the females. But he's well-behaved."

Alka sat quietly for some time and then cleared her throat to say something daring. "You want to consider him in that case?"

"Stop Alka. We've already had a formal ceremony. My social stature is important to me. Sahana can't toss it all away just like that."

He gritted his teeth. "I know what I need to do next!"

The next day, early in the evening, Sahana emailed Ajit and Kartik over her new cost value. Ajit replied in less than a minute and asked them to gather in his cabin.

"It looks amicable now," Kartik said.

"You may need to think again," Ajit said.

"Sahana, I was anyway thinking that HR is in the capable hands of Garima so you can discontinue coming to office," Ajit said.

Sahana was aghast, so was Kartik.

"But Dad, I'm doing good work."

Kartik sat quietly while Ajit continued, "Sahana dear, please let it be."

Sahana was upset over her father's remarks, "You asked me to help."

"And you allowed one of my topmost executives to be insulted in a boardroom."

"Because he wasn't co-operating. You're dragging this issue ever since you've returned. And what does it have to do with my drive?"

"In both cases, you're bossing around without thinking clearly. Please do not come to DataMagica from tomorrow. And I'm sure your silly friends must be missing you," Ajit said sarcastically.

Sahana thumped her fist on the table in anger, "Now, what do my friends have to do with this? You need to stop targeting my people."

"When you'll start listening to me, I'll surely consider your request."

"For me to be listening to you, you have to consider saying something sweet."

Kartik was nervous as he watched the heated argument. It was apparent that a personal tussle was riding on this professional issue. Ajit was being very tough with her and did not even care that Kartik was present.

"I don't care if it sounds bitter. I did ask you and I didn't push you for anything. And now I can't allow you to tarnish my reputation due to any sudden change of your mind or perhaps heart."

Sahana was flustered at what her father was referring to.

"You better sort it before I am ashamed of your existence."

Ajit stared hard at her.

Sahana froze with the fear of complications ahead. She couldn't turn her neck to look at Kartik sitting next to her. Kartik was panic-stricken. He realized he needed to address the issue in less than three days now.

After about a minute, Sahana did gather her emotions and walked out. Kartik sat there immobile, "What about that Australian client we discussed yesterday?"

Kartik's brain didn't even register what his boss was saying. Ajit repeated himself. Kartik's brain was unresponsive.

Ajit raised his voice a little, "Kartik!"

He jumped up in his chair, "Sir you should consider dealing with Sahana a little gently."

Ajit's eyebrows rose, "I think it's my personal matter, Kartik."

"I agree, sir. But she's very sensitive. And as far as this drive goes, I completely support her."

"I think communication has already been sent out for scraping it."

"With all due respect, I believe I should be consulted before any decision like that. Any operational decision needs my approval as well."

Ajit's eyes opened wide at the first ever protest from Kartik. Ajit took a few moments to frame his diplomatic answer, "You weren't around and then being the CEO, if I think it isn't worth it, my COO should support me."

"Vis-a-vis is true too, sir."

Ajit was displeased but couldn't make it very apparent, "Alright then, work with Garima over this and let her drive it."

"It isn't Garima's initiative. Sahana had been working day in and day out over this; she walked around the entire office meeting people personally and in groups to uncover our flaws with people management," Kartik asserted.

Ajit's struggle to contain his displeasure intensified. "I'll think about it," he cut the discussion short. Kartik left.

Final face-off

Kartik called Sahana late at night and found her sobbing. Kartik did many things to cheer her up, but she showed no signs of stopping.

"You know what, being nice is a curse," Sahana said weeping.

"No, darling. You're over-reacting," Kartik tried to pacify her.

"Had that Minisha not called me up pleading, I would have let everyone know about the incident."

"No, you won't have ever considered that. Her calling is irrelevant."

"You know what..."

Sahana was interrupted by Kartik,

"You know what Sahana, I wanted to ask you something."

"What?" She blew her nose hard into the tissue. Kartik took the phone away from his ear.

"Sahana,I was thinking, can we make love tomorrow?"

"What?" she cluttered. "My life is going upside down. My parents make me feel as though I'm the worst thing that ever happened to them. Dad wants me to discontinue work..."

"Hang on, hang on!" Kartik said with silent laughter, "My life is downside up due to you. I look at you like you're the best thing that ever happened to me. And I want to come to office these days only because you're there."

She smiled a little, wiping her tears, "So?"

"So, consider pleasing me. It's been so long that I almost feel like a virgin again."

"What?" she was nettled again. "I'll kill you right away."

"Couldn't ask more out of life."

She blushed a little. "So when can we do that?"

"I don't have an answer," she said hastily.

"Then do this for me to find an answer."

"What?"

"I'm holding on for five minutes, go wash your face first." She smiled and did so.

"Next?" she asked.

"Say sorry."

"For what?"

"For wasting my talktime over a useless issue."

"Almost a fortune,"

They laughed.

"I'm sorry."

"Better. Now walk to your father's room."

"Why?"

"Just do that," he said assertively.

She tiptoed. "He's sleeping. I shouldn't wake him up," she said lowly.

"Okay, but promise me the first thing you tell him tomorrow morning is that I want to talk to him this weekend."

"You sure?"

"Of everyone on the planet, you shouldn't doubt my words."

She smiled and ran back to her room. "I'll be waiting. But what will you talk to him about?"

"Areee. Just told you a few minutes back. I'm feeling sex-deprived."

"What?" she cried, "You're impossible, Kartik."

He laughed out loud, "You still want me to come on Saturday?"

Her snorts answered him.

At the Khurana house, there was brooding silence over dinner the next day. Ajit left after finishing his dinner.

Alka had had enough. She said, "Sahana dear, please consider asking him to speak to your father soon. I can't allow so much stress."

Sahana was taken aback, "What are you talking about, Mumma?"

"You know very well."

Sahana was silent because she had been caught. Alka continued, "You know, he isn't accepted yet. Please let him know that categorically."

"Dad won't appreciate that."

"But you seem to have taken your stand," Alka said. "So please make it easy for all of us."

"You not mad at me?"

Alka smiled. "If you're so sure about your choice, then I'll stand by you. I always liked the boy."

Sahana grinned, "Really, Mumma?"

Alka nodded, smiling. Sahana rose and hugged her mother warmly, "He's coming on Saturday."

Sahana withheld her mother's approval from Kartik so that he didn't mention that while speaking to Ajit. Sahana wanted to use it as a trump card as she was probably the only person on the planet who had some control over Ajit.

◆

Saturday evening arrived soon and with it, Kartik at the Khurana residence. Sahana walked to Ajit's room to inform him.

"Dad, Kartik is here; he wants to talk to you."

"On Saturday! The young man should be partying today."

"He's waiting in the living room." Alka also came over.

"I don't recall any major official issue pending for which he had to come all the way here," Ajit said.

"It's not official, but a personal issue," Sahana said gathering a lot of courage.

Ajit for obvious reasons did not seem pleased, but walked out into the living room.

After formal greetings, Kartik came to the point. Sahana stood gripping her mother's arm.

Kartik cleared his voice, "I'm not sure if I'm the right person to talk about this, but I think I should be the first one."

Ajit narrowed his eyes, increasing Kartik's tension. Sahana shut her eyes being fearful.

"This is about me and..."

"And?" Ajit asked sternly. Sahana dug her nails into Alka's skin.

"And...Sahana," he said with shaking feet. "We would like to be together, with your kind permission."

Ajit smiled sarcastically, "So you finally think my daughter suits you?"

Ajit's statement confused them all thoroughly. Particularly Kartik.

"She's wonderful. It will be my honour," he managed to answer.

"Really Kartik?" Ajit's sarcasm worsened. "She wasn't there until last year. What's so special about Sahana now that makes her a wonder."

Kartik's nervousness deepened.

Ajit stared hard at Kartik, "You didn't know all these years that Sahana likes you? I always shared my life with my wife but could never disclose this only helplessness. Sahana's looking at you admiringly, unconsciously moving her spoon at the dinner table just like you move the pen, accidentally yelling out 'bloody hell'. You never realized how amazing a person she's until recently?"

Sahana and Kartik froze to death.

"You never cared, Kartik."

Ajit's eyes were red with pain, "Alka says that since Sahana had seen me all her growing years building my career on my own caliber, she's unable to be with someone like Rahul. But I know it's not me; it's actually you whom she compared to Rahul all the while. A man she admired all her dreaming years."

Kartik's face gushed with remorse realizing he had not troubled only Sahana, but also his mentor. He was under an assumption that Ajit would not appreciate it if he got into a relationship with Sahana, but on the contrary, Ajit was displeased with him for ignoring Sahana's feelings.

"I have no answer, sir. I thought you won't appreciate it. Because of what you've done for me, I should refrain..." he said fumbling and failed to complete the sentence.

"So this is how you considered returning my favours?"

Ajit was ridiculed, "Admit that you only thought about yourself, Kartik. I've spent more time with you in the last few years than with my family. I could be wrong about my best friend's son. But not about my right hand at work."

Ajit turned to Sahana next, "You are twenty-five now, and can make your decisions lawfully. I don't approve of this alliance for reasons of my own. I don't approve of you being with someone flickering, unthankful, shallow and insensitive. I can't push you into hell again."

Sahana stood aghast with no expressions.

Kartik took two steps backward and turned to leave.

"Wait, Kartik, she may still want to come. Rebelling is her ace art."

"Perhaps you don't know your daughter well enough, sir."

"You don't believe me? Ask her and you'll know."

"I would like to save myself that last nail of embarrassment. Maybe you don't know, but I know which side she'd chosen," he said chokingly and left their house with quick steps.

Ajit moved to his room fuming. Alka followed. Sahana didn't cry; the shock had rendered her numb.

◆

The following Monday, Kartik walked up to Ajit's cabin and handed over an envelope. Ajit was stunned to read Kartik's resignation letter.

"Are you very sure about this?" Ajit asked. "I have no professional issue with you."

"Appreciate that, sir. But I would like to leave."

"No second thoughts? Is this any kind of blackmail?"

"Not even in my wildest dream, sir," Kartik added. "Please let me know whom I need to hand over my responsibilities to. I don't want to serve more than two weeks' notice. I have sufficient leaves to compensate for the three months' notice policy of the company."

Kartik left the room, leaving Ajit behind thinking.

Sahana was dumbstruck since then and had no will to go to office ever again. She came to the dinner table, ate like a bird and did not speak a word. Alka was disturbed, but not Ajit.

"Kartik resigned today." Ajit said abruptly on the dinner table. Sahana did not react. "Did you know that?"

Sahana shook her head.

"But I'm sure he'll shine wherever he goes," Sahana said with a heavy voice.

Kartik worked tirelessly for the next two weeks on all his unfinished tasks. Ajit was still mulling over his replacement, so Kartik transferred his responsibilities to the next in-charge of all departments. Samar was buttering Ajit graciously.

As a final mail from Kartik on Thursday, he cost-adjusted Sahana's drive and again asserted on its benefits. He spent the rest of the day bidding bye to everyone.

"Why are you leaving, Mr Brar?" Prez asked politely during his farewell meet.

"It's a personal matter."

"Are you taking Blues along?"

"No, I'm not that fortunate."

"Did Mr Khurana fire you?"

"I didn't wait to let that happen."

Prez looked at him in amazement, "It takes a lot of courage to do what you're doing."

Kartik smirked emotionally, "This doesn't call for any courage, and even if it does, I draw it from her."

Prez stood humbly silent. Garima was particularly extremely upset with the abrupt end of the beautiful love story.

He finally walked into Ajit's cabin.

"I just wanted to thank you for everything. I've learned a lot from you, and the experience I take forward is very enriching professionally." Kartik said meekly.

"It was great to have you. I still remember our first meeting in Kolkata; your confidence was and still is splendid, and for sure what DataMagica is today is my vision but your focus."

"Thank you, sir."

"Wish you very good luck."

Sahana's phone rang at midnight with a number very close to her heart. She wasn't asleep; just lying lifeless and her voice echoed her emotions as she answered, "Hi."

"Hi, Beautiful. Hope you remember me?"

"I always will."

"I'm departing tomorrow morning. I have a long pending task to complete before that."

"Feel light, you have no pending task," Sahana's voice choked.

"I do and it dates to five years ago. I need to make a long due phone call."

"What's the date today?" he asked.

"It's the 23rd of October, 2007."

"No, it's the 30th of September, 2002. It's just been a month since we returned from Goa."

Sahana cried hard but mutely.

Kartik cleared his choked voice, "Hey! Don't exhaust my talktime, please say something."

Sahana controlled her tears but with very little success, "I'm so glad you called. I thought it was over for you even before it started."

"Do you think you're the kind of girl anyone can get over with; anyone can ever let go?"

Sahana's voice choked, "Then what took you a month to call?"

"I exhausted all my savings on the Goa trip; I had to wait until yesterday for my salary to afford a phone. And the kind of conversation I intend to have can't be made from an office phone or payphone."

Sahana continued weeping without a sound. "Please say something," Kartik asserted.

Sahana curbed her tears to utter, "You tell me what do you want hear."

"Now that's like it." Kartik said, "How's life?"

"Good. Not as great as Goa. How about yours?"

"Good, not as great as the Rajdhani."

Sahana smiled weakly, "That's the only thing you remember?"

"That memory is worth a lifetime."

He paused. "Hey, you were mentioning some Plan Z of your friend jokingly a few days back."

"Silly plan."

"Why silly?" He said, "Let's do that. I'm sure my pregnant Sahana would be handed over to me."

"And I'm sure that isn't how you'd ever want your daughter to be born."

"That's exactly what I always wanted; she'll be coming out of a very hot mother."

"Do you have a plan Y that can be considered?"

After some time, he said, "Let's elope, Sahana. Nobody can love you more than me. I'm worth your entire world."

Sahana's replied sobbing, "How much I wish to but I can't. I don't want my gardeners to be disgusted with the only flower of their garden. I can never step into a new world leaving behind the present one lamenting over my existence."

She gave him one more reason to be proud of her. "I love you," he said.

"I love you too, Kartik." Sahana slipped into distress again, "Take care. Be safe, eat healthy and don't booze too much."

He smiled bleakly, "You too take care, keep smiling. There is somebody for whom it's the world's most beautiful sight. And I called up today so that when we cross paths anytime again in life, you don't blame me for the side you chose."

They heard each other's muffled sobs. Sahana was the one who disconnected the call, unable to deal with the afflicting emotions.

Later the following night, Ajit was standing near the window when Alka walked in the room. "Shall I heat dinner again now?"

Ajit turned at her, "I'm not hungry today." He paused, "Did Sahana eat?"

"Yes, but very little again," Alka said.

"Still home? Hasn't run away yet?"

Alka smirked, "As he said, you don't know our girl well enough."

"I know my fairy very well; I don't have to learn from him."

Alka nodded. "What next?"

"Same as discussed."

"When?"

"Next weekend maybe."

"No," Alka said firmly, "Tomorrow. I won't allow waiting till the weekend."

"That's too early Alka. Try to understand..."

"No," Alka curtailed him. "Now you've got to listen. Throw her out of here at the earliest."

"We will eventually,"

"Tomorrow. We're leaving. I don't want her sobbing face around the house any longer. Also, she had been consuming my husband's attention for years, time for him to focus on me now."

Ajit smiled, "You could have found any other lady to use those words for."

Ajit pulled her closer, resting Alka's head on his chest, "You've been too tough with her, Ajit, too tough."

"I know Alka. Even I haven't slept all these days. But I had to."

Alka said sobbing, "I understand. But tomorrow it is."

"Okay, baba." Ajit kissed her forehead. "As you say. Let's kick her out." They laughed lightly.

Father of the bride

Next afternoon at the Brars' residence, Arminder was startled to open the door to unexpected guests from Delhi – Ajit and Alka Khurana.

He subsided his shock to warmly welcome them inside. Gauri hurried to Kartik's room upstairs after offering them a seat.

"Happy, Sahana's parents are here."

"What?" Kartik said in disbelief.

"Isn't she at her home? Is she somewhere else?" asked a worried Gauri.

"No." Kartik said, immensely worried, "She's home."

Gauri's worry grew, "Is she alright otherwise?"

"Yes."

"Come down soon."

Kartik quickly changed from pyjamas to jeans and flew down.

Gauri quickly rustled tea and some snacks. Alka requested not to bother, but just to hear them out. The doorbell rang one more time and Vinny walked in. Kartik was pleased that he hadn't made his signature storming entry.

Arminder sat in front of Ajit and Kartik adjacently.

Ajit looked at his wife sitting beside him before starting to talk. "I am extremely sorry Mr Brar for dropping in without informing."

"Pleasure is all ours," Arminder said.

"I could have come to pick you from the station or the airport, sir," Kartik said humbly.

Ajit turned his eyes to Kartik, "We've come via road with a driver. And you don't have to address me as Sir now; we have moved past that point. And I am here to talk to your father being Sahana's father; but of course with your kind permission. Just in case you are not very tempted to say get out."

"Absoutely not Mr Khurana." Arminder said even before Kartik could frame his answer, "You are my guest and I urge you not be mad at Kartik. Tell me please, what brings you all the way to my house."

Gauri sat adjacent to Alka. Vinny preferred hearing it from a distance.

"For you to hear my story Mr Brar," Ajit said. Arminder nodded.

"Twenty-five years ago, just like any father would be, I too was super-elated to hold my princess in my hands. Nurses told me that she looked like a fairy, but I defer she looks even better." Ajit's voice was thick with emotion.

"Sahana always hated academics and barely managed to pass her exams."

Everyone smiled.

He cleared his throat, "At fifteen, I urged her to pick science for class eleven. She gracefully flunked to prove to me it was not worth studying and why the hell did Newton bother how the apple fell. Finally the coming year, she repeated class eleven in Arts."

He coughed again. "Ever since then, the battles of Sahana Khurana v/s Ajit Khurana are fought in our family under various titles. 'Nature v/s Technology', 'Aimless v/s Lifeless', 'Mindless v/s Emotionless', 'Jerked v/s Stressed' and weirdest of all 'Passionless v/s Fashionless.'

"I've truly overheard her conversations with her friends being more worried about global warming than their exams."

He paused, "At seventeen, Sahana helped a thirty-four-year-old homeless woman and brought her home. Kauveri serves in our home as a domestic help ever since and bosses around fearlessly, all thanks to Sahana's backing. And my wife doesn't talk to me for three days each time I say it, but it actually feels like there are three ladies at home."

Gauri laughed out aloud but zipped instantly

"Until Sahana was twenty, the friends partied for reasons like a pet's birthday, receiving a voter-id card, etc. She even ran away from her cousin's wedding in Mumbai to let me know that I couldn't get her married at such a tender age. Phew. I wasn't even planning to. She returned home, but a little changed. I was pleasantly surprised at her query on how to get into an MBA college?"

Kartik smiled sweetly as he had much more details about her caprice.

"At twenty-three when she finally made it to B-School, I got my final blow. Ignoring my insistence, she chooses HR over operations. She had her own theories that made no sense to me.

"At twenty-five, destiny plays its role and she gets to peep into my company's issues. And she has a plan that can potentially solve all our personnel issues. Something I could never draft, nor could my very capable COO. It surely needed someone with a beautiful heart to walk down from the seventh floor to the basement."

His voice choked with emotion again, "On her twenty-fifth birthday, I did ask my daughter if she has someone in her life. She stared at me blankly for a while and then shook her head. I did what a responsible father should."

He turned to Kartik and took a deep breath, "But for some reason, the decision doesn't seen reasonable anymore. And until a few weeks back, I've been finding it extremely difficult to deal with her."

"Sorry for interrupting, Mr Khurana, but you're not the only parent who is troubled with the fluctuating temperament of the child. The last one year has been very difficult for us as well." Gauri said, "And until three months ago we didn't even have an inkling of the cause."

Alka turned at Gauri smiling, "All I know Mrs Brar, the proposal should have been brought up much ahead in time."

"Even I did notice Kartik's withdrawal and tried to bring it up at times. He never gave any clear answer, so I assumed it was a highly personal matter," Ajit added.

"Sir, please can I say something?" Kartik said politely, "I anticipated a reaction to exactly what I suffered. Many things were at stake, the top of which being my career and my impression on you. And all my fears did come true. Whatever you said about me was right, but I'm past that. It's not how I was brought up; it's only what time and greed had done to me."

After a brief silence, Ajit said. "Now tell me Mr Brar, how can I be blamed here? The solution to my personal problem at home was in the next cabin at the office, and that of my office was in my adjacent room at home. None considered me worthy enough to discuss that with. What I was told even when Kartik visited Sahana's college in Nagpur was that he didn't happen to meet her."

"I didn't lie, sir." Kartik said instantly, "Sahana didn't turn up to meet me. I kept waiting for more than three hours on the bench in front of the girls' hostel, even making myself a butt of everyone's jokes."

He paused. "It was right after that Pulkit's termination that my mind was tripped. I'm not sure if it was my framed interview with BT lying on my desk, a COO name plate outside my cabin, your trust in me that I deserved all this success, or it had something to do with difference in standard that I assumed exists between me and her when I messed up incorrigibly with her in the last days of internship."

Kartik gushed with emotion, "I deserved all the pain I suffered for one year for being shallow and materialistic. But then it was a lesson for me to learn in this journey called life to realize that I'm nothing but a logically stupid guy."

He paused to clear his throat, "I should have trusted my potential more than my luck. And the worst is that I presumed that it wouldn't be a problem if I didn't see her ever again. My hard work of years can't go for a toss for a girl. That one year taught me every single day, that conquering the moon is fruitless if you have no one on earth to impress and return to. Unlike her, I have always taken my life very seriously. But trust me, when it came to life, the one in your adjacent room at home emerged much more sensible, stronger and clearer than a guy in the cabin next to you."

Alka and Ajit looked at Kartik. They both turned to each other, but said nothing.

"I agree with you Mr Khurana. Kartik should have handled it more diligently. You need to grant some of your kind-heartedness to my son too. It surely is his biggest regret in life," Arminder said softly.

Ajit said emotionally, "Mr Brar, many find Sahana extremely pretty but they are just those who don't know her. For those who know her admire her for her gentleness, tender heart, vivacious personality and altruism."

Ajit cleared his throat, "It will be mine and my wife's immense pleasure if you agree to accept our Sahana as part of your family."

Smiles lit up on everyone's faces, except Kartik, whose eyes were dampened.

Arminder held Ajit's hands between his warmly, "My good fortune, Mr Khurana."

Ajit smiled finally, being relieved. "And as I said, my piece is much defected."

Arminder sniggered, "No one around here is striving for any perfection. We like it that way, imperfectly defective. Keeping life simple, and cherishing one's existence. And from what I heard today, she's a perfect fit to our madhouse."

Everyone smiled warmly. Ajit turned towards Kartik, "I'm sorry."

"Please sir, don't embarrass me."

"Ajit ji, I think you should embrace him," Alka said smiling. Ajit nodded and helped himself up. Sharing a gentle hug with Kartik, Ajit felt ethereal light.

They all mutually decided to keep it a secret and throw a surprise to Sahana two days later at Khurana's Delhi residence.

◆

Ajit and Alka arrived late at night and found Sahana sleeping in her room. They both smiled at their guest of very few days now.

Next morning Alka greeted Sahana, "My dear, a family is coming up tomorrow evening to see you."

"I am not a tourist spot, Mumma," Sahana said bluntly.

"But a beautiful site for sure," Alka said smiling.

"Please put forward your best behaviour. I don't think there could be a better match for you," Ajit said.

"You said that the last time too."

"I mean it this time."

◆

Sunday evening also arrived soon. Alka had called Sahana to her room. Sahana picked up a very average suit and was least interested in dressing up nicely.

Kauveri sauntered in to inform about the guests' arrival. Alka hurried out; Sahana rubbed off the make-up Alka had put on her. Kauveri also hurried to the kitchen to make tea.

"Did Sahana make this tea?" Gauri asked picking up a teacup from the tray.

"No." Kauveri said abruptly, "Sahana baby can't even make boiling water." Alka gazed but Kauveri overlooked. Kartik smiled at the useless help from Sahana's well-wisher.

"Where's she?" Arminder asked.

"She'll be here shortly, she just woke up about an hour back," Kauveri replied.

"Afternoon nap?" Vinny asked.

"No, she returned in the morning from a party."

"Please stop Kauveri!" Alka said with mild anger.

"She's better now ma'am. Just little overhang."

"Hangover," Vinny corrected smiling.

"Whatever!" Kauveri passed a wry smile.

"I'll get Sahana." Alka started to walk to her room.

"Careful mam. There are some broken glasses in the room."

"What happened?" Alka asked.

"You know her temperament. She found her tea too hot."

Alka shook her head and walked inside. Guests laughed mutely over Kauveri's dramatic representation of Sahana.

Gift of a lifetime

Soon, Alka escorted Sahana to the living room. Sahana's eyes were cast down, not with shyness but disinterest. Everyone stood up. Sahana raised her eyes a little to look at the guests. She blinked her eyes to clear the kaleidoscope of water crystals that her moist eyes created. Many small dancing-revolving images of Kartik finally clustered into one big one. She looked at him in disbelief.

And ever before Kartik could pass a smile, she turned to her father.

She walked slowly towards Ajit who was standing at some distance. She whispered lowly, "You don't have to do this Dad, not just for my sake."

Ajit lightly held her hand and stepped few steps further away, "And what if I am doing it for my sake?"

"Dad, you don't have to succumb. I am not adamant."

"Why are you not adamant?"

"Because I love you and don't want you to be shameful about me. It's not something I can fight over and get done against your wish."

He smiled blissfully at his daughter, "When did you grow up Sahana?"

"I am still your little princess Dad, and will always be."
She smiled angelically.

"But it's time for you to be someone's queen. And I
maintain what I said yesterday that I don't think I can find
anyone better."

She waived her head in no. "No you don't."

"He surely loves you, but definitely not as much as you
adore him. Allow me to set things right for you. And I am
very sorry for messing it up."

"Don't be sorry, Dad. His respect for you seconded my
feelings for years. Finally I've won; please don't be sorry at
my life's only victory."

Ajit smiled again, "Let's go; his family is waiting."

Sahana smiled coyly, "Nice people no?"

Ajit laughed lightly, "Very nice, my dear." He gently held
his fairy's face and kissed her temple. Alka dropped a tear
at such an emotional moment even though she had heard
none of the conversation.

Ajit gently held Sahana's shoulder as they walked towards
the family.

"Mrs and Mr Brar, meet my darling Sahana. World's
most wonderful daughter," Ajit said with pride.

Sahana smiled sweetly and bent forward to touch Gauri's
feet. Kartik smiled wide at his most awaited moment; Sahana
greeted Arminder the same way.

Soon Gauri and Alka started talking about the Roka
ceremony to follow next. "Are you okay with that Sahana?"
Alka asked.

"Hmm." Sahana said hesitatingly. "Can I buy an hour?"

"What for?" Ajit asked.

"I want to change my dress," she said softly. Everyone
laughed out, and Kartik too slapped his head.

"What's there to laugh about?" Gauri said. "It's a special day for her; she wants to look her best."

Kartik also expressed his desire to talk to Sahana for a few minutes before the ceremony.

Sahana turned to look at Kartik. "Can we talk?" Kartik asked humbly. She nodded.

Kartik and Sahana walked towards Sahana's room. Sahana sent an urgent SMS from her phone.

They reached Sahana's room and Kartik instantly latched the room.

He leaned on her study table and pulled her close; they embraced warmly.

"Why did you resign?" she asked emotionally.

"Is that the only question you have to ask?"

"No, but the first one."

"I just wanted to go."

"Go? Where?"

"Nowhere, just away, far away."

"So hurt by what Dad said?"

"No,"

"Don't lie."

He snuggled her closer, "I always thought he liked me. He perhaps did too. My blunder was a massive one."

She stroked his back, "You're fine. It happens. Feel light, it's over."

"Sahana, about a year back your father mentioned that he wanted a guy for you who can take care of your three dimensions," he said softly. "First being interest. Now that's the one thing even I don't know. But to the best of my inference is, it starts with L and ends with E."

Sahana smiled and loosened the hug to look up to his eyes. "It starts and ends with K."

He caressed her face affectionately; "Second being tantrums. I beg you to keep throwing those around; it makes my life lively and happening."

She nodded gleefully and asked, "Third?"

His smile weakened, "Expenses."

She shrank her eyes with that moment-spoiling clause.

She rubbed her nose against his. "Heaven's sake, one of the India's youngest COO shouldn't be talking like that. He can have the world at his feet; it's just a matter of time."

"I'm no longer a COO. In fact, I'm jobless these days," he smiled.

"Perfect time to run away to Goa again in that case." She smiled.

He touched her lower lip lightly, "Do you have this shade around in this room?"

"What?" Sahana was a little startled. "What do you have to do with my lipstick?"

"No, you will have to do something with it soon." Kartik playfully pushed Sahana against the wall.

He held Sahana's hand and gently put her two fingers on his lips. He leaned forward to have Sahana's lips on the other side of her fingers. Sahana closed her eyes with mixed feelings of love and nervousness for the most awaited moment of her life.

He slowly pulled her fingers down bit by bit. His upper lip touched hers first, sending chills down Sahana's spine, followed by the touching of their lower lips just a moment later. Kartik held her chin gently with one hand and opened his lips to relish Sahana's. She held him from the waist as they kissed passionately.

Kartik relaxed her lips after some time. "That was your third gift."

"Sahana, your Dad narrated your life's story, but I haven't told mine to anyone ever. Do you want to hear it? Do you want to hear why I reacted like that?" She nodded.

"Next life, please, live my life and you'll have all your answers. Be born in a city where studying is an abrasion."

"It's a cool city. Nobody forces one to study, what else can one want."

"Shut up! And take a loan for higher studies."

"Loan is alright, but studies again!"

"In my growing up years, many girls came into my life. I missed none; none missed me. Love never happened. I just kept running towards my career goals. Then one day I met a man who wanted to turn his dreams into reality."

She put his finger on his lips. "I know the rest. At times, you don't realize the value of the little things in life because they come so easy."

"It's only when they are gone, that you realize they were priceless."

"But I'm such a loser. It took you only five days to woo me, while it took me five years."

He caressed her hair and pulled her close, "My wooing was shameless."

And just when she was about to say something, he interrupted, "I was joking to myself when I first saw you that you look like a fairy. God dammit, you're the fairy of my life. You showered so much love on someone worthless like me."

"Don't you dare call yourself worthless; you're my first, last and only love."

"Sahana yaar, come with me! I promise to make up for all these years."

They shared a warm kiss again.

"Sahana, when shall I give you your fourth gift?" he asked playing with her hair.

"After marriage."

"Really?" he faked disappointment, "That's a very rustic thought."

"Perfect," she smiled coyly. "My rustic husband would like it."

He smiled and raised her chin; love was floating in their eyes. "Do you think you can handle a rustic husband?"

"Yes, he loves me."

He whispered in her ears amorously, "You for sure can handle his love, but can you handle his lust?"

"Are you scaring me?"

Kartik romantically laid Sahana on the bed; Sahana held his wrist to set the time. They giggled to find it was an analog watch. Kartik took out his phone to set the nineteen minutes rolling.

More or less, it was a repeat of the episode in the Rajdhani Express, but with different and stronger emotions. Sahana too kissed him expressing her love.

"Now you'll go and talk to my Dad?" Sahana said at the end.

"Yes for sure," he said as he buttoned his shirt back.

"And, by the way, what will you say?" Sahana took a wet tissue and started cleaning the lipstick marks from his face.

"Don't remove your love signatures from my face. Do I still need to say anything?" Sahana narrowed her eyes faking anger. They smiled zealously.

Kartik left, and Anusha stormed into Sahana's room, and both friends hugged jumping. "I'm so very happy for you my dear." Anusha was excited, "He's so good-looking."

Sahana blushed.

Anusha whiffed around Sahana's clothes, "Before you get ready, take a quick shower."

Sahana narrowed her eyes, "I don't have time to waste. A face wash should do."

"No, you need an entire body wash."

"Do I stink?"

"Not exactly. But a prominent smell, which like me, others may catch too."

Sahana also sniffed at her clothes and was puzzled, "Seems alright."

Anusha passed an elvish smile, "My dear, it's a very strong smell."

"Of?"

"A man's deo."

Sahana passed a coy smile, "Stop making wild guesses."

Anusha then looked at the bed, "And while you take a shower, I'll put things back in order on your bed."

Sahana held Anusha's neck playfully, "I'll kill you."

"One killing a day should suffice; keep me safe for some other day." Girls giggled hard, keeping a tab on the volume.

Anusha after sorting the bed pulled out a dress from Sahana's wardrobe that perfectly suited the occasion. Sahana was touched and within a few minutes was prepared to astound Kartik.

As Sahana walked along with her pal, Kartik's heart missed a beat like it had five years back. The same golden lehenga, but Sahana much dearer, fantasy much howling and moments much yearned.

Kartik and Sahana shared a smile that expressed several feelings. Anusha captured the moment in the camera; it turned out to be one photograph worth a million words.

Kartik then turned to Ajit, "Sir, with you kind permission."

He also bent down to touch his feet. Ajit felt very shy, "My pleasure to have you as family." Ajit embraced Kartik warmly. Kartik then touched Alka's feet to seek blessings.

The Roka ceremony followed where both families exchanged sweets and some gifts. Sahana was very thrilled to see the beautiful sarees Gauri had picked for her.

And sweetest words of the evening came from Arminder's throat, "Ajit ji, we would like to have an early wedding; no later than two months from now."

The Khuranas concurred joyfully.

Kartik and Sahana managed to blanket their excitement.

On Khuranas' insistence, the Brars stayed until dinner discussing the details about the engagement party to be held the coming Saturday.

Perfect Rings

Once they were back in Noida, Gauri and Arminder engaged themselves calling and inviting close relatives for the engagement. Gauri's enthusiasm was skyrocketing.

Kartik was lying on his bed in his room while Vinny was extremely occupied on his phone strolling in the balcony. Kartik was staring at Sahana's photograph taken in Goa when Gauri walked in.

"Happy," she called.

Kartik hurriedly sat up straight, "Yes Maa." The photo, however, refused to slide inside the book entirely.

"Where's Vinny?"

He pointed to the balcony door.

"What's he doing so late on the phone?" she asked. He just smiled lightly to answer. Gauri shook her head. "I wonder how he's managing such long calls from his pocket money."

Kartik chose silence over disclosing on who's paying his phone bills.

Gauri's eyes fell on Sahana's photo peeping out from the edge of the book, "Can I see that?" she asked. He pulled it out to show her.

"Seems an old photo. She has short hair here. Where was it taken?"

"Mumbai," he lied.

"That was when you first saw her?"

"Second. The first time was during her cousin's marriage in a Mumbai hotel. She was wearing the same golden dress that she wore today."

"Ahaa. But she won't have looked as beautiful as today." She smiled a motherly smile, "Is that the only photo you have of hers?"

"No, there are many on my phone. But for some reason, this is my favourite."

"Because she'll always be this for you. The unmatched feeling of first love."

Kartik turned at her with amazement, "Oh! You also know that. Only I didn't know."

Gauri laughed lightly, "I can't wait for her to come home now. Longing for another woman in the family."

Vinny walked in, "And hopefully just one at a time," she teased Vinny and Kartik laughed loud.

◆

In the other part of the city, Sahana also finally made a long due phone call to call it quits on a better note.

Rahul was more than surprised to see Sahana's number flashing on his screen.

"Hi, this is Sahana." She said humbly.

"Of course I know. Haven't deleted your number yet." Rahul too was polite.

"Well, I just called to inform that I'm getting engaged next week. I just thought I owe you a goodbye in a better and little less filmy way." She said and closed her eyes hard, expecting a ballistic reaction from the other side of the call.

"Congrats Sahana. Wish you all the very best for life." His humbleness took her at surprise.

"That's nice of you to say. I was rather worried about this conversation."

"No, and why? I had myself met Ajit uncle three weeks back disclosing the entire matter to him. I tried telling Mumma many times but she was adamant to put us back together. DataMagica is of many's interest. Dad hardly has any say anyway. I had no alternative but to try explaning the incident to uncle instead. Without taking names of course." He said. And Sahana was almost stumped.

"You did, Rahul?" She asked in disbelief.

"Yes. I saw it as the only way out. Nipun was like a brother and I just can't face him anymore. I don't want a wife who'll remind me of the most shameful act of my existence. I want to get over it." He said. "I hope I can trust you with this ugly secret."

"Of course, Rahul. In fact, I hadn't even shared it with my parents. You have my words for life there." She said reassuringly.

"Thanks Sahana, I shall always be thankful." He smiled and heaved easy. "So, COO guy?"

She smirked. "Yah. His name is Kartik Brar. And by the way, he isn't COO anymore."

"Nevermind, he has you. And you have him. Someone you always wanted me to be."

"Not exactly, but yes you aren't wrong too. And I'm sorry too in a way."

"No, I'm glad it's all sorted in time. I could never manage to win an iota of your respect."

"You're nice Rahul. I wish you best of life too." Sahana said, her nicest best.

Before hanging up, she revisited an important piece of information she had skipped to hear properly. "When did you say you met my Dad?"

"Three weeks ago. Why?"

"Hmm, nothing." She hung up soon after. She was perplexed. The incidents didn't appear in a chronological order. If Ajit knew it all three weeks ago, why did he blast at Kartik two weeks ago and made him resign last week? She thought of confronting her dad, but then dropped the idea, considering it inappropriate to talk since Kartik won't be returning to DataMagica anyway.

Ajit and Alka peeped into Sahana's room late at night and found her smiling in her sleep. They both smiled too at Sahana's dreaming light-heartedly.

Reaching back to their room, Alka sat adjacent to Ajit with moist eyes. "Are you sure you won't take him back? You needed him like oxygen."

He finally turned at her smiling, "Yes maybe. But I passed my oxygen cylinder to Madame."

"Things could have been dealt..."

"Please Alka, we've talked about this," Ajit said with mild annoyance.

Alka smirked at his fondness for Kartik, "He'll always be that son for you."

"Now what the hell is this Alka?"

"Be honest. Do you realize it might take Kartik and Sahana years to comprehend why you've done what you've done."

"I didn't do it to win accolades from them." Ajit heaved, "I did it because I could see someone with all the qualities of being a successful entrepreneur, and all these years I was nothing but greedy to keep him for my selfish purposes. But I can't do that anymore. When my eyes opened post-surgery, and I saw them both standing together; I could do anything but not let my daughter have her hankering happiness. I had to ensure he means it. He's wonderful, but a little confusing. And if he can sacrifice his career, then he surely will mean it for life."

Alka said emotionally, "You really love him too. He's that son to you."

Ajit was a little irritated, "What is this 'that son' thing? Even if I had ten sons and all like this one daughter of yours, I would have still hoped for that one son who's ambitious."

Alka flabbergasted, "Don't you dare forget my daughter's obligations to your company."

Ajit smiled wide, rolling his eyes in Sahana's style, "I'm so highly obliged."

His smile broadened into laughter, "Bloody hell, couldn't she find any other guy? Being selfish was not this guilt-inducing ever."

Alka laughed along.

◆

On the evening of the engagement, Sahana had her final kill on Kartik, looking no less than an ethereal beauty draped in a lavish orange saree, causing all the eyes present to dazzle and two to glitter with love.

The rings popped from both sides stamping the approval of the families for the ceremony to follow. As Kartik held

Sahana's hand gently to adorn his lifelong commitment on her finger, he spoke lowly, "I have an urgent thing to ask."

Sahana narrowed her eyes with that badly timed question. "Now?" she said in such a low volume that even a whisper could flaunt its loudness.

He nodded.

"Go ahead."

"Will you marry me?"

Sahana's scintillating blush instigated jubilant cheers in the audience. She nodded back in perhaps a nano-tangential angle visible only to her man.

He smiled back adoringly, and the symbol of his true love made its way to her finger.

Next, Sahana demurely put the ring on his finger.

Celebrations followed merrily. The Amritsaris rocked the Delhi party. Many of the bride's guests picked up a few steps from the groom's side. The newly-engaged couple though avoided to dance and chose to stand at a corner and cheered the ones on the dance floor.

"I have one more important question for you," Kartik whispered to Sahana.

She paused clapping and turned to him, "Choose between London and Sydney."

She smiled and said, "Goa."

He sighed, "How much I wish I could but I can't find a job in Goa."

"Oh!" You were asking about the place where we would live."

"Yes, what did you think?"

"Honeymoon, what else? That's the only thing running, tossing and oscillating on my mind these days." She smiled stupidly.

"Fukri!" he teased. "When it comes to action, you turn chicken-hearted and the rest of the time you talk as if you've produced five babies already."

Sahana couldn't resist laughing, "Whatever!"

He smiled askew, "So tell me, which city?"

"Wherever you have at least ten minutes a day to flirt with me."

He smiled, "That's it."

"Yes, unlike you, I don't have a big list of expectations. All I ever wanted was an absolute sweetheart."

She smiled blithely, "So a little dose of rustic charm daily can keep me alive till eternity."

He turned scarlet, "And for sure your tickling love will also keep me alive till eternity."

"Wow, we'll be modern age immortals," Sahana said funnily. They both laughed.

"On a serious score, a city that offers a better prospect for you should be picked," she said.

"It's the same company; I need to pick between regions as the Marketing Head."

"London, in that case. Let's explore Europe singing romantic duets in Switzerland...Yash Chopra style."

"Great idea. You in a chiffon sari at a temperature of minus thirty degrees, and me in a full-sleeved pullover. Fantastic."

Their titter was humbly interrupted by Honey, "Hey Happy, time for you two to hit the dance floor."

Sahana shook her head but Vinny pulled her to the floor. Kartik was gently pushed too.

Son unlawfully

At the Sunday dinner at the Khuranas' house, the discussion about the eventful engagement was still on.

"So what is Kartik's plan next?" Ajit asked.

"He's joining some company as Marketing Head in London next month," Sahana replied.

Ajit froze, "Are you kidding me?"

Sahana turned at him attentively, "Why would I?"

Ajit's eyes almost busted, "He was a COO! How could he accept anything lower than that? And more importantly, why is taking up any job than starting his own venture?"

Sahana shrugged, "It's his choice."

"Then what are you for?" Ajit dropped his spoon, "You are expected to encourage to progress."

Sahana was flabbergasted. "I don't want to make his career decisions. He appeared content with that offer."

"How can he? He's one wolf or perhaps a lion or..."

"Hang on Dad, he's human," she said sternly.

"And why are you so concerned?" Sahana asked.

"Because I'm still his wellwisher, and will always be."

"Oh really. Please, Dad, he had been unceremoniously shown the exit door at DataMagica. He should only be family to you now, without any professional tie."

"Sahana I'm gonna break you head..."

Alka intervened annoyingly, "Relax you guys. I'm just too tired of turbulent dinners over Kartik. Even though he's family now, I can't allow anyone to storm my family's peace."

Sahana fumed, "He didn't do any wrong to snatch your family's peace. You better tell this man here to stop shouting at people."

Alka turned at Ajit sharply, "And I think she's right. He's none of your business now." She mellowed a little, "Ajit, do you realize Sahana will be leaving us soon. We need to give her sweet memories."

"I'm so glad you said that, Mumma," Sahana said choking. "I hope he realizes that and stops yelling at me for baseless issues." She stood up to leave.

"Sit Sahana," Ajit held her hand and patted it. "I'm sorry my child." He turned to Alka next, "Sorry dear."

"Better," Alka heaved a sigh and the family dinner resumed.

◆

The following week had been professionally exhausting for Ajit. There were severe issues with new assignments, and since departments had split up, there were many people now Ajit needed to coordinate with to know the exact status. He was also irked with Samar's latent incorporation for not declaring him as COO. Worst of all was mass resignations, as associates interpreted 'Climbing Together' drive as nothing more than honey trap.

By Thursday, he had barely slept for fifteen hours in the last four days. Sahana and Alka were very worried for his health.

"Can I help, Dad?" Sahana gently opened the door of his study room at 3.00 a.m. wherein he was struggling to finalize a solution for an unhappy client.

"No my dear. Go sleep and have some sweet dreams." His eyes were clearly pain-stricken.

Sahana still walked inside and sat next to him, "Any major issues, Dad?"

"Many." He heaved a deep breath. "I never thought it would really turn so true; but seems you both were actually body and soul of DataMagica."

Sahana smiled bleakly, "Dad, can I join from tomorrow?"

"No." He turned at her, "You anyway have to travel soon. Brar family is coming next month to fix the date. Don't bother. And trust me, I'll eventually manage." His expressions disapproved with his words.

Next morning Sahana called Garima, who made her aware of the actual gloomy picture. Sahana was disturbed to know of the deteriorating glory of her father's dream.

Another ten days also passed quickly. Ajit's physical condition speaking volumes of the toll he was undergoing. Alka was highly apprehensive, but both ladies couldn't help much.

◆

Saturday evening, Kartik arrived. He had been in Amritsar all this while. Next two weeks were assigned to Sahana before he flew to London.

Khurana ladies' bad mood was quite apparent. "Is everything alight?" Kartik asked Sahana when she sat next to him after exchanging greetings. She nodded gently though her eyes were not sparkling as ever.

Ajit came running out after a few minutes, "I beg for your forgiveness, I had this urgent call to attend." Kartik was stunned to see Ajit's health, which was far decomposed than two weeks ago.

Ajit's phone rang again, he stepped to the corner to attend; call again lasted long. And when Ajit was approaching the family, again he held his head suddenly. Alka freaked out of fright; it was the same red face of Ajit again. Sahana stood up in shock.

They rushed to the hospital and emergency was announced for Dr Sharma. He examined Ajit and was very disappointed. It took him one hour to come out and speak to the family.

"Mrs Khurana, you should know at least," Dr Sharma said bluntly. "It's just been two months since he returned and his stress level is even worse than before."

Alka was just sobbing, "You know he needed proper rest." The doctor continued, "Is he doing that?"

Alka shook her head in refusal, "He didn't sleep more than three hours a day since two weeks." Dr Sharma's eyes were wide open; and even before he could express any displeasure further, a loud noise came from inside the room. Everyone hurried inside.

Ajit was struggling hard to avoid a needle, "I can't sleep, why don't you understand?"

Alka and Sahana tried to pacify him. "Alka, you can't complain this time. You know I can't afford to sleep for hours."

Kartik couldn't resist not speaking anymore, "Sir, your health is above everything else. Please cooperate with the doctors."

"No. I can't." Ajit fluttered vigorously when the nurse made another attempt to insert the injection. Sahana's state of deep shock was apparent; her not crying mounted Kartik's worry.

The nurse finally called two ward boys to help her hold Ajit; she finally succeeded in injecting him. Ajit was still murmuring, "Don't do that. I need to work. It's about 12,000 people. Why don't you understand?" He finally fell asleep shortly.

Sahana stared at her father without a blink; Alka continued weeping. Kartik thought of asking Alka instead, "Mumma, what's the matter?"

Alka almost gagged her dupatta in her mouth to curb sorrow and spoke stammering with grief.

Alka spoke stammering with grief, "DataMagica is drowning." She closed her eyes with pain. Kartik also felt deep scourge.

Dr Sharma walked into the ward, allowing only one attendee to stay with the patient for the night. Alka was the obvious choice.

As Alka walked inside the room, Kartik pulled Sahana's wrist hard to drag her to a vacant room nearby.

"Sahana, how could you do that?" Kartik was mad with anger. She stood quiet.

He repeated his question twice more and shook her arm to bring her to senses, "What did I do?"

Kartik anger's was further fuelled, "Why didn't you tell me about sir's health? And about the company?"

Sahana looked at him blank, her brain was not functioning. "Answer me damnit." Kartik shouted.

"How could I bother you with DataMagica? You've moved on." Sahana answered innocently.

"Sahana, you are almost my wife and I should be privileged not only to share your joys, but your sorrows too." He softened his grip and held her hands. "I should have known this. I asked you several times on calls as well why aren't you sounding happy?"

"Kartik." She said hesitatingly, "You need to understand my dilemma as well. How could I ask for your help? How can I dare to influence your career-related decisions?"

"It's nothing like daring, sweetheart." He kissed her hands gently, "If it's hurting you so deep, it's my responsibility to help you out. And DataMagica is something I can't let sink ever."

Sahana eyes dropped pearls with ferocity, and she nestled her head on Kartik's heart. He embraced her close, lovingly patting her head.

"Kartik, I love you so much. Please save my father; he's killing himself daily. Only you can help. But he won't ask for it. He wants you to move on and start something of your own some day soon. He wants to see you growing. I feel so helpless. And it's not easy to read him and especially how it ended for you at the company…"

"Ssshhh. I'll be always be there for you my Snow white. And you know, sir is even dearer. And if he thinks I can't make out his thoughts behind all his actions in the last few days, then I'm so proud to disappoint him." He gently kissed her cheek. "It'll be fine. We'll fix it. Again."

She cried a little more, he collected all her pearls and kept them safe in his wallet.

Sahana spent the entire night on the hospital bench in her dearest position of resting her head on his shoulder seeking strength. They had a very sound sleep, waiting for a brighter dawn.

When Ajit woke up, the doctor confirmed his stability and allowed the rest of the family to meet him. Kartik waited for him to have his breakfast to start talking.

Sahana and Kartik sat on either side of his bed. Alka stood next to Sahana.

"Sir, do you remember our first meeting in Kolkata?"

"Of course I do. I was never so impressed with a beginner ever before. I was confident that you could run the show effectively. And my budget was also limited then; we were just three hundred in number."

"I got a big answer today on why you risked in handing over so many responsibilities to me. I was feeling proud of myself for nothing; it was only due to low financial resources."

"No way. Your position didn't change even when we expanded to twelve thousand. You deserved to be where you were." Ajit smiled.

"You surely think so?" he asked. Ajit nodded.

"Sir, can I have my job back in that case?"

Ajit turned towards Sahana in mild anger, "How could you do this dear? You weren't supposed to ask Kartik to change his career plan."

Before Sahana could answer, Kartik interrupted, "She didn't. And that's my different disappointment altogether."

He stared at Sahana. She passed him a wan smile.

"Kartik, you don't have to do this. Trust me, I'll manage." Ajit asserted.

"That seems to be the family's favourite quote, 'I'll manage'." Everyone smiled.

Sahana stared at him again, faking anger.

"No dear, you should continue aiming higher," Ajit said smiling. "And now since Sahana has already started shopping for London..."

"I assure you her shopping won't go waste. I'll fulfill her dream of being photographed in 'Juhi Chawla of Darr' style at the Alps."

Ajit insisted, "Please, I beg Kartik, don't make me sound absurd. Let's cut this discussion short."

"I don't get it; if I was doing fine, then why can't I be considered again."

"Consider! It was yours more than mine. I never thought we could grow so big ever. But I don't believe we can grow any further."

"That's again what *you* think, but fortunately not me."

Ajit and Kartik went round in circles. Finally Alka spoke, "Kartik, please come over to the office from tomorrow. It's yours, and you don't need anyone's permission."

"Stop it Alka," Ajit said angered by the discussion.

"No, you need to go easy now." Sahana asserted. "Me and Kartik are no idiots that we can't read between the lines. We know what you wanted to test by pushing him to resign, and I also knew why you were yelling the night after the engagement."

Ajit sighed and then looked around to find everyone staring him, "Just for the time being."

"No, forever. Time to turn this big fish into a whale."

Ajit finally smiled, and his eyes sparkled with pride, "Fine. Let's call Garima to issue an appointment letter."

"I haven't resigned as HR of the company; I have the same authority as hers," Sahana said angrily. "I don't get it why both you men are always 'Garima-Garima' when it comes to HR,"

Ajit smiled, "Oh God! It sounded like if we are heading for a catfight."

"You heard that for the first time?" Kartik said, "Lucky you."

"Because his words aren't as cheesy as yours for her," Sahana stared hard at him.

"Nothing cheesy my dear, as it's what you do to get your work done professionally." Ajit tried soothing her.

"Is it?" Sahana's eyes opened wide, "I never knew that." She made double-quotes in air. "'What would have I done without you?' is professional."

Everyone laughed out loud. Sahana didn't smile and continued to stare at Kartik in fake anger.

"Alright then. Sahana, you get to issue a joining letter for Kartik." Ajit said patting Sahana's hand. "And I also have another task for you, my HR," he paused, "Please take charge of your drive. I was a jerk spurning it."

"Really, Dad?"

Ajit nodded smiling. Sahana gave him a bear hug. Kartik smiled.

"But I have a better name for it," Ajit said.

"What?" Kartik asked.

"Sarhana."

Later in the evening, Sahana printed Kartik's appointment letter as per Ajit's instructions and got it over to the hospital for his signature.

"Are you sure Dad?" Sahana requested Ajit to rethink his decision.

"Very sure," Ajit insisted. "He's my son-in-law now, but he has always been DataMagica's son unlawfully."

This train is bound to glory

Sahana reached Kartik's home early next morning to hand over his appointment letter.

"Good morning." Kartik was very pleasantly surprised to see Sahana.

"Hope you weren't sleeping?" she said walking inside.

"I was dreaming," he held her close. "And the dream came true."

"How do you manage to be so cheesy always?"

"The same way you manage to be so sweet always."

"By the way, I'm here as DataMagica's HR," she pulled out an envelope from her purse.

"Later, first let me greet my fiancé." He hugged her tight.

Kartik opened his appointment letter to read he was being appointed as CEO. He was shocked a little, but Sahana explained that it was Ajit's desire and part of his retirement plan.

Kartik's return was hugely welcomed by the entire office, except one. Sahana issued an email in the first half of the day about the 'Sarhana' drive. Things started getting back on track gradually. All the staff loyal to Kartik worked very hard to bring things back to place. Clients were excited by Kartik's return. At times, one's mere presence makes a huge difference. Few people have catalytic effects, like Kartik on the company and Sahana on Kartik.

Samar resigned a month later, adamant not to accept Kartik as CEO. His position was passed to the next in-charge for finance.

Ajit then on just supervised and offered suggestions occasionally.

Too involved in fixing DataMagica, Kartik postponed the wedding from two to three months later. Sahana devised new ways to take care of Kartik during the courtship period. She almost snatched the duplicate key of his house and ensured that the cook cooked. She didn't cook as a revolt for Kartik pushing the wedding date; she accused him of taking her as guaranteed.

She punctured all his teasing attempts to get to the fourth gift emphasizing on the perks of getting married.

Once she even left a note on the lid of a dish.

"Food tastes chiii. But that is all a bachelor deserves :P."

Kartik peeled in laughter, and even before tasting texted her, *"Nt tht bad, I can manage with it 4 anthr 6 mnths."*

"Go 2 Hell!"

"But on 2nd thght, for dessert aftr dinner 1 shld get married."

"& dare u returned 4m hell!"

"Even heaven without my Snowwhite is a hell 4 me."

"WHATEVER!"

"Will u marry me?"

"NO"

"Sure?"
"Say sorry first."
"I Love You."

For DataMagica's anniversary celebration, Sahana's altruistic heart wanted to extend the five-year celebration to the entire company. She had her first ever official heated argument with Kartik over the approval of mass celebration. She finally had her way.

It was a grand celebration where the invitation was thrown to the entire company and their families in a big farm house near Chhatarpur.

Many couldn't make it because of their personal plans; still there was a huge turnover of around four thousand people. Sahana plied a huge team to look into all the arrangements and ensured no wastage of funds. She worked closely with them for over a month to chalk out all the details. It was shaping up so superbly that even Kartik got immensely excited.

It was a huge ground and celebrations began at around 4.00 p.m. onwards. There were skit and dance competitions among projects to start with. Even Prez and Sahana performed their popular college skit to boost participation.

The DJ rocked the party with cheery music. It was one rocky affair with over three thousand people dancing together.

Before dinner, Ajit wanted to speak to the gathering while giving away prizes for the day's events. He had the key achievements about the company listed to flaunt with pride. Kartik started talking first, completely unaware of Ajit's plan.

"Well guys for the next hour, we'll talk about our vision, strategies, goals, revenue, projections, etc., etc," Kartik said grinning.

"Booooohhhhhhhhh," came a loud hoot from the audience in a chorus.

"I know, I know." Everyone laughed.

"Just one thing from my side, then maybe a quick open house."

He held the mike with both his hands, "Oh well, the best thing that has happened to the company this year is that we've managed to give you reasons to stick around. After struggling through severe attrition for years, we've finally managed to anchor your trust and interest. All I want is to see each one of you here, year after year as we continue to take DataMagica around the globe," he paused. "Now everyone yells loud enough, so our voice reaches the entire globe."

A loud confirmative, 'yes' followed.

"Not impressive. Do that again."

A louder confirmation.

"And now if you disappoint me again, the party is over."

A cheerful loudest 'yes' emanated, loud enough to deafen anyone in the five-miles radius.

"Now that's like it."

"Any questions anybody?"

There originated a murmur at the back. It reached nearer, and someone finally dared to ask it loud, "Sir, when is the wedding?"

Kartik blushed, propelling a loud tehee in the audience. Sahana was relieved she was not on the stage. Kartik offered the mike to Ajit, considering it should be his announcement.

Ajit held the mike on Kartik's insistence. "The ninth of February."

A huge uproar followed the announcement. Kartik looked at Sahana, and they shared a warm smile.

Ajit handed over the mike to Kartik for a few more questions on the growing media presence, expected salary hike, etc. He looked at him very appreciatively. He never had thought a fresher he had hired due to financial constraints would help him churn profits higher than his imagination. He had asked him to be the co-bearer of his dream, but he not only shared the liability all these years, Kartik soared it to the heights beyond his expectations too.

He had only one shortcoming at that time, of not being very polished for the topmost management position. He had all the ingredients of a successful entrepreneur, but having posed with ruthless challenges since the very beginning, his preparations also called for extra rubbing. Rumours had it that Kartik had attended an exorbitantly priced professional personality development course after his first failed client visit with a UK customer at the beginning of the second year of his career.

Nothing irritated and instigated Kartik more than a failure, and he would not rest until he put the ball into the basket. Ajit was shaky standing on the stage, because of the large audience, but Kartik stood addressing the vast mass so effortlessly, exuding confidence, self-belief, energy and above all, positivity.

Ajit moved his vision clockwise and found Sahana standing next to Alka holding her shoulders. Making faces at Kartik and gesturing him to come down instead of boring the crowd. He smiled at his pretentiously silly daughter, he too knew that she enjoyed being silly but was very strong deep down, just like her mother. He felt proud of her choice of a life partner, who had grabbed the opportunity to address her achievement instead of list full of his own.

He glanced through the entire crowd, and one of the facts on his list got visibly asserted: Eighty percent of the company's associates were below twenty-seven years of age. The young blood was taking his company places. They had all reasons to treat the party as college fest, he thought.

He folded his paper and put it back in his pocket; he thought of putting in a presentation and mailing it to all later. As he moved his head a little up, his eyes met Alka's, who had been watching him, reading him flawlessly right at every halt. They shared a smile that was the nectar of their mature marriage. It was now time for Ajit to take a backseat and spend most of his waking time with his wife. Not sure, if DataMagica was a legacy, but that day Ajit had passed it on to Kartik.

Alka turned to Sahana who was gritting her teeth at the prolonged open house; she planned it to be an unofficial one, but these men were on a different track. Her blissful smile broadened, realizing that a few things might fall on Sahana much earlier in life than it fell on her. To have a highly occupied ambitious husband is an incredibly tedious job, but to Alka, Sahana appeared much prepared.

She gently rested her hand on her daughter's hand, blessing her with the strength to deal with the feeling where the husband's work makes you jealous enough to see it as his second wife. And it could perhaps be an only handover of its kind where the mother not only passes this feeling, but also the same second-wife – DataMagica. For sure, Alka had passed on a legacy.

To sir's daughter with love, always

On 9 February 2008, Sahana and Kartik got married in a grand ceremony. Sahana made an immensely beautiful bride, and Kartik a dream-come-true groom.

Kartik surprised Sahana on the wedding night by sharing news of their penthouse. Sahana again insisted that the present house was perfect; Kartik smilingly reasoned that maybe for two of them, but not when their family grew to four.

Kartik tortured Sahana again by postponing their honeymoon; he joined office three days after the wedding and also pulled Sahana along from the fifth day.

Kartik eloped away with his lady love for fifteen days to Goa, followed by Switzerland right after things were green for the company again. He made sure to make it extra-special for the maturity and understanding Sahana offered, wrapped in her stupid pretense.

Just like all other IT companies, DataMagica also suffered financially due to the 2008 recession. But they managed to sail through it successfully.

Sahana also made many attempts to perfect her Punjabi learning from her trainer Vinny.

Sahana always treated DataMagica as another home. She joined and discontinued at her own whims and fancies. She took a summer break, winter break, spring vacations and whatever excuse that popped into her mind. She cherished her life, decorated her home, cooked for her husband and contributed her efforts to 'Ahem Bhumika'. But whenever around, she bossed everyone with high authority. She ensured her drive was under her influence and was always recognized as the best thing that ever happened to the company. Being stupid is blissful! Earlier, people would occasionally criticize Sahana's way of working despite being the CEO's daughter, but now no one would dare to offend the CEO's wife.

On a late afternoon in September 2008, Garima and CFO Prahlad were sitting in the CEO's room discussing two issues.

"So, what are the two ideas that Sahana proposed?" Kartik asked.

"She directed that we should give away a one-month salary as Diwali bonus this year," Garima said.

"Little financially infeasible in my opinion," Prahlad added.

Kartik contained his smile, "We should include her in this discussion to get it sorted."

"Even I wanted the same," Garima smiled. "But before leaving yesterday she said that the festive season is coming up, she has a lot of things to take care of and hence won't be able to shell out time for office in the coming month."

Kartik nodded and blushed lightly, "Well, we know her philanthropist beliefs, so something could be done as it is festival time."

Garima's smile broadened, "A small gift for all?"

"Good idea. Look into options." Kartik said. "And second?"

Garima and Prahlad looked at each other visibly hesitant to speak. Kartik noticed and was expecting a big bomb.

"She insisted that an associate's leaves shouldn't be deducted if it's for marriage," Garima said beaming.

"Not only a philanthropist, Mrs Brar appears to be highly romantic too," Prahlad added.

Kartik scratched his nose to cover a coy smile. "Is it workable Garima?"

"I'm afraid no."

"But we can give a week's time off at least."

"Depending upon their length of service with the company. For new associate, it's a clear no."

"That sounds good. See if we can come up with some formula."

Garima stared at her old friend and nodded. Prahlad left the discussion; she had some more things to discuss.

"Why the hell did you get Prahlad?" Kartik asked her.

"So that you know the financial impact too."

"I don't need him to tell me that. Why do you put me in such situations?"

"Because I love the way you handle them," Garima laughed out loud.

Kartik shook his head smiling.

"But still, isn't that just too sweet?"

"I handle because I see all her acts from a different perspective. You have to agree that if we can really implement whatever she suggests, the world will be a better place."

"Awww. But it has costs associated with it."

"Yes and we can always tweak it a bit to suit the budget as well. I just don't want to tweak her thoughts."

Garima nodded admiringly, "Do such ideas keep flowing in your house too?"

"Yes they do, and they make our house beautiful."

Sahana was very thrilled to open the door to Kartik much earlier. He took her out for dinner, followed by a long drive for ice-cream. Cuddled her all night, shielding her innocence from the malignity of the world that surrounds.

With the global economy improving in 2009, DataMagica also picked up again.

As nicely as he took care of his 'Sir's' company, Kartik cosseted his daughter. All her interests and tantrums were handled decorously. Sahana proved to be a very mature homemaker. In less than two years' time, the couple could pay off their hefty home loan.

As it happens to most home-buyers, there was a terrible delay for possession. A home that was promised to be delivered in 2009 finally celebrated its house-warming ceremony in 2011.

The first steps in the house were those of Sahana and Kartik's two-year-old little fairy Suhani. A perfect replica of her mother, looking at her, Kartik could ask for nothing more out of life. But Sahana wanted another child and her wish was granted a year later. Kartik Jr entered their life in 2012. And on Kartik's insistence, Alka got the honour to name the boy what she'd preserved for hers. Everyone, particularly Vinny found the name 'Nirvan' super cool.

It was Nirvan's first birthday party and Vinny's special guest for the evening irked Gauri. The idea of 'Vinayak weds Dhanalakshmi' was beyond her, but not Arminder's "Cut it short, let's get the girl."

"How could you, Arminder ji? You should also be mad at Vinny," Gauri said.

"Mad? Why? He had done a better job than your elder one who had been sobbing for a year over his lady love."

Vinny and Sahana smirked. Kartik passed a wry smile.

"What will everyone in Amritsar say?"

"Invite them over for idlis."

"Be serious, please."

"And anyway, no one in Amritsar likes the names of our kids. We were always teased as a South-Indian family."

"Come on, Maa, besides that idli factor, how did you like the girl?" Sahana asked.

Gauri's smile finally gave in. "Of course she's sweet. And so lovely that a guy can spend his entire life..." Gauri bit her tongue midway as a riot of laughter followed.

Sahana teased her over the old family joke, "Why Maa, you don't want any more grandkids?"

Sahana convinced Gauri that Dhanalakshmi would help her Shiva family look more complete. Gauri finally ceded.

◆

The super-busy CEO today has a hectic travel schedule and four offices running in the NCR region. The family however still is his priority, and Sahana ensures to make most of the time he spends with them. She keeps teasing him, saying that she ponders whether he is a better boss or a better father, but a poor husband for sure. It's her self-invented style to send him a reminder of her ten minutes of rustic charm.

Kartik gets extremely emotional watching Sahana playing all her roles so effectively – a dedicated wife, a good daughter-in-law, affectionate mother, flawless homemaker, warm host, and the list goes on.

Despite the two tadpoles at home, Kartik still gets butterflies when he sees Sahana.

Even today, Kartik has only one question for Sahana:

"Poori duniya mein tujhe meri hi gaadi mili thi bhagne ke liye!!

Recommended Reading

When the Heavens Smiled
Ritesh Arora

Sarthak meets Sarangi through a common friend and love blossoms. But when things seem to be falling on track, like a bolt from the blue, Sarangi is diagnosed with a medical condition that leaves her with only three months to live. With no visible solution at hand, nothing but fate seems to be holding power. Explore uncharted realms of life and beyond with Sarthak as he takes it upon himself to alter Sarangi's destiny.

Ritesh is an author and columnist and works as a management consultant with a global business consulting firm.

ISBN: 978-9382665526; Price: ₹ 195/-; Pages: 168; Binding: Paperback.

You are the Best Wife
Ajay Pandey

This is a story of two people with contradictory ideologies who fall in love. This is a true inspiring story of the author and his struggle with life, after his beloved wife left him halfway through their journey. This heart-warming tale of a boy and a girl who never gave up on their love in face of adversities, ends on a bittersweet and poignant note as Ajay comes to terms with the biggest lesson life has to offer.

An engineer by degree, Ajay works in the IT field and loves to read and trek. He has immortalized his life story through this book.

ISBN: 978-9382665540; Price: ₹ 175/-; Pages: 248; Binding: Paperback.

Keeping the Promises

Dhruv Gajjar

Dhruv had almost lost himself when M brought him back to life with her promises. Dying from a dreadful tumour, every night before they went to sleep, she took a portion of his heart and soul as promises. For better or worse, he'd have to keep the promises for the rest of his life. What were those amusing, surprising and painful promises he kept? Can you live and die…both at the same time?

Dhruv is a doctor by profession, and passionate about working on his fitness using advanced bodyweight training and all kinds of sports.

ISBN: 978-9382665519; Price: ₹ 195/-; Pages: 200; Binding: Paperback.

Love on 3 Wheels

Anurag Anand

A young and ambitious girl misplaces a parcel carrying a large amount of cash. She doesn't want to take help from her suitor who seems to have a whole lot of skeletons in his closet. She doesn't want to lose her job either. What can she do?

This is a saga of love, lust, aspirations and trickery that unfolds over a period of three days, propelling those in its midst into an unmindful frenzy.

Anurag holds a Master's degree in business, but loves to read and explore new places. He has ten books to his credit.

ISBN: 978-9382665588; Price: ₹ 175/-; Pages: 168; Binding: Paperback.

Guru with Guitar
Vikrmn: (CA Vikram Verma)

In spite of his great job and hefty pay package, Viktor didn't feel the sense of contentment. Then he met Kim, his lady luck. This story is his journey through life-changing experiences in India and USA – ranging from writing his first book to becoming a coach for cancer patients, and then a motivational speaker, to finally becoming the Guru with Guitar. The book has 11 heart touching songs, 8 lovely poems and 111 life-changing quotes scripted by the author.

Vikrmn: is a multi-talented person with a knack for numbers, chalk carving, oil painting, spreadsheet programming, photography and obviously, guitar.

ISBN: 978-9382665533; Price: ₹ 250/-; Pages: 264; Binding: Paperback.

A Silent Promise
Namrata Gupta

Avantika's rose tinted glasses grow hazy as she steps into college with a broken heart. She is instantly surrounded with a whole lot of drama from people around her. But slowly, the DU campus life charms her and makes her forget the suffering from her past, especially by bringing her to her soulmate Keith. Everything seems fine, till her nightmare comes to haunt her in real life.

Namrata is a management student with a degree in literature. She loves travelling, exploring new things, and wishes to leave an everlasting impression with her writing.

ISBN: 978-9382665496; Price: ₹ 175/-; Pages: 168; Binding: Paperback.